BLACK RIVER

A RUN AND HIDE THRILLER

JJ MARSH

PREWETT
BIELMANN

Published by Prewett Bielmann Ltd.
All enquiries to admin@jjmarshauthor.com

First printing, 2021
eBook Edition:
ISBN 978-3-906256-07-8

Paperback:
ISBN 978-3-906256-08-5

To Ellen Durkin, for being a friend in deed

1

onday and Tuesday were the quietest nights of the week. Obviously you'd expect Friday and Saturday to be crazy busy, but often it was Sunday too. The good thing about Sundays was they wanted to be tender. Only when the men went back to work on Monday did the girls find a few days' peace.

The plane flew in every Wednesday and that could go any number of ways. Sometimes they were homesick and missing their wives; maybe they had something to celebrate; or they brought her presents. Hard to tell what kind of a mood they'd be in.

If Alexandra had any hope of succeeding, it had to be Tuesday. It had to be tonight. She lay on her bunk, visualising every stage of her plan, trying to convince herself she could pull this off. Her pulse sounded like a gong in her ears and she stroked her hands over the butterflies in her belly in a reassuring caress. The camp lights went out at midnight. It would take another hour before the last stragglers had left the bar, returned to their bunkhouses and the camp was asleep.

Just before one o'clock in the morning, Alexandra slid out

of her bed and onto the wooden floor. She waited several minutes for any change in the breathing patterns of her three roommates, then lifted her bag from beneath the bed. The weight simultaneously comforted and concerned her. She had everything she needed. Her clothes, a few gifts from her regulars, her toiletries and a blanket to protect her until dawn. But it was so heavy. How could she run carrying such a burden? She steeled herself. She had no choice.

With nimble fingers, she lifted the latch and bore the weight of the door with her arm. She'd practised the move a hundred times but never in the dead of night. As expected, it swung open with no more than a whisper. Alexandra slithered through the gap like a ghost and closed it behind her.

Night air came as a relief after the stuffy room filled with the breath and overly perfumed bodies of four young women. She waited a moment until her eyes adjusted to the starry but moonless sky, breathing in the smell of sawdust, chopped timber and diesel fumes. Nothing moved other than the jungle trees swaying in the warm winds. Everyone was asleep, dreaming of tomorrow and what the plane might bring. Alexandra focused on what the plane might take away.

With one last look over her shoulder, she crept away from her sleeping co-workers. When they awoke, her roommates would assume she'd gone out early with her best friend. She wouldn't be missed until five o'clock that afternoon, when she was expected to turn up for work. By the time they came looking, she would be far away where no one could touch her. Despite her qualms, Alexandra sensed a bubble of triumph.

Her planned route was longer than necessary to avoid Dona Candida's sleeping quarters. Why that *bruxa* needed sleeping quarters, Alexandra had no idea. If Dona Candida slept, she did it with her eyes and ears open. The slightest sound of conflict or fear in any of the rooms or huts and she arrived as fast as her broomstick could carry her. Usually to punish the girls.

The long way round involved passing the other girls' bunkhouses, circling the medical shack and tiptoeing past the brothel to the priest's place. Wandering around in the half-dark, Alexandra knew one false move could prove fatal. The camp was littered with life-threatening objects and machinery. Vigilance was a hard-learned lesson; she had the scars to prove it. One cautious step at a time. After all, she had all night.

The Rio Negro camp was roughly divided into four uneven sections. Logging work took place at the westernmost point. Chainsaws screamed, earthmovers rumbled and trees crashed with such force into the undergrowth, you could feel the vibrations beneath your feet. North was where the loggers lived, in portable bunkhouses like the one Alexandra had just escaped. That quadrant, the other side of the solitary road, also housed the canteen-church-cinema building, occasionally used as a meeting-room for pay disputes or safety problems.

East lay the cargo area, where pyramids of felled timber awaited the river boats or long-haul trucks. Huge yellow machines with grab hooks and caterpillar tyres sat under a semi-circular shed when not in noisy use. Beyond that ugly mess of torn-up earth sat the landing strip, the only way in or out, unless you were dead wood. The weekly plane delivered provisions, letters, or sometimes people. It represented a distant promise of escape. Because everyone wanted to escape this hellish confusion of mud and metal and its relentless assault against the natural world.

Alexandra and her colleagues were quartered in the south, on a scrappy section of barely-cleared jungle. Southside, as the inhabitants called it, was what passed for infrastructure in this far-flung corner of the Amazon. Three rows of three buildings provided all the camp could desire. Row one contained a shop and two bars. The bars were differentiated by entertainment:

one had a TV, the other a jukebox. Behind them lay three buildings: the doctor's clinic to the left, the priest's surgery to the right and in the middle, Alexandra's own workplace, the brothel. The rest was four basic bunkhouses. Three for the girls and one for their hateful shrieking boss.

Never show weakness! You may not get sick, have a period or contract anything which renders you unable to work. Nothing can interrupt our business. Three months working these camps and you'll have more money than you can ever imagine.

If Alexandra was honest, she could imagine a whole lot more cash than the bundle of notes wrapped tightly inside her bra. Another week's pay was owed her but Dona Candida could stuff it. She suppressed her own aggressive thought as if that evil witch could hear her. Fewer than fifty metres from where Alexandra stood, her boss was lying awake, ears cocked for any hint of an escapee.

If everything worked out, this would be the first time one of Dona Candida's girls had succeeded in getting away. It *would* work out. The alternative was unbearable. Alexandra paced behind the bunkhouse, testing each step before putting any weight on her foot, along to the second hut where Juliana was sleeping. The thought of leaving her friend behind constricted her throat, but she pressed on. One girl would have a chance. Two? Forget it. Juliana only had a few more weeks to go and they would be reunited at the beach. *Please God.* She missed the sea almost as much as she missed her family.

Not a single light shone from any of the buildings. Alexandra took a wide detour, closer to the bars and the shop, aiming for the priest's hut. Her intention was to hide, wide awake if she could manage it, beneath his place until morning. Everyone knew he used earplugs to get to sleep. When the plane landed, she would wait until the pilot had unloaded his cargo and gone to the canteen for some food. His routine was so predictable, Alexandra knew exactly what he'd eat. While the men filled their bellies, she would run like the wind, cross the landing strip and bury herself somewhere in the cargo hold. The pilot would finish his meal, load whatever needed taking to Manaus and, if she got lucky, by sunset Alexandra would be home.

Or as close as she could get. Assuming she didn't get caught, she could walk from Soure Airport to Praia do Pesqueiro. What happened after that was anyone's guess.

Juliana's voice echoed in her head. *Don't waste the present worrying about the future.*

Her own voice responded. *But it's not just my future anymore, is it?*

She edged around the final corner and judged the priest's hut around ten metres ahead. Almost there. Before she took her next step into the shadows, a repetitive noise made her stop. Beneath the wheels of the hut where she planned to hide, a silhouette of spiky ridges and steady scraping indicated an iguana had got there first. Generally, she wasn't afraid of iguanas or any other reptile, but had no intention of sharing two square metres with a huge lizard. She squatted on her heels, reassessing her plan. Patience.

A watery sound preceded an unpleasant smell. Piss. Strong beery urine with an overtone of black tobacco assaulted her nose. The association rang alarm bells before he lit the match. The sulphuric glow illuminated his face as he took a drag of his cigarette and gave her a lopsided leer.

Alexandra didn't hesitate. She whirled around and ran straight back the way she came. No more guarded paces but a blind bolt from danger. When she passed the final bunkhouse, rather than turning left to her own cabin, she ran into the jungle. No matter what predatory creatures lay in wait, she'd take her chances. Anything was better than Bruno.

· · ·

Her breath short, she stumbled her way along the path, her arms raised and crossed in front of her face for protection. The ground was dangerously uneven so she slowed and controlled her panicky panting, balancing hazards ahead and behind. Bruno's crunching boots had slowed to a halt. The stupid lump knew better than to approach the girls' cabins or he'd be banned for another month. Drunk and unimaginative, he would never think she had run into the jungle. In ordinary circumstances she would never attempt such a crazy move, but what was the alternative?

Alert to every sound and ready to leap from harm, she moved along the path like a cat. A derisory snort escaped her nostrils. *More kitten than cat.* She was no nocturnal panther or jaguar prowling its domain but a terrified teenager in total darkness with all the jungle savvy of a domestic tabby. Alexandra took several deep breaths, calming herself. Stress was not good.

If she could find it, the pool would be a safe place to hide until daylight. Their pool. Even the thought of it soothed her nerves. Juliana, always the braver of the two, had gone exploring and found a little stretch of limpid water, just a short way into the jungle. A minuscule beach between two huge rocks hid them from everyone and everything. It was nothing more than a collection of pebbles and silt, really, but they named it Copacabana and called it their own. The two of them sneaked off there as often as they could, sure no one would follow. Two silly girls swimming, sunbathing and talking about the future. Such plans! Such dreams! Four more weeks and if she was lucky, those wild imaginings might come true for Juliana. For Alexandra, it was too late.

On bright sunny days, it took the two girls around ten minutes to walk to the pool. How long it would take at night, Alexandra had no idea. Mosquitoes pierced the skin of her neck and the damp dripping of condensation from the trees began to penetrate her clothes. She stopped, wondering if it might be wiser to turn around. Her plan was still achievable; she had to believe that.

A sound up ahead caused her to freeze. It wasn't a voice, more like a sigh, but it didn't sound human. Something freakish was coming along the path, soft-footed and making a gentle hum. She dropped to a squat, her eyes wide. What kind of animal hums?

Alexandra clutched her belly, frozen in a petrified crouch. Her stomach began to cramp. She peered ahead, searching for the yellow eyes of a jaguar, demon or *cuca*. The spasms got worse, all caused by fear. She had to relax and get control of herself. The hum grew louder. Rigid with fear, she took long steady breaths on all fours, her head swivelling to make out any kind of shape in the darkness. The tone, alien as it was, didn't seem threatening. It sounded like a lullaby.

A dim glow, no bigger than a firefly, floated towards her. She was crying now so didn't trust her vision. Two human figures approached, carrying a ball of light. Their faces, in shadow, looked like Mexican sugar skulls.

Alexandra scuttled backwards until something sharp and painful stabbed her knee. Her observers didn't move, simply watching as she whimpered and keeled over.

The generator showed the diesel level had fallen to just below a third. Her consumption in the past month had been ridiculously extravagant and Ann resolved to be far more prudent in future. No more lights in the evening; she would go to bed and get up with the sun. The only things she really needed electricity for were the icebox and her rickety hob, where she was cooking black beans for a poor woman's *feijoada*. No pork, no chorizo, no bacon. Her only concession to tradition was some dried buffalo strips to add flavour, while worrying about the fuel situation.

The only place to get diesel was Soure, and lugging a jerry can ten kilometres in this heat would be no joke, even with her bike. When purchasing the noisy generator, she'd paid extra to have it delivered and filled. This was the first time she'd needed to top up. She stirred the beans and considered her options. Persuade Zé to give her a lift in his pick-up on his frequent trips into the city? But to find him, she'd need to cycle into the village, which she was still trying to avoid. It might be worth doing if Zé could be persuaded to buy the diesel and deliver it to her end of the beach, for a few extra reais. That would be ideal. She really did not want to walk the streets of Soure for fear of bumping into Gil Maduro.

Since rejecting the police inspector's advances, she'd kept a low profile. She stuck to her own end of the beach, stayed away from the village, and wild horses couldn't drag her into Soure. Daily she asked herself if she should leave this tiny corner of Brazil. Her heart said no. But her heart had proven unreliable on more than one occasion. Emotions were not to be trusted. Once again, she stirred the beans and tried to solve her logistical problem. Get diesel without making human contact. In the end, the solution came via the dog.

Branca, the stray mutt who had adopted her, had the appetite of a hyena. All day she went out hunting or begging, Ann had no idea which. As the sun set, she returned to wolf down a plate of dog biscuits, drink like a camel and fall into a flatulent sleep.

On Monday morning, the dog had barely moved. Everything about her drooped. She got up when Ann opened the door and went down the steps to vomit on the path to the beach. Hunched and miserable, she crawled into the shade beneath the stilts supporting the beach hut and lay with her head on her paws. Ann followed her with a water bowl, a handful of dog biscuits and a precious piece of chicken, but Branca showed no interest.

Not now, please. I've no idea how to find a vet and if I buy medication as well as diesel, I'll have to use some of my savings.

Accessing her stash would require a trip to Belém and a visit to Western Union. That was not part of the plan. Ann left the dog to rest, pacing the veranda with another cup of coffee. *Go local. There must be natural remedies.* She washed up and locked the shack, taking a second at the top of the steps to absorb the view through her sunglasses. Directly in front of her, the Atlantic Ocean shimmered and thundered, a diva owning her stage. White sands stretched left to right while palm trees reached out from the jungle like supplicants to the sun. Seabirds of more varieties than she knew names for glided along the coast, ready to scoop up whatever the fishermen discarded. Ann tiptoed down the steps and peered under the stilts to see Branca curled on her side. For a second, Ann held her breath until she saw Branca take hers.

The nearest hut a kilometre up the beach belonged to Fátima, who was not a dog lover. Nevertheless, Ann started there. She might know someone who knew someone because Fátima always knew someone. She set off to walk along the tree line, keeping out of the strong sun.

As usual, her neighbour was on the veranda, in a violet top and denim shorts. She caught sight of Ann and waved.

"*Olá*, Ann! Come here, I want to ask your opinion."

"And I want yours." Ann trudged through the sand. "Branca is sick. Is there anyone who can treat animals in the village? Or maybe a vet who makes house calls in Soure or Salvaterra?"

"You're asking me for advice on dogs? Yeah, well, I was about to consult you on fashion and look at the state of you." She shook her head and rolled her eyes. "I guess it's a fair exchange. Coffee?"

"No, thanks, I already had too much." Ann climbed the steps and flopped into a canvas chair. "I'm not built for this heat."

Fátima held up a magazine. "Look at this dress! I want to get something just like that for my next date. It could have been designed for me." The image was of a TV star at an awards ceremony, wearing an ombré gown, grading from puce at the hem to a peach neckline.

"She looks like a Knickerbocker Glory," Ann said in English. Then she reverted to Portuguese. "Not to my taste, although I agree the colours would suit you. Where are you going to wear a dress like that around here?"

"On my date! I'm meeting a man at a hotel in Salvaterra on Wednesday and I am going to blow his mind. If only I knew someone who could sew. As a neighbour, Ann, I have to say you're useless. You can't even make cocktails. What's wrong with the dog?"

The enjoyment of their mutual teasing faded and Ann couldn't hide how much Branca meant to her. "She won't eat or drink and she's puking." Her voice shrivelled to a choked squawk. "I have to do something to help."

Fátima rolled her eyes again. "Sentimental. That's why people take advantage of you. That cop is a prime example! All right, all right, we don't need to go over that again. Feed your scabby dog rice and nothing else. If she's not better tomorrow, come with me to the village in the morning. Zé is doing a trip to Soure so I can buy something for my date. Well, it's not just for me. He's fetching some herbal supplies for Tia Maria. She's the person to ask. Whether it's people, dogs or buffaloes, she always knows what to do."

"Tia Maria, of course. I should have thought of her. I'll start with rice, good idea. Fátima? If you're going to Soure, is there any chance you could get me some diesel?"

Fátima sighed and shook her head in exasperation. "You'll have to face him sooner or later. OK, I'll get your diesel but it'll cost you at least a piña colada. In a posh bar, I mean, not something knocked together in your crappy shack from whatever fell out of the jungle. And I want the diesel money up front."

"Deal. I'll buy the cocktails and give you the diesel money right now. *Tá bem?*"

"*Tá bem.* What's a Nickybocky Glory?"

Half a bowl of rice with chicken stock was all Branca consumed in twenty-four hours, but at least she kept it down.

The following morning she was equally listless, her stomach tucked up as if she was in pain. Ann had never put the dog on a lead or tried to persuade her into obeying any orders, so was wondering how to take her to the village when a truck rumbled down the beach shortly after sunrise.

Zé's arm waved from the cab like a college pennant. "*Olá*, Ann. You're coming to Soure with us, right? I thought you might need a ride if you have a sick dog."

The village grapevine could sometimes be a game of Chinese Whispers. Ann opened her mouth to refuse but Tia Maria was already exiting from the passenger side, giving Zé instructions. He drove away and the village healer rolled up the path with her swaying gait. "Let me see her first before dragging the poor thing to Soure. Most times they've eaten something bad and need to puke it out. I brought some herbs to make her better. She's only a young dog and very healthy, thanks to you. Yes please, a coffee is exactly what I need."

She knelt beside Branca as Ann made coffee, muttering gentle words and running soft hands over the animal's flank. The dog accepted the attention without resistance, a sign Ann found worrying. She made coffee and placed two cups on the table.

Tia Maria was shaking her head, tracing her fingers over each leg in turn. "She's been poisoned."

Ann let out a little gasp. "Who would do such a horrible thing?"

"Not who, what. A snake bite is my best guess. I'm trying to find a puncture wound." She tilted Branca's rear leg to the morning sunshine. The dog twitched and pulled away. "Ah, here we are!"

Ann bent to look at the limb but saw nothing to indicate an injury. Tia Maria was taking different packages from her leather holdall.

"Boil some more water. I'll make an infusion we can place

on the inflammation to draw out the toxic stuff. I warn you, it may not work. Depends on how badly she was bitten. But it can't have been too serious if she's still here and fighting. The last thing she needs is to be jolted about in Zé's truck. I'll give her something to keep her calm. Leave her here and come to Soure. You must find that French dentist and convince him to give you an anti-venom shot. It'll cost you, but it should fix the problem. How about that coffee?"

Ann handed over the cup. The older woman began combining dried plants in a bowl, then poured hot water over the green, brown and yellow leaves. The scent filled the shack, faintly medicinal and also familiar, like a whiff of marijuana when passing a pub garden. Maria's capable hands crumbled some powdery lumps into Branca's water, as she nodded to herself with a smile. She took out several strips of what looked like an old T-shirt and soaked them in the herbal mixture.

Something about Tia Maria gave Ann the sense this woman was different to the other villagers. Her confidence and knowledge were comforting and her maternal nurturing seemed natural; why else would everyone call her 'Aunt' Maria? Yet there was something else. As Ann watched her wrap the cooled strips around Branca's hind leg and drip water into the dog's mouth, she understood what it was.

Silence. Since coming to Praia do Pesqueiro, everyone she met wanted to talk and Ann struggled to keep up. Not just with the language, but the stream of words and chatter. Tia Maria listened and instead of speaking, she reacted with action. It was refreshingly calm.

Whatever was in the water seemed to take effect in minutes. Branca's taut, miserable curl relaxed into her usual horizontal posture and her breathing slowed to a snore.

Tia Maria finished her coffee and patted Ann's hand. "Ready?"

"I don't really want to go to Soure. Is there any way I could pay you to ..."

"No, there isn't. Come and do the right thing for your dog. Sooner or later, Ann, you'll have to face Gil Maduro. You cannot hide forever. Thank you for the coffee. Let's go."

Ann locked up, wondering if there was anyone left in the village who didn't know she'd rejected Gil Maduro.

3

Three women, three men. On one side of the flatbed truck sat Ann, Fátima and Tia Maria. On the other, two fishermen heading for the hospital with injuries and an overexcited adolescent going for a job interview. Between them lay six bags of coconuts and an outboard motor due for repair. Waves of humidity billowed from the jungle and the sun was relentless. By the time they entered the city, Ann's back was damp with sweat and her stomach in knots.

Zé parked opposite the hospital for the convenience of the wounded. His passengers clambered off and scattered to the four winds. Fátima heaved a bag of coconuts over her shoulder before yelling a reminder about where to buy the cheapest diesel. Ann gave her the thumbs-up and tugged her baseball cap over her eyes against the glare of the day. Standing on a Soure street made Ann feel vulnerable, exposed and stupid. *When you made your decision, you chose to run and hide. Yet here you are, standing right out in the open.* Her paranoia was at its height, convincing her that behind every window, people were watching.

Hiding. A remote Brazilian beach was supposed to guarantee anonymity. She hadn't reckoned with the curiosity factor of the local villagers or becoming embroiled in a bloody drugs bust. Now she was practically a celebrity, the last thing she needed. In some ways, she'd have been more anonymous if she'd stayed in London. There, she could move in the shadows, leaving barely a footprint. But that was not an option, with the net closing in. Her choice was stark: run or suffer the consequences. One way or another, they would take her down. *Keep moving*, said a voice in her head. It sounded like her sister.

Ann shook herself and put one foot in front of the other. In the city of Soure, everyone had somewhere to be. Ignoring the pull of the Internet café, she strode in the direction of the river. Tia Maria's instructions to locate the dentist/vet were somehow both specific and vague. She had to ask a passer-by for help, who sent her back the way she had come. When she eventually located the Frenchman's small practice behind a repair shop for farm vehicles, she had a different battle on her hands.

Persuading the man to sell her an anti-venom shot took patience and determination. He was arrogant in the extreme and his assistant clearly took her cue from the boss, giving Ann a snooty once-over.

"I don't just hand these things out like candy, you know. I need to see the patient and assess the right course of treatment. For example, what kind of poison it is will dictate which shot to administer."

"I'm sorry, I don't know exactly. But a local expert said it was a snake bite and told me to come to you as the only person who could cure my ... friend."

"Snake bite? Local expert? Bring the patient to the surgery and I will give you my professional opinion."

Humility and profuse apologies weren't cutting it, so Ann slapped a hand on the counter, held out fifty reais with the other.

"That is impossible, I'm afraid. I must insist you give me the medication and I take full responsibility for the consequences." She stopped short of saying 'Do you know who I am?' because she hoped they didn't, but gave every impression of having some kind of authority they should respect. She knew she had no chance of getting the antidote if she told them this urgent medicine was not for a young child or elderly relative, but a stray dog.

An elderly man entered the porch which passed for a reception desk and broke the impasse.

"*Bom dia*," he croaked.

The assistant gave him a pleasant smile. "*Bom dia,* Senhor Alonso.*"

The dentist waved a dismissive hand in Ann's direction. "Give her the dose. The price is fifty-five reais. I have work to do." With a twirl of his white coat, he returned to his surgery. Ann gritted her teeth and paid the money. In the worst-case scenario, that Branca was already dead, at least she had an emergency anti-venom shot should she ever be bitten by a toxic jungle creature. She left the surgery with a brief smile at the old man, hoping he would have better service than her.

With the precious medication in her rucksack, she set about procuring the rest of her essentials, starting with diesel. She was on the way to a supermarket when once again she sensed she was being watched. This time she was right.

Her instincts elevated her adrenaline alert to emergency until she saw the figure of Gil Maduro emerge from behind the dentist's building. Adrenaline kicked in on a different level. Her stomach flipped as she saw the police detective saunter across the scrubby grass. His blue shirt unbuttoned at the top to reveal a hint of chest hair, he walked towards her, unhurried but confident. Behind his sunglasses his expression was unreadable, but his lips curved into a faint smile. Everything about him made her simultaneously nervous and aroused. Cops should not be allowed to be this sexy.

"Toothache?" he asked.

Ann tried to suppress a blush and failed. "No, not toothache. Branca was bitten by a snake and I needed an anti-venom shot."

He raised his sunglasses to look into her eyes. "Is she going to be all right?"

His concern for the dog was one of the reasons Ann liked the guy so much. Another reason she had avoided him since the last time they met more than a month ago.

"Fingers crossed, she will be. I should do the rest of my shopping. My lift won't wait. Nice to see you again."

Maduro gave a light laugh. "Zé never leaves until midday. You have another hour and a half before you need to catch the truck. Have a cold drink with me. I won't ask any questions, unless it's about the dog. Come on, Ann, I have some news."

They sat on a terrace in the shade. Maduro related the progress of his current case with much enthusiasm and Ann sensed his pride. Part of her thrilled at the news he was spearheading the case against a serial killer, yet she restrained herself from asking too many questions.

"That's fantastic, Gil. On several counts. Not only are you taking down a racist psychopath, but this must surely earn you huge kudos in the eyes of your superiors, no?"

He waved his head from side to side, his eyes on his glass of guaraná. "Yeah, I'm the poster boy of the moment. That brings its own pressures. Until this comes to court, they're sending me to investigate a missing person case. One I cannot solve." The animation left his face and he stared at the floor.

"What you mean?"

"Never mind." He lifted his eyes to look directly at her.

"You told me you were leaving Ilha do Marajó. But you're still here."

Ann drained her soda water. "For now, I'm still here. To tell the truth …"

"The truth?" He raised his eyebrows.

She allowed him a reluctant smile. "To tell the truth about my current situation, I'd like to stay in Brazil, as long as I feel safe. That can change at any moment. For example, when our village medic told me Branca had been poisoned, I assumed it was an attack on me. It wasn't. Only a snake bite. As soon as she gets better, I really should think about moving on."

He folded his arms and shrugged. "You need to do what you have to do."

Neither spoke for several minutes, but every time their glances met, bolts of electricity shot across the table. She had to get away from this man, although every fibre of her body urged the opposite.

Ann revolved the ice cubes around her glass and directed the conversation onto a polite neighbourly plane. "How is your injury? The burn?"

"Better than the last time we spoke."

She flushed again, recalling the evening he limped up to her shack with a bottle of wine, ate ceviche and kissed her. "I am happy to hear that. Thank you for the drink and all the best with your cases."

He took the arm of his sunglasses out of his mouth. "How much have you seen of Brazil? I'm not enquiring about your past, not this time. Here's an idea. I have to fly up the Amazon to Manaus and Rio Negro for this missing person's case. If you want, you can come with me and see part of the interior." He gave an awkward grin. "I know you're not interested in a relationship and I respect that. A small plane, a special city and a flight up the river almost to the border with Venezuela is an exceptional opportunity. Consider me your friendly tourist guide. Or fellow explorer. It's new territory for me, too."

Ann heard the plea in his voice. This was something different to the currents that flowed between them. He was asking for help. "Sorry, Gil, I can't. What with a sick dog and trying to keep my head down, well, you know. Thanks for inviting me, though." She heaved her rucksack over her shoulders. "Good luck with your trip."

"The plane leaves at eight on Thursday." He put his sunglasses on and left some coins on the table. "Just in case you change your mind." He strolled away in the direction of the police station and Ann watched him go before shaking herself to get on with her errands.

At the garage, she haggled for ten minutes, settled on a price and agreed to collect and pay the vendor on her return. The last thing she wanted to do was lug a jerry can of diesel around Soure in this heat. In the supermarket, she could only remember half the things she'd wanted and hurried through her shopping, concerned about getting back to the truck in time. What was she thinking, wasting her first city visit in ages by spending time sitting around with a cop? Her head was muddled by the effect that man had on her equilibrium. Not one of the men in her most intimate circle had ever confused her to such an extent. It was a sign in flashing capital letters: KEEP AWAY.

Zé dropped her at the jungle shortcut. With the load she carried, Ann was grateful and picked a tentative path between the trees of the dense, moist canopy. A flock of macaws screeched out of the trees, their calls and colours electrifying the greenish gloom. Her sense of urgency increased as she spotted the beach through the palm trunks, but she still took care to check every step for spider webs, snakes or reptiles in the undergrowth. Once clear of the trees, she dragged her jerry can at a lumbering run towards her shack, muttering a breathless mantra. *Please let her live, please let her survive.*

The beach was like quicksand, slowing every step and forcing her to sweat under the unforgiving sun. Ann powered on, the jerry can thumping against her leg, beating bruise upon bruises. She passed the palm trees and her hut came into view. Relief and exhaustion almost made her cry. The white heron perched on the roof, her veranda with its tomato plant and inside, a tatty white dog. *Please, please, please, let her still be alive.* She wasn't sure who she was praying to.

Regardless of the pressure of anxiety, Ann ensured all her markers were undisturbed before unlocking the hut. Branca lay in the shade in the same position as Ann had left her, still breathing. She opened her eyes but neither lifted her head nor wagged her tail. But she had drunk some more water and Tia Maria's poultice was still wrapped around her leg.

"Branca? Good girl. Stay still, this won't hurt." She took out the syringe, pinched a piece of the dog's thigh and injected the serum. Branca tensed for a second, and then relaxed under Ann's soothing hand. The two of them stayed in the same position for twenty minutes until the animal fell asleep. The act of injecting an injured body and waiting for it to take effect triggered a memory.

The kid. A teenage drug-runner who 'lost' a consignment of Peruvian cocaine and swore he'd been mugged. He wouldn't change his story, no matter how much they hurt him. She stepped in, partly because she couldn't stand the violence any longer, partly because she had a better idea. Sodium thiopental, otherwise known as a truth serum. She should have known by his terrified reaction that it was a bad idea. He was too young, too easily influenced, and under the influence of a sedative and relaxant he would tell his interlocutor whatever she wanted to hear. *Damn fool.* The judgement was aimed as much at herself as the teenager.

That was when she learned the punishment for employees with sticky fingers. She hunched her shoulders to her ears, trying to push away the image of his white face and bloodied hands. Even now, she believed he'd been telling the truth until she injected him. Then he lied, agreeing with her version of events, and in doing so lost two fingers.

Her memory was horribly accurate on some counts and vague or absent on others. For example, the kid's name. Kev? Kenny? Kai? Whatever he was called, he recovered and he continued to work for them after his hand healed. But whenever she walked into a room, he found an excuse to leave. She understood. He could never forgive her. She could never forgive herself.

She stroked Branca one more time then scrambled to her feet to unpack her rucksack. *That was the past*, she told herself. *You did things differently then.*

4

Her encounters in the city, the walk through the jungle and unwelcome recollections left Ann feeling hot, bothered and uncomfortable. While Branca was sleeping, she decided to swim, cleansing her body and clearing her head. Her mind was a maelstrom of unreasonable thoughts, not just the deep-seated terror that her past was catching up, but even the beach, the jungle and the sea seemed filled with hazards. She slipped on a pair of diving socks rather than swim barefoot. Were she to tread on a stingray, its barb would whip straight through the neoprene. But it offered some protection against jellyfish and snakes. She waded into the surf, launching herself immediately into the next wave.

The salty water was rough and abrasive against her skin, the current muscular and unforgiving. It was exactly what she needed. She swam out to the point where the water changed from the colour of mouthwash to a profound, intimidating navy blue. Where the land fell away like a cliff was her limit. To go further was to invite trouble from what lurked beneath and Ann had more than enough trouble in her life. She swam for half an hour, alternating breaststroke, crawl and backstroke.

Unlike in the lido in Hackney Fields, backstroke was not the lulling rest she used to enjoy in the pool. She employed all her muscles to counter the drift, determined to swim in parallel to the beach and not get washed ashore like so much flotsam.

Finally she gave in and allowed the waves to carry her over the shallows and onto the sand. Under other circumstances, she would lie on her towel to recover and dry off, but her concern for Branca propelled her home. While swimming, she never secured the hut with such rigour as when she cycled to the village or went into Soure. In fact, this afternoon she'd left the door open to invite a fresh breeze. As she reached the end of the path leading to the porch steps, she saw Branca sitting on the threshold, sniffing the air.

"Hey, girl, how are you feeling? Hungry? Let's get you some food."

The dog wagged her tail and softened her ears. She was over the worst. Ann retracted all the hateful curses she had mentally hurled at the French doctor and sent him embraces of gratitude instead. Branca ate a small portion of dog biscuits and drank an entire bowl of water, then on wobbly legs came to stand beside Ann. She looked up, her brown eyes expectant.

"Better now? You can't have any more, we have to take it slowly. Oh, right, you want to go out. I'll carry you down the steps but you mustn't go far, Branca. Do your business and come right back, OK?"

Branca's tail thumped the wooden floor. Ann scooped her up, one arm under the dog's chest, the other under her hindquarters. She carried her down the steps and set her onto the sand, where the dog shook herself and took a few paces down the beach. She barked once, more in recognition than warning. A slight figure was approaching the property from the direction of the village. Branca's tail was already weaving from side to side.

Serena. The teenage surfer had turned up for one of her

irregular English lessons, her fist raised in some kind of girl power salute Ann didn't understand, so she simply waved in return. It didn't matter. Serena was already on her knees in the sand, stroking Branca's fur.

"She got bitten by a snake, I heard," Serena called up to the veranda.

Village gossip, as efficient as ever. "That's what Tia Maria said. Luckily the anti-venom stuff is working. I've not seen you for a while. How are you?"

"OK, I guess. You got time for an English lesson?"

"Sure. Come on up."

Ann watched as the girl patted Branca's neck and released the dog, who promptly squatted to pee in the sand.

"I think Tia Maria has saved the life of every creature in this village," said Serena, bounding up the steps. Her brown legs in cut-off denim shorts moved with energetic leaps, her surfer's physique lean. "I wouldn't be here if it wasn't for her. *Olá!*" She kissed Ann on both cheeks. She smelt of coconut oil and sunshine, and could have walked straight out of a shampoo commercial.

"*Olá*. How did she save you?"

"When I was a baby, I wouldn't feed. And because I wouldn't eat, I wasn't putting on any weight and just getting weaker. My mother was desperate. Tia Maria took over nursing me and within one week I was consuming almost a bottle a day. I don't know what she did, but I do know she saved my life. Now my mother's desperate again, but this time to get rid of me."

"That's not true. I know how panicked she was when you went missing in June."

Serena shrugged. "That was then. She's got a new boyfriend and he's round our place ALL the time. I pretty much live on the beach. It's great she's happy but ..." She mimed sticking two fingers down her throat and retching.

"You should be pleased for her. She's been alone a long time, devoting her whole life to raising you. It's her turn to enjoy life."

"Yeah, I know. Hey, I've never seen you with your hair down before. It's beautiful."

"Thank you. I just had a swim and haven't had time to put it up yet. What you want to study today? It might be a good idea to go over past tenses again. Do you want some tea?"

Serena shook her head. "Can we practise conversation? There's an American guy who comes to Praia do Céu. He's cute. He tries talking to me but I'm too embarrassed about my English."

Ann laughed and wrapped her hair in a towel. "I see. Today's lesson is going to be all about flirting. Go inside and take a seat. I'll just get Branca and then we can begin."

Around two hours later, the heat of the day subsided and a cooler wind floated through the house. The two women relocated to the porch with a jug of lime water, followed by the dog. Serena had given up on English and was now relating the morning's drama at the padaria. Ann was only half listening, toying with the idea of offering English lessons for paying customers. Buying diesel and Branca's medication had used up her budget for the week, so it would be helpful to have a few reais to spend on food. Serena continued her story and said a word Ann didn't understand.

"What is a *balseira*?" Ann interrupted.

"The women who work the boats. They're prostitutes too, but they often stick to one man. It's not an easy way of making a living. The river people start girls young."

"Hang on, what's that got to do with the women in the bakery?"

A voice called out from the beach. Fátima was heading in their direction, waving something in a canvas bag.

"Ah ha, it must be cocktail hour," observed Ann.

As usual, Fátima started talking long before they could hear her. "... decided to keep them both because if this date works out, there will be a second. And if it doesn't, I need a different date and I can't always wear the same dress, can I? That dog is better, I see! Anti-venom works like a charm, if you can afford it. But wasting that much money on a stray animal? It's not the first time I said this, but Ann? You need your head examined. *Olá*, Serena, *tudo bem*? Did Ann tell you I've got a date tomorrow night? His name is Alberto and he is a scientist. Can you imagine me with a scientist? I'm not sure how much money he earns, but at least he'll be clever. I brought some rum so we can try out a few cocktails. You thirsty, ladies?"

Serena smiled. "Hi, Fátima. I don't drink alcohol, but thanks anyway. Did you bring your new dresses to show us?"

Fátima stomped up the wooden steps and dumped her carrier bag on the table. "If I'd known you were going to be here, I would have. But I already showed them to Ann and everybody else on the back of Zé's truck. They are beautiful, aren't they, Ann? I can't bear to part with either of them because they suit me so well."

"They're stunning. Both are very you." Ann was telling the truth. The silver-pink halter-neck and the raspberry maxi were far louder and more attention seeking than anything Ann would ever wear. But for her flamboyant neighbour, the two dresses represented her personality to a T. "Alberto is a lucky man. I only have Coke and soda water as mixers, so it's mojitos or Cuba Libre."

"Let's have both." Fátima plonked herself at the top of the steps and peered at Branca. "No more puking, dogzinha? Good, because I brought something for you too." She jerked her chin at the bag. "Buffalo jerky for the dog, plus papayas, a coconut and a pineapple for you. But I'm taking the rum home with me, you understand? Hey, Serena, did you hear what happened at the padaria this morning? Do you know those girls?"

"I was just telling Ann about it! No, I don't know them but I've seen them at the beach."

Ann thanked Fátima and took the bag into the kitchen, leaving the two villagers to gossip. Branca was right on her heels, as if she knew there was something in there for her. She accepted the slice of jerky in dainty jaws and took it onto her bed to gnaw. While Ann made three cocktails, one without rum, she heard snatches of the conversation from the porch.

"... says nothing and just keeps crying."

"Tia Maria says it's grief and maybe PTSD. She's got medicine for that."

"… the other one?"

"God knows." Serena's voice dropped to a respectful whisper. "I'm afraid to even imagine."

"Her father went to the police, you know? He told that cop, the same guy…"

Ann looked up to see Fátima glance over her shoulder in Ann's direction.

"Inspector Maduro?" Serena was wide-eyed. "Can he do anything?"

"Anything about what?" asked Ann, carrying the tray of glasses out onto the veranda.

If there was one thing Fátima enjoyed more than nuts with her cocktail, it was lurid local gossip. "Some local girls came back from Rio Negro last week. They spend three months up there, working as prostitutes, earning serious money. But when they returned this time, one girl was missing and another won't speak. She just lies in her room and cries. The father of the missing girl reported it to the police. I don't know why he bothered because the cops can't do anything. It's not in their jurisdiction. If you ask me, that man couldn't care less about his missing daughter, he just wants her earnings."

Serena prodded the ice cubes in her virgin mojito. "They were a pretty close group of friends, Maria, Juliana and Alexandra. Poor Juliana is still up there. If Alexandra died or ran away, of course Maria's going to be devastated."

"Ran away?" Fátima shook her head and lowered her brow. "Where to? She's dead, that much is certain. She either died at the camp or if she ran, the jungle took her. What do her family think the police can do?"

Ann sipped at her cocktail, thinking about Maduro's assertion that he had a missing person case he could not solve. "I'm not sure they can do anything but the police are planning to investigate." She related Maduro's words and mentioned his offer to show her the interior.

Serena and Fátima were agog. "You're so lucky! I don't know anyone who's ever been to Manaus, leave alone up Rio Negro." Serena breathed, her eyes shining. "It's one of my life goals."

"That guy is smitten! I knew it when I first saw him hanging around here." Fátima slapped her hand on her thigh. "Well, he's not the worst-looking guy in the world, apart from the stench of cop. When do you leave?"

"I'm not going. I turned him down."

The two women shrieked in disbelief and outrage, demanding an explanation.

"For several reasons! One, I have a sick dog. Two, I don't want to give Inspector Maduro the wrong idea. Three … three, I have poems to write."

Fátima snorted and Serena immediately put forward a counter-argument.

"Branca is no longer sick, look at her." The dog was gnawing at her chew, looking more content than Ann had ever seen her. "I can come down here to look after her because she trusts me. Poets need inspiration, no? Going up the Amazon, seeing Manaus and travelling almost as far as the border with Venezuela will fill you with ideas! You can't say no, Ann." She repeated herself in English. "You cannot say no."

"She's right. Turning down such an offer? You're crazy, but I told you that already." Fátima took a large swig of her drink. "Tell the cop you're coming with him on one condition – he stays out of your pants. See? Problem solved." She gave Ann a sly look. "Unless, of course, you don't want him to stay out of your pants."

Ann released a deep sigh as Fátima and Serena burst into knowing giggles.

5

The nightmares had become so infrequent Ann almost believed they'd stopped. Monday and Tuesday nights proved her wrong. In the small hours of Tuesday morning, ignoring her vow to save fuel, she was sitting at the kitchen table with all the lights on, trying to calm her breathing. She didn't dare close her eyes in case those infernal visions of men in animal masks returned to torment her. The worst part was that she knew who they were and whatever punishments they intended to inflict were nothing more than she deserved.

Tonight, she decided, to hell with it. She would have no night terrors, because she intended to get blind drunk on cachaça and the hangover would be worth it.

In Wednesday's pre-dawn blackness she was in exactly the same position, huddled over a cup of peppermint tea, wiping her tear-stained face with her T-shirt. The third time she'd awoken, heart thudding and body tense, she'd given up on sleep, resolving to sit at the kitchen table until the sun came up. Her rational mind told her dreams of trying to rescue her sister from drowning were nothing more than her subconscious processing the near-loss of Branca. Her realist mind told her she would never escape the guilt of abandoning Katie, who might well be metaphorically drowning, all on her own.

Ever since they were small, she'd protected Katie. Her sister was nervous and wary, alarmed by everything, not only for herself but her older sibling. The rope swing over the river, such a thrill when she was alone, lost all its joy while her sister gasped, trembled and cried on the riverbank. Even as adults, they had an unspoken agreement never to discuss the reality of Ann's profession. The vaguest allusion would give Katie the heebie-jeebies. Yet strength manifests itself in less obvious ways. During their mother's long illness, it was Katie who sat by the bedside, who took over the role of carer and stood stoic in the face of death. Not once did Katie blame Ann for being 'busy with work', instead comforting their father, organising the funeral and responding to each message of condolence personally.

Now Katie was alone, abandoned to look after their remaining parent, with no idea whether her older sister was alive or dead. Katie's tendency to imagine the worst must be giving her sleepless nights, worse than Ann's own nocturnal bad dreams. As the sun rose over the horizon, Ann vowed to make a call or at least send an email. For Katie's sake. She wanted to be sure her little sister's head was above the water line. She wanted Katie to know she was sorry. A cryptic email from a fake account or maybe a bunch of flowers with a card only her sister would understand.

She crawled into bed for another few hours' sleep, in the full knowledge she would do neither.

When she emerged from under her mosquito net at dawn on Thursday, her hangover was a waking bad dream. She showered, drank half a litre of mineral water and still felt like crap.

Two parts of her personality were having an endless circular argument in her head. Every five minutes, she changed her mind.

When will you have such an opportunity again? You're going to have to leave Brazil soon and I think you know that, in your heart. The likelihood of your returning to this country is minuscule. So make the most of it! See a little bit more of wildly different geography than this tiny beach. Take the flight upriver with Maduro and enjoy his company. He promised not to ask any intrusive questions, didn't he? The dog has recovered, your shack will be fine, and the chances of anyone recognising you in such a remote location are nil.

She packed her rucksack with some toiletries and a few clothes, wondering how long the trip would take. Two days, maybe three? Where would they stay overnight? Her stomach thrilled with a sense of adventure and she found herself humming a song she used to sing with her father.

What are you thinking? You knew when you left London that this was not going to be a holiday. By leaving your entire life behind, you saved your skin and the only way to protect yourself is to remain out of sight. This is not a gap year where you can learn a language, explore a country and meet strangers. You are in hiding and if you want to remain alive, you will stay that way. Because if they catch you, it's game over. A jolly trip into the Amazon interior with a professional police officer, a pilot, airport security and no end of CCTV cameras is the precise opposite of keeping your head down.

Abashed, she unpacked her rucksack and brewed some coffee. The best place for her was right here with Branca, listening to the call of the heron on her roof and watching the light glint off the waves until the sun sank and darkness claimed the beach. There were enough dangers right here without going in search of more.

She shared her breakfast of stale bread rolls dipped in milky coffee with the dog, whose appetite appeared fully restored. Then she opened the house for Branca to roam the sand, with a stern warning about hunting in the jungle. As if the dog would take heed, even if she did understand. Ann drank a second coffee on the porch and absorbed all the beauty of another morning at Praia do Pesqueiro. Why would anyone want to leave such an idyllic spot?

Only when she turned to go inside did she see the paper bag hanging from her front door handle. Immediately on guard, she stared at the object, unnerved that someone had come so close to her home without her noticing. The bag was too small to be one of Fátima's random presents and who else would come all the way down the beach in the night? She peered inside and saw some documents zipped inside a plastic folder.

Ann never took chances. She went inside to find a pair of rubber gloves before even lifting the bag from the door handle. The plastic folder contained a press pass in her name, an itinerary for the journey upriver and a press release, stating the reason for her trip.

Soure police, in collaboration with the Manaus force, are investigating the disappearance of a young woman from the logging community located on the banks of the Rio Negro. Alexandra Lemos was working as a prostitute in one of the logging sites, due to return to her home on Ilha do Marajó at the end of July. Fourteen of the fifteen women who left at the beginning of May came back. Alexandra Lemos did not. Enquiries at the timber company have produced no satisfactory results. Therefore, two detectives and a freelance journalist are travelling to the camp with the intention of ascertaining what happened to the nineteen-year-old from Praia do Pesqueiro. All enquiries to Inspector Gil Maduro.

Without a watch, phone or any means of telling time other than the sun, Ann had no idea if she could still make it. She repacked her rucksack, locked up the hut, heaved a bag of dog biscuits onto her bicycle and set off up the beach.

Fátima was drinking coffee on her porch.

"What time is it?" Ann yelled, aware she'd picked up her

neighbour's habit of beginning a conversation from a distance. "The flight leaves at eight!"

"Ten to seven. So you're going, then? I knew it!"

"Yes, I'm going. It looks like I'll be away for a couple of nights. Can you feed Branca for me? Or ask Serena to do it." Ann dropped the bag of biscuits on the sand.

"Sure, I can feed her. Don't you want to know how it went?"

Ann blinked, confused. "Oh, your date! I forgot! Well, how did it go?"

Fátima looked like the cat who'd got the cream. "He is a gentleman. He paid for everything, told me I am beautiful and when we said goodbye, he kissed me here and here." She touched the corners of her mouth. "I'm seeing him again on Friday."

"Sounds wonderful! Hopefully I'll be back sometime on Saturday, so I'll come round to hear all about it. Thank you for minding Branca for me. I have to run if I'm going to make it."

"Yes, let's discuss our luck with men over a cocktail on Saturday. Have a great time and don't worry about the dog. Take plenty of photographs!"

"I don't have a camera."

"What? Wait there." Fátima went inside and returned with a digital camera the size of her hand. "Now you have no excuse. Plenty of photographs and if you lose that camera, don't bother coming back to Praia do Pesqueiro. *Tchau*!"

When she arrived at Soure airport, her head thumping, body sweaty and legs tired from her mad bicycle dash, Maduro didn't seem in the least surprised.

"Good morning. So you got my message? How's your dog?"

"Better. Yes, I got the message. Why didn't you knock?"

"I wanted you to make up your own mind. Come, you're just in time because the plane is ready. Remember, you're a freelance journalist doing a story about a missing person. That's all."

She followed him across the tarmac to a small aircraft. There was a group of around eight people climbing the steps to the plane. She and Maduro brought up the rear. Inside, there were twelve seats, four rows of two and on the other side of the aisle, single seats by each window. All single seats were taken, as were the first four near the front. Maduro chose the last two, beside the entrance, for himself and Ann. At the front, two pilots were visible, one checking instruments and the other speaking into a headset.

They buckled themselves into their seats and the aircraft door closed behind them. Maduro released a sigh and glanced at Ann. For a second she wondered if he was nervous, but saw it was relief the two seats in front of them would remain empty. The engines started, vibrating under their feet and after a few moments, the little plane taxied down the runway, turned and accelerated.

Only moments after the engines reached screaming point, the ground dropped away and they were airborne. With a swell of gratitude, she realised Maduro had given her the window seat so she could appreciate an aerial view of the journey. The city of Soure fast became the size of a farmyard and Ann marvelled at the scale of the jungle surrounding it. Trees blended into a green ocean, rippling and bending in the winds like tidal movements, impossible to comprehend. The aircraft climbed higher and the landscape of rainforest resembled the contours of a brain, with ridges and valleys and silvery veins. The sight was as alien as the surface of another planet, but made up of elements Ann knew as intimately as her tomato plant. Fascinated and in awe, she stared at the canopy, elated by a perspective on nature she had never seen.

The pilot addressed them over the tannoy, but due to the noise and his casual delivery, Ann understood about one word in ten. Maduro gave her a reassuring nod, which she took to mean he would explain. She relaxed back into her seat, gazing out at the endless acreage of forest below.

They had been in the air for twenty minutes when Maduro pulled his wheelie case from beneath his seat. He unzipped it and took out two bottles of water and a paper bag containing two *pães do queijo*. She accepted hers eagerly. Her throat was dry as the beach and it had been a long time since her morning coffee. She drank with as much enthusiasm as Branca and about as much sophistication. Then she bit into a cheesy roll and listened to Maduro's explanation.

"The flight to Manaus will take almost three hours. There, we are meeting a local officer to catch a second flight upriver to the camp on Rio Negro. Same as everyone else, Inspector Rocco Delgado believes you're a journalist covering the story. When we get to the location, you need to stay by my side the whole time. Ann, please listen to me carefully because I want you to understand. These camps are like nowhere you've ever seen and they operate under their own rules. We're talking cowboy country. I've been several times and even with the authority of the law, I'm uncomfortable about going into a place like this. They don't like the police or any other government agents. I know we're not popular at beaches like Praia do Pesqueiro either but trust me when I say this is a different level of hostility. Officers have disappeared while investigating illegal mining or logging companies."

"The camp's illegal?"

"No, this one is government approved. Though the attitudes are pretty similar wherever you go. Anyway, we're not there to interfere with their activities, but to find out what happened to that girl. You must hold your tongue, no matter what you see. That goes for anything Rocco does as well as what you see at the timber company. Just remember, whatever you think, keep your judgement to yourself. You're an outsider."

His words stung Ann. She wasn't some crass tourist who expressed her loud opinions on the way other people lived. She had undergone cultural awareness training and appreciated other people had different ways of doing things. However, she didn't argue. Something about Gil's intensity gave her the feeling she had very little idea what she was getting into. Instead she focused on practicalities. "Will we be staying at the camp or returning to Manaus overnight?"

She looked past her out of the window at the sandwich of sky: clouds above and the endless vista of greenery below. "That remains to be seen. I trust Rocco's take on the situation. If he says it's too risky to stay at the camp, we'll fly back to Manaus. As if that hasn't got problems of its own. A lot will depend on how these people react to our presence. I'm going to play it by ear and make decisions on the ground. All I ask is that you don't question me and do exactly as I tell you."

"Yes, sir," Ann muttered under her breath, but she nodded her understanding. Inside, she had already changed her mind about this trip. She heard Fátima's words again. *You need your head examined.*

6

Anticipation, dread, unease and a feeling of foolishness were no match for three sleepless nights and a hangover. Her stomach filled with cheesy bread and the sense of protection lent by the presence of Gil Maduro lulled Ann into a doze. The first thing to penetrate her consciousness was the voice of the pilot announcing their imminent descent to the city of Manaus. She opened her eyes, aware of a stiffness in her neck due to the way she had been leaning against the window.

She sat up, self-conscious, and glanced at Maduro. He too had his eyes closed and arms folded, resting his head on the back of the seat, but somehow Ann knew he was not asleep. The glow of his skin made her think of autumnal ripe fruit and his lips looked like milk chocolate. The impulse to touch him was so strong she blushed and shuffled upright to absorb her first views of this enormous jungle city. Such a spread of urbanity and industrialisation in this far-flung location stretched her belief. A mirage shimmering out of the steamy rainforest could convince you this was an implausible fantasy of your own imagination, yet the vision below refused to be dismissed.

From the air, it seemed the muddy Amazon was dividing into two, like a snake shedding its skin. To the left, the same iced-coffee colour they had followed for the last two hours expanded to the breadth of a swollen anaconda. While to the right, a lithe black serpent peeled away to slide past the city and continue northwest. Contrary to what her eyes told her, she knew the opposite was true.

The most famous phenomenon of Manaus was 'the meeting of the waters', where Rio Negro met the Solimões. Rather than a separation, it was actually a conjoining. At this distance, this blending didn't look like a river but the start of an ocean, with lighter coastal water mingling with the deep blue sea. Except this was the wrong way around. Black water hugged the curvatures of the city after its long journey from Colombia via Venezuela and through Brazil's Amazonas state until it encountered a river equal to itself. Two mighty bodies of water flowed alongside for several kilometres before mingling and becoming the legendary Amazon. To witness this marriage of heavyweights after having seen the fruits of its union bursting into the ocean made Ann uncharacteristically emotional.

"Mother Nature. Nothing can compete," said Maduro, his voice close to her ear.

She didn't turn, unwilling to let him see her watery eyes. Before she could compose herself to reply, the city of Manaus hove into view.

A vast spread of urban grid, factories, skyscrapers, football stadiums, parks and lakes, this could have been a jigsaw piece which fell out of a North American puzzle and tumbled south to land in Brazil. Between the two banks of the Rio Negro stretched an incredible span bridge, a feat of technology Ann could scarcely believe. The pilot dipped the left wing and circled the city in a flight pattern towards the airport. Swimming pools, wide avenues, churches, a port and colourful roofs gave Ann the urge to explore this breathtaking city and stay a while. She gazed at the city as if she might never see such a sight again, soaking it all in. Because this plane would land at the airport and all she'd see of Manaus was a stretch of tarmac before she boarded another light aircraft to fly two more hours north west. Destination: Upper Rio Negro. Ann had already come to the conclusion she preferred beaches and cities to remote parts of the jungle.

How Gil Maduro navigated the chaos of Manaus airport was beyond Ann's ken. But somehow, he did. One minute, they were pushing through crowds of excited families; the next, he drew her aside, pressed a code on a door and entered a private area for security staff. Ann was reaching for her journalistic credentials so tuned into the atmosphere a beat late.

The second the door closed behind them, this loud room full of security guards, customs officers and police withered into silence. Everyone stared at the newcomers. No one moved. Ann caught all the meaningful glances as the tension in the room intensified. A little woman in a cleaner's uniform lifted an arm as if she were about to answer a question from the school-teacher. Instead, she prodded the shoulder of a man with his back to them.

All eyes swivelled to the huge hairy individual. He took at least four steps to turn around. Well over two metres tall and built like a buffalo, the man had skin the colour of dark rum while his eyes were blue as an ice cube. He didn't favour Ann with a glance but focused all his intensity on Maduro.

Ann's toes curled and fists clenched as the man took slow, deliberate steps towards them, no hint of a smile escaping from his bushy beard. One step away from Gil Maduro, he stopped and gave him a scathing once-over.

"You got old."

Maduro returned the contemptuous look. "You got fat."

The big man threw back his head and roared with laughter, grabbed Maduro in a tight embrace and released him to shake his hand.

Everyone in the room relaxed and resumed their conversations. Maduro's accent changed and Ann found the conversation almost impossible to follow. After several minutes, they took their attention off each other and Maduro introduced her.

"Ann Sheldon, Rocco Delgado."

"This is the journalist?" asked Delgado. "Hello, city lady, and you're welcome. Your first time upriver, right? Let me tell you this. It's an experience you won't forget. Stick close to us, only take photographs with permission and ask no questions, OK?"

Ann assumed an expression of humility. "Of course. I'm grateful to be here and I will follow your lead. My aim is to ..."

"I know what your name is and you can call me Rocco. Look, the plane isn't ready. Technical problems. The mechanics say they can fix it by the morning. I booked us some rooms in the airport hotel so we can get up early and fly to the camp. Maybe have a few beers tonight, huh, Gil?"

Ann ignored his mishearing and checked Gil's expression.

His eyes were sharp. "Shit. So another day passes before we start searching for that girl?"

"You think we'll find the girl? Ha! She's been missing two weeks already. We'll be lucky if we find one of her fingernails. Listen, I'm as pissed off as you are. But what can we do? Let's make the most of a bad situation and catch up on each other's news."

"Looks like we have no choice. If we have to stay overnight, though, I don't want to sit in an airport hotel. Let's go into the city. Ann's never seen Manaus before."

Rocco flared his nostrils. "Entertaining tourists? You're getting soft. Whatever. We'll go to the other place."

The other place had seen better days. They drove past many grand façades along the wide boulevards and Ann kept hoping one of those might be their lodgings for the night. With the palm trees, heat and noisy traffic, they could have been in Seville or Faro. She had to remind herself she was in South America, not Europe. Rocco navigated his way through the shopping district, parked up a side street and pressed the buzzer on a nondescript gate with a battered sign saying Apartamentos Shangrillá. The gate swung open into a court-yard. Once upon a time, this place must have had fountains, fairy lights and lush greenery filling the air with the scent of tropical flowers. Now, it was neglected and barren, the only scent being fetid rubbish and urine. Rocco didn't notice the looks of consternation on his guests' faces and marched across the shady yard.

An old woman in widow's weeds sat under an umbrella, listening to the radio. She didn't look up as Rocco approached but all three cats sunbathing around her feet gave the visitors an unfriendly stare. As Rocco raised his voice to be heard by the elderly lady, Ann attuned herself to his accent. He addressed her by name, Dona Lidia, and asked about her son, her health and some family member currently in jail. Her replies were impossible to follow. The woman's accent was impenetrable and her voice barely a croak. Rocco counted out several notes from his wallet and received two keys in exchange. He wished her a good afternoon.

They walked up a flight of stairs to a stone corridor, with one side open to the courtyard below. Ann tried to imagine the place with lemon trees and honeysuckle, but could only see dust and termites. Rocco stopped at a door and thrust a key at Gil.

"Here's yours. You two want to have a shower or whatever? Then let's get some lunch and talk about what the hell we're going to do about this case."

Gil nodded. "Yeah, OK. Where's the other key?"

Rocco looked from his hand to Gil, his expression puzzled. "That's yours. This is mine. Our rooms are directly opposite. Give me a knock when you're ready."

"But what about a room for Ann?"

For a second, Rocco looked from one to the other in total bewilderment. Then he let out a huge belly laugh. "Right, now I see. She really *is* a journalist. Sorry, I thought you two were shagging. OK, OK, give me a second and I'll get us another room. Here, Ann, you take mine."

Without daring to look at Maduro's face, Ann took the key and announced she was going to rest. She'd catch up with them later. Considering she expected the worst when unlocking the room, the accommodation was basic but clean. There was a single bed, a table and a wardrobe, with a small sink in the corner. It was rather like being in a monastery. She pulled down the sheets and examined the pillowcase. There was no trace of a previous occupant. Out of habit, she tried the lock and tested the strength of the door. Both seemed capable of withstanding a chance intruder. She closed the blind and lay on the bed, confused and unsettled. In a matter of hours, she had lost control of her life, faking yet another persona. One of these days, she'd forget who she really was. She closed her eyes, planning a ten-minute power nap with no room for nightmares.

. . .

A knock on the door woke her and for a second she completely lost orientation.

A voice came from the corridor. "Ann? It's Gil. Would you like to see some of the city?"

She swung her legs off the bed and calmed herself. "Yes, please. I'm hungry and I'm curious. Give me two minutes to organise my rucksack."

The afternoon heat was like nothing Ann had previously known. Air on the streets seemed thick and moist, like second-hand breath. At the same time, humidity made sweat break out everywhere. She ran a sleeve across her forehead and top lip, only to start sweating again. She walked beside Maduro over the *calçada* pavements and through the crowds towards the shopping centre. It was a long time since she'd been in a city this size and found it overwhelming. Her initial protest, that she wanted to eat local street food, was forgotten as she stepped into the air-conditioned mall.

Cool draughts lowered her temperature and buzzing stress. Maduro led the way to a food court on the mezzanine level, where one could eat anything from buffalo burgers or *churrasco* to caiman steaks. Ann opted for something less challenging – a fishy soup called *tacacá*. They found a table overlooking the shoppers below where Ann could eat her food and Gil could drink his beer. Oddly, for a soup, the vendor had only offered a two-pronged fork as a utensil. On seeing her confusion, Gil explained the fork was to pull out the fish and the vegetables. The soup itself should be drunk directly from the gourd.

She followed his instructions, still feeling foreign and off-kilter, and asked Gil about his meeting with Rocco. For a moment, he didn't reply, his gaze ranging over the other restaurants. The soup was extraordinary; sour, spicy, tingly and hot. The numbing sensation Ann recognised as *jambú* leaves and for the first time, grasped a sense of familiarity.

"Something's not right," said Maduro, pressing his fingers

to the corners of his eyebrows and staring at his bottle of beer. "He's scared. Let me tell you, never in my life have I seen Rocco Delgado afraid of anything."

"Scared of going upriver? You think he's lying about the plane?"

"No, he's scared of staying here. The plane is undergoing technical repairs, that much is true." He looked her from the corner of his eye. "I never believe what people tell me, no matter who they are. Rocco and I are old friends, sure, but I did the same training as Paolo, our pilot. So I found the guy's number and asked him to tell me what's going on. His plane is in the shop, hopefully fit to fly tomorrow."

Ann studied his expression. "If Rocco's telling the truth, why do you say something's wrong? I don't understand. This whole situation is bizarre and I feel like a fish out of water."

"You're not the only one. Ask yourself this: Rocco has a great apartment and a steady stream of girlfriends. He lives just over a kilometre away from our hotel. The plane is defective and we have to say overnight. Why would he book an airport hotel? And when I suggest we stay in the city, he organises a one-star hostel for us and himself. Why not go home? He's nervous and doesn't want to be seen. You know where he took me for lunch? A *tasca* three doors away. Then he went straight back to his room and locked himself in. As I said, something is very wrong."

By this time, Ann had scooped out all the prawns, cubes of fish and leaves from her soup. She picked up the gourd and took a greedy gulp of the flavoursome liquid. "This is the most beautiful soup in the world. I must find a recipe. Look, if you two are old friends, can't you just ask him what's the matter?"

Gil lifted his gaze to hers for the first time. "Trust a woman to find a simple solution. Yeah, maybe that's what I should do. We planned to have a few beers tonight at the hotel bar."

"There's a bar? Where? Somewhere between the cat shit

and the rubbish bags?" Her tongue was numb but her tone was sharp and she was surprised to see Gil crack a smile.

"That place gets a whole lot livelier in the evening. Just wait and see. I know it's not the Hilton, but Rocco chose it because it's a safe place. In a place like Manaus, cops need to know which of these joints they can rely on. You know, if you want to make *tacacá* at home, you should buy some *tucupi*. Don't try making it yourself or you'll end up poisoned. When you're ready, it should be cooler outside by now. Would you like to see some of the sights? The opera house is a must."

"Yes, please. Just don't ask me to make scintillating conversation. My tongue is dead, like I've just come out of the dentist. But that soup, oh, that soup!"

Gil laughed, his face relaxed. "They say it's pointless to kiss a woman after she's eaten a bowl of *tacacá*. You can't feel a thing, can you?"

As they left the shopping mall, Ann's lips were numb but her imagination was on fire.

Gil hailed a taxi and this time, Ann didn't protest. Of course the best way to see the city was on foot, but while the heat remained at sauna temperatures, the cab would do. They drove down broad boulevards, took side streets and emerged alongside an enormous square, housing an edifice Ann could not quite believe. It reminded her of London's National Gallery on Trafalgar Square. To see a Renaissance-style building on such a scale after flying over a thousand kilometres of jungle robbed her of breath. "Eldorado," she whispered, in awe.

The cabbie rattled off some statistics about Italian marble, the number of German tiles on the dome and how many Murano chandeliers it housed, before name-dropping its most famous performers. Then she steered out of the square.

"Wait, we're not stopping?" Ann asked, craning her neck to take in the whole structure.

Gil dabbed at his forehead with a handkerchief. "Not now. It's crawling with tourists and far too hot. The best time to see Teatro Amazonas is at night. You wanted to see the 'real' Manaus, no? We're going to the market and that's as real as it gets. I hope you like bananas?"

After another drive-by past the Palácio Rio Negro, another jaw-dropping construction as yellow as the theatre was pink, they pulled up outside Mercado Adolpho Lisboa. The entrance with its Art Nouveau façade and clock tower gave her pause. This city made no sense and confused her concept of Brazil. Nothing like Rio de Janeiro or São Paolo and a world away from Soure, this was the most implausible place she'd ever seen. Gil paid the driver and wished her a nice afternoon. The market was madly busy, with cars blowing their horns at delivery trucks, tourists snapping pictures and residents going about their grocery shopping with woven baskets.

Inside, the assortment of souvenir stalls, eateries, spice sellers, vegetable merchants and range of handicrafts were bursting with life. Scarlet wooden parrots, feathered dreamcatchers, yellow signs assuring customers they could use their credit cards, pink dolphins printed onto blue beach towels and multi-coloured bead necklaces created a kaleidoscope of colour. The air was filled with the aromas of cooking and the pungent odour of herbs. A jewellery stall drew Ann's attention, with woven leather bracelets, silver earrings, baskets of polished stones, straw hats and carved masks. The owner showed her a tray of necklaces made of shells and hustled pretty hard until she gave in and paid him five reais for a pair. Gifts for Fátima and Serena, as a thank you for dog-sitting. Gil haggled and ended up buying a black leather bracelet and a pair of silver earrings. Ann was curious. Who was he buying presents for? Her pride refused her permission to ask.

They wandered between the stalls, pointing out everything that intrigued or amused them, such as fresh herbs in plastic bottles and a kilo of Viagra, headdresses and gourds, an array of fruits Ann didn't recognise and more bananas than she'd ever seen in her life. Twice Ann considered digging Fátima's camera out of her rucksack, but for some reason did not. Sweat darkened her T-shirt and dampened her hair. The second section of the market, containing meat and fish, came as a welcome relief, as refrigeration and ice were essential for the produce. Ann bought them each an ice-cream and they consumed flavours of chocolate and coconut while gazing at hills of prawns and slabs of dried fish the size of a mainsail.

"Let's go to the Alfândega. You'll like it. They imported the bricks from England."

Ann wrinkled her nose, but with no real antipathy. "I'm not an instant fan of everything British, you know. And a customs house isn't usually on my list of top sights in a new city."

"This one is special."

He wasn't wrong. She stood on the quayside, taking in the lighthouse and crenellated roofs of the vast building which resembled a prison or police headquarters. With the floating dock at her back, she could have been in Cardiff, except for the heat, rainforest, insects and humidity. Manaus, she acknowledged, was like nowhere else in the world.

"Once again, Inspector Maduro, you surprise me."

A grin crept over his face and he came to stand beside her. "As I said, I'm a pretty good tourist guide. Back to the hotel?"

When they exited the cab outside the other place, Ann hesitated for a second, wondering if they'd come to the right other place. The place had transformed from crappy backyard to welcoming bar. The gates were wide open, multi-coloured bulbs lit the trees and around the courtyard were a dozen tables and chairs. The steel shutter behind the old woman they had met earlier that afternoon was now raised to reveal a fully stocked bar with its own set of spotlights. Music streamed from hidden speakers and all the rubbish bags had been removed. Cats lounged on low walls, windowsills or on chairs meant for guests. No people as yet, but the scene was set for hospitality. Ann's imagination filled in the gaps and she saw dancing, laughter and fireworks.

Gil was laughing at her open-mouthed astonishment. "I told you so. Let's freshen up and meet down here at eight. There are only two dishes on the menu, whatever they got at the market, so I hope you're not tired of fish."

"Tired of fish? Never. Listen, Gil, I thought you wanted to have a private conversation with Rocco and I don't want to intrude. Just to give you some time to yourselves, I can arrive late or leave early."

"That's not necessary. I'll fill Rocco with beer and goodwill then ask him what the hell is going on. By the way, if he offers you a cocktail, say no. He's a great guy but thinks everyone can drink like him. I can't and neither can you. See you at eight."

"See you at eight. Thank you for showing me the city."

"My pleasure." He pulled something from his pocket. "These are for you." He handed over a little tissue-wrapped packet.

Ann peeled it open to see the silver earrings from the market: one a macaw, the other a dolphin. For a woman with almost no jewellery, this was a precious gift. "These are just gorgeous! I'll wear them tonight. Thank you!" Her green-eyed monster put words into her mouth. "What about the bracelet? Who's that for?"

He couldn't quite hide his smile. "It's for me. A memory of Manaus."

7

The noise from the courtyard grew livelier as more people filled the area below. Voices echoed off the walls and the sound of chinking bottles engendered uncertain and at the same time eager anticipation in Ann, as if she was a student going to a freshers' ball. She reassured herself, exactly as she had done in university. She could leave whenever she wanted and return to her room.

Her rucksack contained no make-up and only one dress. She always packed the same way. Practical basics and a plastic rain jacket. Medication, toiletries, flip-flops for unsanitary showers or beaches, a swimming costume and one cheesecloth dress for special occasions. Scrunched-up into a ball, the dress took up less space than a pair of shoes. All she needed to do was let down her hennaed hair, wipe some Vaseline over her lips and she was ready to dance the night away. But now she had a beautiful pair of earrings to show off. And show off she would.

Since running from her old life/lives, she had no use for a watch or mobile phone. To her surprise, she had embraced the release from the tyranny of time and living her life according to natural rhythms. Get up at sunrise, nap when the day was at its hottest and light one candle after dusk. When that burnt to a stub, it was time for bed. Unless the nightmares made an appearance.

Here, she navigated time by the church bells. When they struck eight, she was sitting beside her window, watching the scene below. Rocco was already in the middle of the action, feinting punches at two men and laughing his unmistakeable laugh. Nowhere in the crowd of people was Gil Maduro. She watched for another minute and gave in to the impulse to join the throng. This was the perfect time of night, warm enough to be relaxing, cool enough to be pleasant. She stuffed her essentials into a canvas and macramé bag, useful for maintaining the hippie poet persona, left and locked her room. The door opposite opened.

Gil Maduro took in her dress and hair. His eyes widened but he covered his reaction with a polite smile. "You look nice."

"Thank you. I like that shirt." The inspector did not officially wear a uniform, but Ann had rarely seen him out of a light blue shirt and black trousers. Tonight, he wore a green and cream patterned short-sleeved shirt made of some thin material over wheat-coloured trousers. Without his boots and belt, he looked somehow softer. "You ready? Somewhere down there, a gin and tonic is waiting for me."

"So is Rocco," said Maduro. "I could hear him laughing even as I was under the shower. Remember what I said about his cocktails."

Any hope of remaining inconspicuous was dashed as Rocco saw them emerge. He lifted his arms into the air and roared. "Finally! My old pal Gil is here, all the way up from the coast, with Ann, his lovely lady. Dona Lidia! Two cocktails for my friends!" He opened his arms to embrace Ann as if they'd met far longer than a few hours ago. Ann kissed him on both cheeks, aware that Gil was sneaking off to advise the old lady behind the bar. Rocco introduced Ann to the two men at his table and then promptly abandoned them.

"We have some catching up to do," he called over his shoulder, as they relocated to a table nearer the building. "Gil, if one of those pathetic gins is for me, you can blow it up your arse. I want a proper drink."

"This is a proper drink, you big-mouth. Gin and tonics for us, while you get one of your old favourites; Death in the Afternoon."

Rocco's jaw snapped shut. "You got me a Death in the Afternoon? Are you insane? Do you know how much a shot of absinthe costs around here?"

Gil slid the glass in front of him. "I do now. You'd better damn well appreciate it, you old bastard. Cheers!"

Rocco's grin split his face and he cradled the glass as if it were the Holy Grail. "Cheers!" He took a sip and closed his eyes in bliss. "Now I'm happy!" He looked at Ann with a huge beam then spotted something over her shoulder. All the joy left his face and he seemed to physically shrivel.

"You OK, big man?" asked Gil, scanning the courtyard for what had attracted Rocco's attention.

"Yeah, yeah, all cool. Thought I saw someone I didn't want to see, that's all. My mistake. *Olha*, Ann, I owe you an apology. The reason I introduced you as Gil's girlfriend is because that offers you protection. No one will try anything with a cop's chick. Of course I know you're not his girl and to my mind, that's a pity. You two would make a lovely couple. OK, OK, I've said too much. One second, I need a piss. Don't let anyone touch my drink."

He scraped back his chair and strode into the building. Ann studied Gil's face.

"He's jumpy, isn't he?" she asked.

Gil's eyes were on the door where Rocco had disappeared. Without responding, he relaxed into his chair, folded his arms and looked around the crowded courtyard. Not once did he give an indication he'd seen anything of interest and returned his focus to Ann with a smile.

"This is not a trick. Come closer so I can whisper. Pretend we're lovers, just for a minute."

The tone of his voice convinced her he was serious. She smiled and leaned towards him. He reached up a hand to stroke her cheek and brushed his lips against her ear.

"There's a man by the bar in a black shirt. I've no idea who he is but I'll bet everything I own that's who frightened Rocco. I'm going to the bathroom to make sure my friend isn't alone. Stay here and watch the drinks. Don't let anyone come within spitting distance of our glasses. If we aren't out in fifteen minutes, tell Dona Lidia to call the police. No matter what happens, don't come into the bathroom. Just don't." He cupped her chin. "Tonight, you look so beautiful it hurts." He kissed her gently on the lips, got to his feet and walked casually through the same door as Rocco.

Ann kept up appearances, assuming a dreamy-eyed face which belied the bolt of tension up her spine and melting sensation in her stomach. How was she supposed to know when fifteen minutes was up? Usually she was pretty good at estimating the passage of time, but with all her senses scrambled, she didn't trust her guess to be accurate. Their table was a good two metres from the next, so the only way of someone interfering with their drinks was for a person to approach her. She let her gaze drift over the various occupants of the bar, alert for any eyes focused in her direction. Lifting her chin, she looked up at the fairy lights decorating the trees above their heads and in her peripheral vision, she located the man in the black shirt.

Ann sipped at her drink, trying to project an air of relaxation, and calculated five minutes had passed. A young girl with long black hair came through the gateway and made a beeline for Ann's table. Just as she was about to come close enough to touch, someone shouted, "Marina!" The girl turned and raised her arm, swerving away from Ann's chair to greet her friends.

Ann let out a tense breath. When she checked the bar, the man in the black shirt had gone. The music changed to some kind of samba and several people began to dance in the centre of the courtyard. It must have been more than ten minutes since Gil had left. Ann looked across at Dona Lidia, rehearsing what she would have to say. In another part of her mind, she was counting. Eleven minutes. Two of the dancers came close enough to bump into Rocco's chair but held up a hand in apology as Ann steadied the drinks. Twelve minutes. A loud shout behind her made Ann jump and she whipped around to see two men embracing and slapping each other on the back. As she counted thirteen minutes and glanced at the door to the bathroom, Rocco and Gil emerged. They stopped in the doorway, surveying the area. Rocco was talking earnestly while Gil nodded. He caught her eyes and gave her a reassuring smile.

"Sorry, Ann, we were very rude to leave you here alone. Let's drink these and have a dance! I love this song!" Rocco took a hefty slug of his cocktail and reached for Ann's hand.

She let him lead her onto the dance floor. What Rocco lacked in skill, he made up for in enthusiasm, spinning her this way and that, and twirling her under his arm. The difference in their heights made it easy for Ann to pirouette and lean backwards with his hands on her waist. She threw herself into the dance with great enthusiasm, a by-product of her relief, and found she was enjoying herself. Two dances later they returned, laughing and exhilarated, to the table.

Gil patted his hands together. "You two looked pretty good out there, except for when Rocco trod on Ann's feet. I hope he didn't hurt you."

"Ignore him, Ann, he's only jealous." Rocco picked up his

glass and finished his cocktail in one gulp. "More drinks! The night is young."

They had another cocktail at the bar then Gil insisted they find some food. Rocco did not want to stray too far from their accommodation so they chose a café nearby which served *frango piri-piri*. By that time of night, after two gins and some energetic dancing, the spicy chicken was exactly what Ann needed. She refused to give in to Rocco's persuasive coercion and opted for a can of lemonade. The men drank beer and related some of the cases they had worked as fresh graduates from the police academy; stories neither had forgotten but both enjoyed the re-telling. Ann, as their audience of one, was encouraging and enthusiastic with one eye on Rocco's body language. He was an entertaining raconteur, yet nervous tension made him frequently check the door and bounce his leg under the table.

When they returned to the courtyard for a nightcap, Ann seized her chance and made her excuses, leaving the two men to chat. Rocco complained bitterly about being deprived of her company, but Gil simply wished her goodnight and reminded her to lock the door. She said her goodbyes and climbed the stone steps to her room. Despite the constant sense of danger, she'd had fun tonight. She undressed, washed, secured the room and got into bed. Only then did she replay the feeling of Gil Maduro's breath on her ear and the touch of his lips to hers.

The next morning, she woke early and stared at the ceiling, barely able to believe the complete absence of nightmares. She used the shared bathroom to shower before the rest of the building stirred then dressed in a clean T-shirt and faded jeans. By the time Gil knocked on her door, she was all packed and looking forward to flying up the jungle. Her new earrings,

wrapped in tissue and stashed in an interior pocket of her rucksack, would stay there until it was safe to wear them again.

Downstairs, Dona Lidia placed a pot of coffee and a stack
of paper cups on the bar. The elderly lady ignored her guests
completely and commenced feeding her cats until Rocco
bounded down the stairs. Only then did she offer glazed croissants, guava juice and a fruit platter.

"*Muito obrigado!*" he boomed, tipping a coffee down his
throat and grabbing a croissant, a banana and two slices of
pineapple. "Come, people, we have a flight to catch. *Tchau*,
Dona Lidia, *até a proxima vez!*" He blew her a kiss and stomped
across the courtyard, Gil and Ann in his wake.

On the drive to the airport, Rocco seemed none the worse
for wear considering all he had consumed the previous evening.
While Gil was quiet and looked rather tired even in his freshly
pressed white shirt, Rocco was in an excellent mood, joking
and eating and delighted to be leaving the city behind.

Until he couldn't.

The pilot, Paolo, broke the news with an apologetic face.
The repairs to the aircraft were incomplete. One of the
replacement parts that arrived yesterday afternoon didn't fit.
He had ordered another which would be arriving today. If all
went smoothly, they could leave for Rio Negro in the morning.
Rocco's jovial good nature switched to raging aggression in an
instant. He demanded another plane. The pilot said this was
the only one available. Rocco swore at him, cursed the charter
company and told them he and the entire police force would
find a more professional alternative in the future. Paolo apolo-
gised again, but assured Rocco he was one of the few people
who could fly to the camp in question. They really had no
alternative but to wait till tomorrow.

The Manaus inspector was the only one disappointed by
the news. Ann had told Fátima she might be away for a couple
of nights. Now with this unexpected stopover in Manaus, that

could easily become four. Perhaps she should cut her losses and find a flight back to Soure. She was about to voice these thoughts when Rocco let out a spitting curse and punched a metal cabinet in the workshop. Tools clattered onto the floor and the other mechanics looked up from their work to gawp in shocked silence.

Gil stepped up to place a hand on Rocco's shoulder. "OK. If that's the situation, we have to deal with it," he said, his voice soothing and reasonable. "Thanks, Paolo. We'll see you tomorrow morning. Come, Rocco, let's get out of here and have some breakfast. We need to talk." He guided the big man away from the hangar and Ann followed at a distance, allowing them to converse in private.

They were around ten paces from the car when Rocco stopped and bellowed, his voice ringing off the airport buildings. "NO!"

Ann halted in her tracks.

Rocco dropped his voice to an angry growl through clenched teeth. "You don't understand anything about it! I have to get out of Manaus. If I go back into the city, I won't be flying anywhere tomorrow morning. You want to know why, Gil? Because they'll cut my throat."

8

"I have an arrangement with a certain organisation."

The three of them sat in a roadside café, drinking coffee and eating toasted *pão francês* with butter. Ann stirred her coffee, keeping her eyes on her breakfast. Gil said nothing, giving his colleague space to speak.

"It's different here. You either work with these people or you get nowhere. It's just the way we get things done." Rocco tore off a piece of bread with his teeth, his expression defensive. "All I'm saying is, don't judge me. You don't know what it's like."

Gil shrugged. "No, I don't know what it's like. I'm not judging you, Rocco. All I can see is that you are scared shitless and desperate to get out for a couple of days. I don't understand who's after you or why and until I do, it's going to be hard for us to trust each other. You can't give me names, I know that, but paint me a picture."

Rocco chewed and added two packets of sugar to his *pingado*. Then he looked directly into Ann's face. "And you? A juicy story about police corruption would do your career a whole lot of good, no?"

She gave him an even stare in return. "The reason I'm here is to report the story of what happened to the missing girl. I thought this would be a couple of days upriver investigating the circumstances of her disappearance. Staying over in Manaus wasn't part of the plan and neither is any kind of police exposé. But I appreciate you don't want to explain your circumstances in front of someone you've only just met. I'll go for a walk and come back in around half an hour."

Rocco reached out a hand and placed it on her own. "No, you won't. You sit right here. I'm being an asshole and I'm sorry." He closed his eyes for a second to compose himself. "As I said, I have an arrangement with a certain organisation. Between us, we manage what goes on in the city. I turn a blind eye to some of their activities, they help me with some of mine. Occasionally there will be an incident I cannot ignore. That's when they tip me off so I can arrange to be out of the city while they do whatever they have to do. Obviously, this is one of those times."

Gil tipped his head to one side, his eyebrows raised. "You're serious?"

"Come on, Gil, be honest. There's no way I would investigate the story of a missing prostitute from a logging camp up Rio Negro under normal circumstances. But because she came from Soure, my old mate Gil's patch, plus the fact I need to get out of town for a couple of days, it seemed like the gods dropped a solution into my hands. Yesterday's delay was bad news. But I hoped we could fly out this morning, guaranteeing my absence this afternoon. If I'm in the city today, I've broken my end of the bargain. These people don't do negotiations or explanations; they act."

They sat in silence for several minutes until Gil spoke. "Do you trust Paolo? I mean, you believe he's telling the truth?"

Rocco looked astounded. "The pilot Paolo? Hell, yes! He's not stupid and he understands how important this is to me. Or if he didn't before, he does now, after I left a dent in his tool cabinet. The plane isn't ready, I know that. It's not Paolo's fault, it's not the company's fault, but under no circumstances can I return to Manaus tonight. Look, why don't we stay here? I'll screen my calls and we can hide in an airport hotel. Tomorrow we fly out, if the gods are smiling, and when I get back, it's someone else's problem."

Ann looked at Gil, who was studying Rocco. She cleared her throat. "Can I say something? It's been an adventure for me to travel to Manaus. The thing is, I only planned to be away for a couple of nights to get the background for a story. If you don't mind, I'd prefer to take a flight home to Soure today and skip the Rio Negro. Sorry, Gil, but I'm trying to keep out of trouble and this situation has trouble written all over it."

Gil rubbed his face with his hands and threaded his fingers behind his head. "Yeah, that's probably best. I came here thinking it was a genuine investigation, but it turns out my friend just needed an excuse to leave town. I'll stay and fly upriver tomorrow to do my best for Alexandra Lemos. If I find anything or hear anything, I'll let you know."

Rocco bowed his head and shook it like an old cow wearing a bell. "Ann, the only risk here is me. Why don't you stay? You and Gil can take my car, go into the city and enjoy the festival. Go back to the same hotel; they always have rooms. Tomorrow morning, we fly upriver, ask our questions and fly back the next morning. Not a couple of days, but overnight. What do you say?"

Ann finished her coffee. "What difference does it make, Rocco? Why on earth does it matter to you if I stay or if I go?"

He shaded his face with his hand, hiding his expression from Gil. With a theatrical widening of his eyes, he indicated Maduro and batted his eyelashes. "I'd like you to stay, Ann. But to somebody else it makes a whole lot of difference."

Gil groaned in embarrassment and held out his hand. "Just give me the goddamned car keys."

Some of Gil's brittle tension could be explained by his driving a strange vehicle on unfamiliar roads. Some of it could not. Ann made no attempt at small talk and allowed him to negotiate the route into the city with full concentration. He used the Satnav to find the odd little hotel from the night before. He parked in the same alleyway as Rocco had done and Ann hauled her rucksack from the back seat. Gil left his case in the boot while they went to arrange rooms, but Ann never let her pack out of her sight. They returned through the same gates to see Dona Lidia listening to the radio, surrounded her cats. The sense of déjà vu was eerie. Until she looked up. The minute Ann saw her face, she knew something was wrong.

Gil greeted her politely and enquired about the rooms. Ann observed her body language. The old lady shook her head sorrowfully, opened her palms and placed a hand on her heart. Gil's gestures became more and more agitated until finally he turned on his heel and stormed back in Ann's direction. His face was thunderous.

"She says the hotel is full and we can't stay here tonight. Some people got to her and I think I can guess who they are. This is insane. We'll just go back to the airport, lock ourselves in our rooms and fly out in the morning. It's the only thing to do."

"*Com licença, o senhor?*" The elderly lady came down the path with something in her hand. Her hand shook almost as much as her voice. "You cannot stay here, I'm sorry. But around the corner is an apartment which belongs to my sister. She's away for the festival so you and your lady are welcome to use it tonight. Drop the keys in the post box tomorrow morning.

Please, *o senhor*, for your own sakes, don't come to Shangrillá this evening. Keep away."

Gil took the keys and began to thank the woman but she backed off, scuttling up the path to her cats. He glanced up at the windows overlooking the courtyard and strode out of the gates. Back on the street, he handed the key to Ann.

"It's over there." He indicated some wrought-iron gates. "Wait till I get my case and we'll go in together." She stood on the street watching Gil fade into the darkness of the alleyway, alert to every window and doorway from where she could be observed. Instead of the sound of a wheelie case on the cobbles, she heard a shocked curse. "*Filho da puta!*"

Even as she ran across the street, Ann was reaching for her knife, wishing she had something more effective at her disposal. Her eyes took a moment to adjust to the overshadowed alleyway. Gil was standing with his back to the wall, staring at his vehicle. Ann crouched, her weapon at the ready and called to him.

"What is it?"

With a haunted expression, he pointed a finger at the spot where Ann's pack had been sitting around ten minutes ago. She crept closer, conscious of alcoves and balconies where people might be lurking.

Gil took out his phone and illuminated the torch, taking the guesswork out of deciphering what was inside. In the back seat of Rocco's car, leaning against the window was a human shape with a black hood over its head. As Gil drew the light down the vehicle, Ann's breath caught when she saw rust-coloured blood seeping down the window.

A snapping sound drew her attention. Gil was donning plastic gloves. He handed her his gun. "Cover me. Whoever it is might still be alive."

Ann scanned the alley in both directions and looked up and behind her. Not a window was open nor a balcony occupied.

Gil opened the car door and the body tumbled out, hitting the stones with a dull, nauseating thud. Rather than pull off the hood, Gil checked for a pulse. He shook his head, snapped off his gloves and pulled out his phone, muttering. "Of course he's dead. No one wearing a black silk hood is likely to live. Goddamn you, Rocco Delgado."

The furious telephone conversation between Gil and his Manaus counterpart occupied only part of Ann's attention. She circled the car, gun cocked, making sure there were no other surprises inside or out. With extreme caution, she opened the boot, jumping back as the door opened. Inside was Gil's suitcase and standard police equipment, but nothing else.

Gil's voice rose in agitation. "*Por amor do Deus*, Rocco, I'm a police officer! I can't do that! All right, all right, but only until you get here. We'll take cover and I'll send you the address. You'd better get here fast because this bullshit is your responsibility and you're going to clean it up."

He discarded his gloves, scanned the alleyway and held out his hand for his weapon. Ann gave it to him, asking questions with her eyes.

"I don't know," he whispered. "I just don't know. We have to leave things as they are until Rocco arrives. Thank you for covering me and now let's get off the street." He taped off the entrance to the alleyway and created another police barrier three metres behind the car. Then he led her out of the gloomy back street, checking for any signs of pursuit. Ann looked over her shoulder at the pile of rubbish and the dead body just dragged from Rocco's car.

"Gil?"

"Rocco's problem, not ours. I have reported it to the authorities and we should keep our distance. Let's get inside. I should never have brought you to this place."

He unlocked the gate with a little fumbling and led the way to a ground floor apartment towards the rear. Unlike their accommodation last night, this courtyard was well-tended and filled with vibrant greenery and ostentatious blooms. The neighbourly atmosphere calmed Ann's nerves and locked gates added to that sense of security. The apartment itself was cool and shady and when Gil opened the shutters, it revealed its true colours. Every wall was painted a different shade. Carmine, bottle green, buttercup yellow and ochre, with a scattering of glazed tiles gleaming from the kitchen wall. If this had been a holiday apartment, she would have loved it. But this was no holiday.

Ann dumped her rucksack beside Gil's suitcase and took a profound inhalation. The apartment had a feminine touch and as such lent a sense of protection. As much as anyone could feel safe after finding a dead body in a recently vacated vehicle.

"Gil?"

He returned from checking the rest of the apartment. "Yes?"

"What the hell is going on here?"

He reached a hand behind his head to massage his neck. "My theory, but I hope to God I'm wrong, is that Rocco has made a pact with the devil." He sat down at the dining table and Ann joined him. "Various organised crime gangs operate in Manaus. Some have infiltrated factories, others control supply boats, and of course several of them manufacture and distribute drugs. Only one has a finger in every pie and a reputation for ruthless punishment of its enemies. Based on Rocco's description of his arrangement with 'a certain organisation', I believe he's working with O Cabrito."

Ann recognised the name with a chill shiver but pretended she didn't. "A goat?"

"*The* goat. The man who covers his victims' faces with a black silk hood. If they're lucky, he shoots them in the head. The people in his network are everywhere, all wearing black silk shirts. That guy Rocco saw last night? He was a warning."

"No wonder he's terrified. To get a body into his car that fast, they must have been following us."

"Did you see the way the body fell?" Gil asked.

"Yes. Limp, mobile and still warm."

"Exactly. Whoever it was, they killed him while we were in the other place talking to Dona Lidia."

"Which means they're likely to be outside right now."

Neither spoke for several minutes.

Gil rested his chin on his hands. "Whatever happens tonight, you must stay here. If I'd known Rocco was entangled up in all this crap ..." He groaned, closing his eyes for an instant. "I'm sorry. You shouldn't be here. Tomorrow morning, we take a taxi to the airport and you fly home to Soure."

His expression was sombre. Ann didn't argue. "Why doesn't Rocco tell you the truth? You obviously know what's going on and you're old friends. Surely he trusts you?"

Gil exhaled a humourless laugh. "The beach bumpkin who rides a water buffalo instead of a police bike? The inspector who spends his summers fining people for littering? What do I know about organised crime?"

"The fact you nailed a serial killer no one else in Brazil or the States could touch makes you a bit more than a litter cop, I'd say."

"That's because you know the background. Rocco and his colleagues have no interest in our part of the country. In their eyes, they police a vast, dangerous city while I swing in a hammock eating ice-cream. But at least I'm not under the ..."

A buzzer interrupted him and Gil found the intercom.

"*Sim?*"

"Let me in, Gil. Now!" Rocco's voice was panicky and urgent. Gil pressed the button to release the external gates. When he turned to Ann, his face had lost all its colour.

9

R occo was on his phone when Gil opened the front door. He rushed inside and locked the door behind him. With a quick scan of the room, he continued his conversation in hissing, angry tones.

"No, of course I don't take him for a fool. I just need to explain why … no, listen to me, for the love of God. The plane will be ready tomorrow and I'll … of course I can't take a boat! I don't have that much time to waste on a missing whore. Just call off those bastards and let me speak to him, OK? What do you mean? Now you're taking *me* for a fool and … what, now? OK, OK, I'll be there in an hour. Call them off, you hear? I said I'll be there. Yes, alone." He ended the call and went into the kitchen to wash his face and swallow two glasses of water.

Ann and Gil watched him from the doorway, waiting. He wiped his mouth and went to speak but the beep of his phone interrupted. He read the message, exhaled a huge breath and kissed the screen. When he opened his eyes, his expression of relief changed when he saw Gil's face.

"I know and I'm sorry. But I've fixed things. No more bodies in the car, no more aggressive tails, it's all good. A friend of a friend will get rid of the dead guy and clean up my car while I have a conversation. My associates want to talk and I'm meeting them in an hour, but I have to go alone. Then we stick to the plan and fly out tomorrow, OK?"

Gil's voice was icy. "You're telling me an inspector from the Manaus force is going to meet a gangland boss on his own and expects to walk out of there unscathed? Where's your goddamned head? Wake up, Rocco! Whatever deal you made can be cancelled in a heartbeat. So can you. Who was the guy in the back of your car?"

"How should I know?" Rocco's shoulders reached his ears. "Some nobody, I guess. I didn't see his face under that hood. Could have been anyone." His gaze was evasive.

"Remember who you're talking to, *Inspector* Delgado. That nobody was wearing a black silk hood? I know as well as you do what that means. These aren't amateurs who snatch any old beggar off the street, kill him and shove them in the back seat of your car. This is the work of O Cabrito. Drop the outrage because I already worked it out this morning. Whoever the dead man was, he had some significance to you. That was a message and you understand it only too well. Who was he?"

Rocco's expression was mulish and he kept his mouth closed.

It was Ann's turn to speak, if only to save time. "Here's an educated guess. The guy was a grass, someone you've been leaning on for information. He probably didn't know all that much or what he did know was deliberately fed to him. They sussed he was a leak and used him to funnel false information in your direction. Killing him and leaving his body in your car serves three purposes. They let you know they were aware of his role all the time, plus they disposed of the grass and frightened the shit out of you. These guys are pretty good."

"What kind of a journalist are you?" Rocco scowled, his brows knitting.

Gil answered in her stead. "A smart one. Listen to me, if you're going to meet this man, I'm covering you."

The fear returned to Rocco's eyes. "Not in a million years, *amigo*. This is my mess and I accept the consequences. But dragging you in means you'll end up dead. Not might, not maybe, not possibly, you *will* end up dead. I'm doing this on my own, I mean it."

The ensuing battle of wills raged on for another fifteen minutes. Ann went into the kitchen and made coffee. While she was there, she noted the kitchen door. Another entrance. Or exit. Just as a precaution, she took the key out of the lock and put it in her jeans pocket.

She took the tray of coffees into the dining room and Gil tipped his down in one.

"I'm leaving now to position myself on Rocco's route. We've agreed I should follow at a distance. He's going to leave here in around half an hour and walk to his meeting. My role is to hover nearby and only intervene if there is no alternative. Ann, I know you can handle yourself but I have to ask you to stay out of things this time. These people are not a bunch of small-town Praia do Pesqueiro drug farmers. We're talking an international cartel with a reputation for violence. I can only devote my full concentration to covering Rocco if I know you're safe. Will you promise me to stay here until we return?"

She looked from one man to the other. Rocco was seated, wearing a creased and sweat-stained black linen shirt, stirring sugar into his coffee. Gil stood, his white shirt as pristine as if it was still on the mannequin, his hand resting on a dining-room chair. Both stared at her intently.

"Relax, guys. I know when I'm way out of my league. If I was stupid enough to try tailing Rocco, that could put both of you in danger. You don't have to worry, Gil, as I told you before, I can obey orders."

"Thank you." Gil's gaze was intense and she could not be sure if he was projecting gratitude or testing her veracity.

"We should be back in around two hours," said Rocco. "If not, wait until seven o'clock, then call Dona Lidia and tell her what happened. She knows what to do. Gil, it's time to rock 'n' roll."

Interesting. Dona Lidia's hotel and bar were just around the corner, but the advice was to call her, not to go in person. *It's almost as if they planned to lock me in.*

Like a true method actor, she could play Etta Place to their Butch and Sundance. She gulped and clasped her hands at her throat. "Please take care, Gil. And you too, Rocco. I'm going to be pacing the apartment until you walk through that door safe and unharmed. Don't take any risks, you hear." It was all she could do to avoid the Texan accent.

Rocco finished his coffee and pushed back his chair. "We're professionals, Ann, we know what we're doing. Anyway, I need a shit. *Tchau*, Gil, and thank you for being a true friend." He went into the small bathroom and closed the door.

For a moment, Ann's eyes locked on to Gil's, trying to express all she wanted to say through her gaze. Then from the bathroom, Rocco let out an explosive fart and the tension was broken. She crossed the room, grabbed Gil by the shoulders and kissed him on the lips.

"Come back," she whispered. "That's all I ask."

He stared into her eyes for another beat, then gave a quick nod and was gone. She locked the door after him and looked at an oil painting of the Madonna on the opposite wall. "Take care of him," she whispered. "He matters."

When it came time for Rocco to leave, there was no such emotional farewell. He punctuated his instruction with a finger pointed at her and said, "You. Stay. Here," as if she was a

Labrador. To her complete lack of surprise, he took the keys and locked her in. She instantly dropped to the floor, looking through the five millimetre gap between the ground and the door. Two shadows indicated Rocco was standing outside, listening. Ann performed her role as expected. She reached up and tried the door handle, once, twice and then released a little pathetic cry. She sniffed and faked some sobbing sounds, her face turned from the door. Then she flattened herself to the ground to watch the two shadows pacing away. In a second, she was on her feet. She grabbed her backpack, pulled out the key to the kitchen door, unlocked it and left. She was gambling on the fact that the iron gates permitting street access to the leafy compound had some kind of egress button.

She was right. The clanging of the gates still echoed after Rocco's departure and Ann scuttled into the shadows, leaning to see which direction he had gone. His tall frame was visible a hundred metres down the pavement. Due to his height, he wasn't hard to spot and Ann could afford to hang back a little. That was handy because she needed to know Gil Maduro was ahead, not behind her. Ann would be hyper-alert for anyone else following the big man. She tucked her hair under her white baseball cap, pressed the button to release the gates and stepped out into the street.

As soon she was in the presence of other people, she altered her posture, keeping her head down and trudging heavily as if weighed down by her weekly shopping. She stopped by a fruit stall and bought some bananas, with a quick look over the vendor's shoulder to judge Rocco's progress. It took another three crowded streets before she spotted Gil Maduro at a café table, reading a newspaper. Inside, she smiled at his mussed-up hair and man-spreading posture. He looked like every other guy in the café. A poster advertising a concert caught her attention and she stood, half hidden behind a placard, reading but not reading.

If she could keep Maduro in her sights, she had no need to watch Rocco. She crossed the street and asked two teenagers for directions to the Opera House. As she listened to the explanation, Maduro folded his paper, left a coin on the table and sauntered off down the street. Ann thanked the girls and walked back the way she came, as the girls had advised. Once out of their sight, she crossed the road and followed in Maduro's footsteps. It was not ideal, as the sun beat down on this side of the street, leaving her exposed. As soon as she spotted Maduro, strolling past café tables apparently absorbed by his phone, she crossed to the shady side. Her intention was to keep the tail in view at all times. That was when she spotted the tail's tail.

A man in a black T-shirt and black jeans with a shaggy mane of hair was examining tourist trinkets on a street stall. A blind man galloping by on a horse could have seen that guy was not a tourist. His attitude was dismissive when the stallholder offered his assistance and he rotated his head to assess his surroundings as if he was Robocop. *I see you, but you won't see me.* Ann bought a slushy smoothie which acted as part of her disguise and added its own cooling effect.

The domino effect was not wasted on her. Rocco in black, tailed by Gil in white, followed in turn by the hairy guy in black, with a woman wearing white on his heels. *Who's watching me?* she wondered, bearing in mind they might be wearing any colour of the rainbow. She waited until the shaggy-haired guy moved on, trying to keep both him and Gil Maduro in sight. Rocco had melted into the crowds. Ann picked up her pace, overtaking the guy in black and powering on until Gil Maduro was a stone's throw away. Only then did she march into a restaurant, as if she was late for an appointment.

She stood in the doorway, pretending to look for her imaginary friend and then turned to look through the window. Sure enough, the black T-shirt guy paced by at speed. Ann noted the tattoos. A waiter asked if she wanted a table and Ann told him she was waiting for a friend. She stood there another sixty seconds, her eyes assessing every pedestrian as a likely gangland employee. Not a single individual in the street aroused her suspicions. It was risky to wait too long or she would lose her mark. She thanked the waiter, left the restaurant and hurried after the man following Gil who was following Rocco.

A sharp-eyed scan of the street told her he'd disappeared. Up side streets, on the opposite pavement, even behind her she could see no trace of the man in the black T-shirt. Panic was her enemy and she breathed deeply to remain calm. She stood under the dappled shade of a palm tree, her head bowed as if she were gawping at a phone, and collected herself into a state of focus. Without actively looking, she absorbed the vibrations in her environment. That was much more easily achieved on a deserted beach, but even here, in the melee of downtown Manaus, stillness opened her mind to whatever impulses would come.

Traffic noise and people's chatter flowed in waves, like the sound of the sea, and her sense of smell was all but overpowered. Still as a human statue, she extended her awareness like a radar, seeking areas of intensity. Not the taxi driver yelling at a motorcyclist, not the teenage boys posing in front of the café, not the argument at the bus stop, but other knots of tension. Her attention was drawn to a young woman, slumped against a wall, her eyes dull and her agony tangible. Ann recognised the desperation of a drug addict and tore her gaze away.

Something over the street caught her attention and she replaced her sunglasses. A white shirt emerged from behind some street musicians, moving fast and with a purpose. Gil Maduro walked past a pizzeria called La Concettina and slipped into an alleyway between the restaurant and a hairdressing salon. The guy in the black T-shirt detached himself from the shadow of a bus stop and melted into the same darkness where Gil had disappeared.

She made a series of calculations and walked past the pitiful girl, dropping a few reais into her skirt. *"Boa sorte,"* she whispered. *Good luck.*

The move served two purposes: a professional tail would not stop to donate to a beggar and now this destitute woman had enough money to buy whatever she needed. Ann walked to the next crossing and waited, her hands supporting her rucksack, as if it was a piggybacking child. The pack was not that heavy, but any attempt to slash it and she would wield her own knife. A swell of people crushed beside her as they waited for the lights to change. Her vulnerability and raw naïveté drew her down a vortex of memory, when she'd stood in front of six men, each one ready to kill her. All she had then were her wits and that was all she had now.

Quick thinking had served her on multiple occasions, but this was a whole different landscape. If Rocco was meeting O Cabrito or any one of his lieutenants, the Manaus inspector had as much power as a fly in spider's web. Unless he was useful to them, he'd never escape alive. Nor would anyone who followed him. The lights changed and the crowd spilled over the tarmac. Ann walked at a leisurely pace, past the pizzeria and hair salon without a glance. Then she took a right, found the service lane behind the businesses and switched her white cap for a black beanie.

The rubbish-strewn alley was silent. Not even feral cats chanced their luck. Ann tuned into her environment, all senses alert. A ventilator hummed at the back of the pizzeria, wafting cooking smells into the air, a pleasanter scent than the putrid stench of garbage bags. From the open windows of the hairdressing salon, female voices chatted and laughed above the blast of a hairdryer. The pizzeria was a more likely venue for a rendezvous – surely they had watched *The Godfather* – so Ann paced silently past the hairdressers, keeping close to the wall in the shade of a fire escape. She noted the number of cigarette butts around her feet and paused to observe the pattern. If the smokers had come from the hairdressers, it was more likely that the butts would be closer together and nearer the wall. The scattered and random configuration suggested they had been thrown from higher up.

Ann stepped away from the building, looking up at the fire escape. There was a platform on the next floor with a chair in the corner and an open door. She strained to make out any sound coming from within, but the buzz of conversation, the ventilator and the clattering of crockery from the pizzeria made it impossible. She put a foot on the bottom step, testing whether her weight would cause the metal structure to creak and give her away. There was the slightest ring, but barely audible amidst the rest of the noise.

Cat-like, Ann ascended the steps, her attention divided between the open door above and potential observers below. Six steps from the platform, she crouched so that only her eyes and the top of her head were visible, and peered over the edge. The interior was dimly lit and she could hear no sound. She counted to sixty and then eased herself onto the platform, still in a runner's crouch. From that position, she could see the door led onto a kitchen. There was a coffee machine, a cooker and a large Formica table, cluttered with cups, glasses and a packet of Marlboro Reds. She took a step in, her breath shallow. On the right of the cooker was another door. This one was closed but through the thin wood, a bass voice was audible and a sudden burst of male laughter frazzled her nerves. Ann crossed the room on tiptoes and knelt to look through the keyhole. She could see a patch of sunlight and part of a man's back, but precious little else. The bass voice rumbled again and she judged the speaker to be on the other side of the room.

With a slow and steady hand, she depressed the door

handle, easing it open a millimetre at a time. The voice continued and the rumble became coherent words.

"... only as good as his word. Therefore we must assume, seeing as your word is worthless, so are you. Not only did you fail to keep your end of our agreement, but you assured Toni you would come here alone. Instead, you brought along another cop. I'm disappointed, Delgado, very disappointed indeed. This afternoon, my boys must dispose of two bodies when they should be out enjoying themselves at the festival. It's a shame you've spoilt their fun."

In the silence after his speech came a muffled protest, followed by more male laughter.

"I didn't quite catch that, Delgado. But if I take off your gag, you'll only splutter the same old excuses and I have heard enough. The situation is quite simple. I told you to get out of town two days ago. You are still here."

Ann inched open the door so she could peer through the crack. Her breath caught as she took in the scene. Half a dozen men stood with their backs to her, watching the owner of the bass tones pace around two people sitting in chairs. Ann couldn't see their faces because both their heads were covered with black silk hoods. One big man in a crumpled black linen shirt, the other shorter and wearing white. She froze, recalling Gil's words. *No one wearing a black silk hood is likely to live.*

The speaker continued to pace and as he faced his audience, Ann got her first look at O Cabrito. For someone with such a reputation for ruthlessness and brutality, he had the air of a kindly uncle. The silver streaks in his black hair glinted in the sunlight, and his tanned skin made his teeth seem even whiter as he smiled. "You see my point? As a case of failing to obey orders, it's clear cut. One might even say it's black and white." The watching men, all wearing black shirts, burst into laughter. "Now, ordinarily I wouldn't even waste my time explaining why we must execute you, because I would have thought it was obvious. But there's something I'd like to know. Toni."

The shaggy-haired man Ann had seen in the street moved behind the two chairs and removed the bag from Rocco's head. Ann bit her lip. His nose was bleeding and his eyes wild. Toni unbuckled the ball gag and Rocco heaved for breath. O Cabrito jerked his chin towards Gil and Toni repeated the procedure. Ann could see no visible signs of injury but pain was evident on his face. Both men's arms were tied behind their backs.

"I have a question for you. Toni tells me you are travelling with a woman, a *gringa*. Tell me who she is."

Rocco shot a glance at Gil who gave his interrogator a dead-eyed stare.

"She's a journalist," blurted Rocco.

"Is she really? How fascinating. And her name?" His question was met with silence.

Again Rocco looked at his friend, but Gil kept his mouth shut. Rocco filled in the gaps. "Her name is Ann Sheldon. She comes from Soure, like my colleague. She's covering the story of a girl missing from a timber camp in Rio Negro."

"I see. So she's a friend of yours?" He addressed Gil. "Or perhaps more than a friend? Toni said you two seemed rather close."

Gil kept his focus on O Cabrito and said nothing.

"Forgive the personal questions." O Cabrito flashed his white smile again. "I just wondered how well you knew the young lady."

Finally Gil spoke. "It's none of your business."

His words caused consternation among the group of men, but O Cabrito simply rubbed his hands together and nodded. "None of my business. No, strictly speaking, it isn't. But if she is who we think she is, some professional associates of mine would be very interested in locating her."

"I will never tell you where she is."

O Cabrito laughed, his head thrown back and mouth open to the ceiling, gesturing to Gil as if he was the greatest wit on the planet. The henchmen joined in, roaring their mirth until their boss silenced them with a flick of his hand.

"Oh, my friend, you are quite the comedian. We know exactly where she is and as soon as we have finished with you, we're going to invite her to join us. Don't you worry, we'll take good care of her until my associates get here. After that, I'm afraid, I cannot say. All I wanted for you was confirmation of her identity."

"It isn't her." Gil's voice was tight. "I know what you're thinking because I thought the same, but I can tell you for sure it is not the same woman."

Rocco's head snapped between the man in the suit and Gil Maduro.

O Cabrito steepled his fingers beneath his chin. He'd obviously studied every Bond villain's gestures in preparation for his role. "Perhaps you didn't ask the right questions. Or maybe you lacked the right kind of inducement. Whereas Toni is an expert at getting answers. As you're no use to us, we'll say goodbye to you now and ask the lady in question. Toni, replace their hoods, if you please."

Toni stepped forward, the gags and silk hoods in his hands.

In the space of a second, Ann evaluated her options. She'd been here before and she'd never forgotten how it felt. Leaving a colleague to the mercy of a sadistic gangland boss haunted her nightly. Never again. She pulled off her beanie, released her hair and swung open the door. Holding out her arms as if she were about to burst into song, she spoke in a loud, clear voice.

"What do you want to know, O Cabrito? Because the lady in question is right here."

10

Seven men pointed a gun in her direction. Ann kept her arms open wide. Not hands in the air, like a supplicant, but broad and confident, like a diva stepping into the spotlight. In her peripheral vision, uncertain looks flashed around the room but she kept her stare fixed on the man in the suit.

He stared right back. The silence stretched long enough for Ann's arms to tire. Eventually, he broke into a shit-eating grin.

"Well, hello there. Please, come in; sit down and thank you for dropping by. Toni, a chair for our guest." He gave his henchmen a filthy look and his tone turned scathing. "Put those guns down. That's no way to greet a lady. What kind of idiots are you, locking the door *after* the house is robbed?"

Ann floated her arms down to rest at her sides and waited till all weapons were holstered before walking into the room, her chin held high. O Cabrito gave her the full once-over with an approving nod then his face twisted into a scowl as Toni dumped a wooden kitchen chair next to Rocco.

"Not there, you donkey! Give it to me." He placed the chair beside the window, facing away from the two prisoners, dusted it with his handkerchief and invited her to sit. With an expression of disbelief, he glared at Toni, who dashed into the kitchen and brought out another chair for his boss, wiping it with the hem of his T-shirt.

Without a word of thanks, O Cabrito sat opposite her and crossed his legs at the ankle. "If I had any doubts, now I am convinced. No one else could or would walk in here like that. You're pretty comfortable in a lion's den, no?"

"Lion, wolf, goat, it's all the same to me. Not one of them is immune to snake venom." Ann held his gaze, amused to see he wore coloured contact lenses. Green with gold flakes. A man who took his image seriously. Presumably the next step would be rectangular pupils.

"A snake." He stroked his chin. "Yes, one bite and you slither away to hide under a rock, leaving your victims to die a slow, painful death."

She controlled her breathing and reminded herself who she was talking to. "From what I've heard, I'd say that is more your area of expertise."

He tipped his head, as if acknowledging a compliment. "And here you are, out in the open, like a fruit falling from the tree. It's been a long time since luck walked in through the back door."

"Ha!" She forced a laugh and clasped her hands together. "Come on, *o senhor*, you're smarter than that. You think I'm here to offer myself in exchange for those two?" She grinned and jerked her head in the direction of Rocco and Gil. With her right forefinger, she pulled down the lower lid of her right eye. "You're a businessman and I'm here to do business. When luck strikes, the greedy or the stupid snatch what's on the table. Those with patience and brains play the longer game. Luck is not lightning, it can strike more than once."

All fidgeting and shuffling in the room ceased.

O Cabrito's green-gold eyes assessed her and his lower jaw

moved back and forth as he thought. Now Ann understood how he'd earned his moniker. Each time his jaw slid forward, his bottom teeth protruded, exactly like a ruminant.

"Why would I do business with a poisonous snake when I can earn the reward for her skin?"

"Toni?" Ann spoke with authority. "In the kitchen, you'll find my backpack under the table. It's OK, none of the explosives are triggered. Bring it in here, will you?"

The shaggy-haired goon was already on his way before he remembered to check with his boss. O Cabrito gave an irritable nod.

Ann leaned forward, directing all her energy into those green-gold eyes. "My skin is valuable. That much we know. But another part of me is a goldmine." She tapped her temple three times. "What if I told you all I know? What if I told you the routes, the connections and the gatekeepers? What if I gave the goat the advantage over the lion?"

She reached out a hand to accept her backpack from Toni, who held it at arm's length. Ann grasped it and placed at her feet without breaking eye contact with the old goat. Several henchmen drew their weapons, but O Cabrito held up a hand to stall them.

"*Esperem-aí*! Toni!" He directed his right-hand man to stand behind Ann and she heard the click of his safety catch. This would be either the performance of her life or her swansong.

She reached her arms behind her head, interlacing her fingers and leaning back to stretch her neck, making herself as vulnerable as she could. The message would be read as the opposite. This woman was not afraid. Therefore she had a secret weapon.

"You're a success, *o senhor*, and I respect that. You have many admirers and also plenty of envious enemies. People in powerful positions always do. What keeps them in position is knowledge. That's where I can help." She tapped her foot to her backpack. "In here, I have a little black book which contains all you need to know. Now, what's stopping you from shooting me and taking the book? I'll tell you. Without me, that information is meaningless. Only I know the logic behind the system and how it connects. So what's it to be? Sell a cow or take over the farm?"

Ann sensed eyes boring into the back her head. Although she couldn't see him, she felt the heat of Gil Maduro's gaze like a laser.

O Cabrito's jaw worked as he dropped his head to stare at Ann under his brows. "You would work for me?"

"Let me be clear. I'm moving on. I will tell you all about my ex-employers because they damn well deserve it. You're no fool, but neither am I. Once you've milked the cow for all she's got, you could call the slaughterman." Ann shook her head, smiling. "No, O Cabrito, I don't work for anyone but myself. The deal is this: you get the little black book. When I'm at a safe distance, I'll give you the key. The information is useless to me, but for you, it's a seam of gold. I'm happy to trade that for a safe passage out of Brazil."

The old goat shook his head like a pendulum. "As you said, I'm no fool. What, you hand over a piece of shit and fly away like a pigeon? I don't think so. There's no information you can give me I don't already know. Good bluff, I credit you with that. Before we say goodbye, tell me your real name."

"Names. Real names. I'm sure I wrote a poem about that very subject." Ann raised her hands to the gunmen and pointed to her backpack, raising her eyebrows for permission. O Cabrito beckoned the men closer and Ann inched her fingers into the front pocket, drawing out a little black book, filled with snatches of poetry. She held it up and rotated it in the air, demonstrating its innocence. She flicked through the pages and stopped near the end. She read the words in English and repeated them in Portuguese.

"The lady knows her poison
And what she can afford
The lady wields her weapon
Like a Damoclean sword"

It was a woeful ditty, improvised in desperation and Ann hoped never to repeat it.

O Cabrito sneered, unimpressed. "Very nice. And this is how you prove your worth?"

"You haven't heard the title. In English, it's called 'The Wandering Spider'. Or in Portuguese, *A Aranha Errante*."

A hush fell over the room. Someone behind her swallowed.

"No information you don't already know, O Cabrito? If you're familiar with the true identity of *A Aranha Errante*, then I have nothing to offer. Go ahead, call them and name your price for my head." She closed her book and clasped it to her chest as if it contained prayers.

He lowered his head once more, his teeth jutting below his top lip. "Word on the street is The Wandering Spider is dead. Shot in Fortaleza in an ambush."

"Word on the street is wrong. I can tell you who she is and where to find her. Your worst enemy, delivered on a plate. That must earn me a caipirinha, at the very least. Come closer, this is for your ears only." She wrapped her arms behind her chair and clasped her hands together, indicating she was defenceless. She leaned forward, face tilted upwards as if ready for a kiss.

O Cabrito flicked a glance at Toni and the rest of the muscle-bound macho men then bent towards Ann.

"*Quem é?*" he murmured.

"Lusita Ferra is alive and well, managing her operation as well as she ever did. She's scaled things down since the Fortaleza bust but she's rebuilding her empire. Last I heard she was in Barcelona. No, she's not enjoying a sangria on the Ramblas or gazing at a Gaudí. She's a little over two thousand kilometres away from here in Venezuela. They say she spends the weekends on her island and she's still catching flies. You're welcome."

She sat back and folded her arms.

The green-gold eyes sparkled and his face cracked into a genuine, rather than showman smile. "Put those guns away. Let's celebrate a new partnership! Come, 'Ann Sheldon', we are going to have a party! Toni, call A Tasca and tell them we want a *feijoada* for ten."

"Twelve," said Ann, nodding in the direction of the two cops. "Let's face it, who wants to dump a body on a Friday afternoon when we could be drinking aguardente instead? They're far more use to us alive. Tell me something, did you ever meet El Chapo?" She swung her backpack onto her shoulders as if the fate of Rocco and Gil did not concern her, keeping her gaze on the boss.

"Yeah, OK. Let them go, we've got better things to do. Delgado, you'd better learn a lesson from this. Next time you let me down, you'll end up meeting the waters." He accepted the applause at his own joke. "*Vamos*, let's eat. Toni, if you don't lock that kitchen door in future, I swear I'll use a *martelo* on your balls." He held out an arm and Ann slipped her hand into the crook of his armpit. "Not El Chapo personally, but I met Coronel twice. Like you, she's very smart for her age."

Ann let her little black book fall to the floor and knelt to retrieve it. "Oops, we wouldn't want to lose that, would we?" She looked up at O Cabrito.

He smiled down at her as if she was his favourite daughter. "No, we wouldn't. Because that's your insurance policy. Without that, you're nothing more than a bargaining chip. Are you hungry?"

11

The waiters at A Tasca bowed and scraped as if their party was visiting royalty. A large table was set with a white cloth in the centre of the room and O Cabrito took his place at its head, with Ann on his left and Toni to his right. All the aggression towards Rocco and Gil seemed to have been forgotten, and one of the gunmen offered them both a seat, patting Rocco on the shoulder. Ann was careful to avoid Gil Maduro's eyes.

Wine and beer flowed freely and it took two men to heave a huge pot of black beans into the centre of their table. One of the waiters took each guest's plate to add a ladle or two of the thick bean stew. Then the side dishes arrived: white rice, *farofa*, slices of orange and some wilted greens. Finally, with great ceremony, the main course made its entrance. Three waiters circulated the table with huge skewers of roasted pork, beef and goat, each half a metre long, slicing off pieces directly onto each diner's plate. In combination with the *chouriço*, smoked bacon and air-dried salt beef in the stew itself, Ann was about to consume more red meat in one meal than she had in a year.

O Cabrito lifted one finger and the owner was at his elbow

in a second. He muttered an instruction. Two glasses of aguardente appeared and a waiter scooped out some bean juice from the stew to fill them up.

The old goat lifted his glass and spoke softly, just to her. "To you, *a ruiva*, and here's to a great future for both of us!"

"To our future!" Ann knocked the chunky little shot glass against his and drank. It was potent alcohol warmed with feijoada stock and exactly what her stomach craved after the stresses of the last twelve hours. "It's not real, you know."

His head whipped in her direction, his voice harsh. "What's not real?"

Everyone at the table tensed.

Ann brushed her hand through her long coppery locks. "The hair, O Cabrito. That's all. I'm 100% real, but this is henna."

His expression softened and he reached out a hand to stroke her hair. "Real or not, it's beautiful. I have a soft spot for redheads." He became aware of the whole party staring. "Eat your food, you morons!" He cut into a slice of pork belly. "This is one of the finest restaurants in Manaus, you know. We have Michelin-starred places everywhere, but this joint is authentic. Even though the décor reminds me of a urinal."

With a glance around at the blue-tiled surroundings, Ann laughed. "At least it doesn't smell like one. The food looks incredible. And the aguardente is as authentic as it gets."

"Are you sleeping with him?" O Cabrito waved a knife in the direction of Gil Maduro. "He's got that possessive air when he looks at you. What kind of a woman sleeps with a cop?"

Ann put down her cutlery and swung her torso to face this vain old brute. "As he already told you, it's none of your business. Understand this: I will give you inside knowledge in return for letting me go. That is all. Whistle as long as you like, but I'm not one of your sheepdogs."

On the opposite side of the table, Toni gave her a furious

stare as he gnawed on a slice of beef. She could see they'd never be friends but she had to show him respect.

O Cabrito chewed on like a ruminant. Ann returned to her meal, hoping the roasted flesh she was eating was another old goat. She was on dangerous ground and if she stumbled, she'd take Rocco and Gil down with her.

"Here's the truth," she lied. "All my life, I've wanted to visit Manaus. It's an incredible city. I mean it. *Incrível!* Everything about it is hard to believe; rivers, jungle, architecture, landscape and infrastructure. We were supposed to go upriver and those two were furious when the plane broke down. But me? I was delighted! I get to explore a little of Manaus. You're lucky to live in such an extraordinary location. Toni, have you always lived here?"

He seemed startled by the question and shook his shaggy head. "I come from the south. Bahia."

"Do you miss the sea?"

Toni gave her a crooked grin. "I miss the surfing. Coming out of the water with salty skin, the air on the ocean, it's special. Here, the rivers are exciting, but yeah, I do miss the sea. My brother is …" He broke off at a look from his boss.

The beans and rich meat weighed heavy on Ann's stomach so she took another slug of red wine, smiling at everyone down the table. Rocco's seat was empty. She helped herself to another portion of orange slices to enable her to look out of the window. Rocco's distinctive large, bearded physique was visible, pacing outside as he talked on his mobile.

"How long were you a snake in the grass, Ann Sheldon? To know so much, you were part of the inner circle, I think?" O Cabrito refilled her wine glass.

This slice of goat was extra chewy. Ann nodded, her mouth full, aware of Rocco re-entering the room. He grabbed a beer and glugged it all in one go, to the applause of O Cabrito's men. He held up a hand, fingers splayed in acknowledgement and fell into his seat. His eyes locked on to Ann's and he held his arms out, wobbling from side to side, and then gave her the thumbs-up.

She got it. The plane was ready.

"Yes, I was. You could say I used to be part of the family."

"The family." O Cabrito waved the waiter over for another aguardente. "You weren't a blood relative, but married into the clan, unless I'm mistaken."

"You're not mistaken." They chinked glasses and Ann downed hers in one. "It's a long story and one for your ears only. People talk," she said, her gaze sweeping the table.

"I like long stories. After lunch, we'll have coffee in a quiet spot and you will find me an eager listener."

A dozen or more festival-goers passed the restaurant, all in costume. Whistling and singing, many of them carried the red, white and blue state flag.

"What's going on? Is there a football match?" she asked, watching the group dance-walk out of sight.

Incredulous, Toni spoke with his mouth full. "It's the Festival Amazonas!"

"You don't know it?" asked O Cabrito. "A three-day celebration of the state and the highlight of the year. Musical concerts, samba bands, acrobats, costume parades, dancing in the street, it's our pride and joy."

"Oh, wow! I wanted to catch some local culture and it sounds like I timed my visit pretty well. Can we go? Oh, please, O Cabrito, let's all go and dance!"

O Cabrito smiled at her enthusiasm. "Why not? We'll go to Teatro Amazonas and watch from the balcony. Toni, call ahead and tell them to put some champagne on ice, then bring my car around. Those two," he pointed at the police inspectors, "are not invited."

"How wonderful!" Ann met Gil's eyes for a fleeting second,

but couldn't risk a hint at what she was planning. He and Rocco would just have to trust her.

Wherever O Cabrito went, he seemed to have VIP status. On arrival at the mighty opera house, cordoned off to all visitors, Toni ignored all the No Entry signs and parked right outside. He ran around to open his boss's door, leaving Ann to fend for herself. O Cabrito indicated the balcony at the top of the sweeping steps. "Our viewing platform, the best way to enjoy this festival."

"Stunning!" Ann breathed, exaggerating her wide-eyed wonder. "Are we allowed to go inside?"

He snorted. "Allowed? I'll get someone to give you a guided tour. But first, champagne!"

Ann followed him up to the building, flanked by two of his henchmen. She stopped to take in the view and they stopped with her. The square around the opera house was filling up with party people and a samba band started up. "You know what, I'd love to dance!" She placed a hand on O Cabrito's arm. "Dance first and then champagne?"

He cast a glance at the building crowd. "I don't do street level. But you go ahead. Toni will accompany you." He yelled over his shoulder at his driver. "Toni! Dance with the lady and meet us on the balcony. Give me your backpack, Ann Sheldon."

"Thank you so much! No need, I can manage."

"It wasn't an offer. I will keep your pack until you return."

"Fine. If that's what you want." Her expression remained calm, as if it was unimportant, and she slid the weight from her shoulders. One of his heavies took it. "Back soon! Come on, Toni!" She ran across the *calçada* patterns and into the melee, bouncing and swaying as if she hadn't a care in the world, while her mind raced to find an escape route.

Toni caught up with her, gyrating and grinning at her and the other revellers. He looked like he was having fun. In another life, she could actually like this guy. She clapped her hands over her head in time with the rhythm, already slick with sweat. Every second she spent separated from her rucksack added to her panic. Twice she twirled away into the throng to see Toni shimmying after her. Some teenagers squealed with excitement and let off a string of firecrackers. An idea occurred and she looked around the square to get her bearings.

She leaned forward to shout over the music. "That was great fun! Thank you for dancing with me!"

He gave a mock bow, his face red and sweaty.

"Wanna go drink some champagne?"

He nodded and pointed at the thinnest area of the crowd. She started weaving her way in the direction of the huge ornate theatre. When they extricated themselves from the dancers, she wiped a forearm over her brow.

"I love samba music! Is it popular in Bahia too?"

He mopped his face with his T-shirt. "It's popular everywhere in Brazil. We're born knowing how to dance."

"Ha ha! I used to go to salsa classes in ..." She spasmed, widening her eyes. "Oh no. Not now." She looked around wildly. "I must find a bathroom."

His brow creased. "You don't look so good. Temporary toilets are over there."

She didn't need to check where he was pointing as she'd spotted them while dancing. "Quick, I have to hurry. Oh God, my stomach!"

"This way! Too much rich food at once, I guess." He took off around the edge of the crowd and in the direction of the flimsy roofless stalls. She hared past him, dived into the first available one and locked the door. Instantly, she stood on the toilet, and heaved herself up and over the wall, dropping onto the ground the other side. She pulled a scrunchie from her pocket and tied up her hair. Too bad the beanie was still in her rucksack.

Keeping to a low run, she threaded her way to where she'd seen the teenagers shrieking. She ran over and offered them twenty reais for two strings of firecrackers. She pressed her finger to her lips and winked. The tall kid in a tight T-shirt took the note and handed over two yellow strings. She grabbed them and ran, ignoring the howls of laughter at her paying 100% over the going price. *If you only knew how much they're worth to me*, she thought, taking a direct route to the rear of the Opera House. Once inside the building, she worked out how to get to the balcony O Cabrito had indicated. It was at the opposite end. She set off at a run along the corridor until she was close enough to make out the party through the glass doors.

Sure enough, there he stood, holding a glass of champagne and lecturing another suit with a wagging finger. Ann drew closer. The henchmen were lounging around, looking out at the celebrations below. A waiter carrying an ice bucket came through the open doors and gave her a startled glance.

"Hey there, could you help me?" She spoke in English with an exaggerated American accent. "When I got here earlier, I left my rucksack while I went outside to dance. Now I can't find it. It's dark blue and kinda dirty. You seen it anywheres?"

He leaned back to look through the doors. "There's a rucksack just here, against the wall. Is that the one?"

Ann had no plans to go any closer for fear of being spotted, so smacked a palm to her forehead. "I'm such an idiot. Of course I left it with my friends. Too much cachaça, you know what I mean? Thank you and please take this." She gave him two reais. "Oh, you got a match? Now I've found my pack, I can have a cigarette."

"Thank you, ma'am. Yes, of course." He took an Opera House matchbook from his waistcoat pocket. "You can keep that. I hope you enjoy the festival!" He walked away, the melting ice cubes tinkling in his bucket.

The timing was tight. O Cabrito and his party were at the right-hand side of the balcony along with her rucksack. When the firecrackers exploded in a cloud of smoke, his goons would act fast. First defending their boss from attack and then going after the perpetrator. She'd have to set the crackers at the very end, so they would be looking in the wrong direction. By the time the smoke cleared, the first thing O Cabrito would look for was her rucksack. Which meant she had less than two minutes to grab it, flee the building and run into the street to flag down a cab.

Her mouth was dry after the afternoon's alcohol and dancing in the heat. Pity the waiter had gone or she could have drained his ice bucket. No time to hang about. Any minute now, Toni's suspicions would overcome his manners and he'd break down the door to that toilet stall.

Like all the other pairs of glass doors, those at the end were framed by a thick set of curtains. Ann used them as a shield, prodding the string of mini-explosives beneath the velvet and across the threshold. When she was ready, she clenched her fists, tensed in a runner's crouch and lit the fuse.

In an enclosed space, the bangs were far louder than they had seemed outside in the square. She took off instantly, ducking through the middle doors and grabbing her backpack. The shouts and confusion at the other end were exacerbated by the sounds of breaking glass and a woman's scream. Ann sprinted down the length of the building, dashing past a tour guide and her flock. Ann's all-out pelt towards them caused a flurry of alarm, which she used to her advantage.

"Terrorist attack!" she screamed as she ran past. The ensuing panic would add an extra obstacle to anyone in pursuit.

Outside the building, it was impossible to keep up her pace.

The crowds had grown into a mass of bodies, moving in a steady flow towards the bands. Ann wanted to go the other way. It was swimming against the tide so her only option was cut across. She swung her rucksack to her front, cradling the top of it against her shoulder with her right hand. If no one looked too closely, they would make the obvious assumption she was holding a child. By saying '*Com licença*' about a hundred times, she bumped and nudged her way onto the pavement beside the main drag.

Taxi after taxi passed, all occupied, and the conviction her pursuers were closing propelled her to keep moving. The traffic on a day like this was impossible. Even if she did manage to get a cab, it would be at a standstill for hours. A pizzeria occupied the corner with a trio of delivery motorbikes standing outside. She stood there staring for a second then scanned the street behind her. No way to tell if someone in that crowd was stalking her. A guy talking on his mobile came out of the shop carrying two flat boxes and put them into the pannier of the first bike. He rang off and stuck his key in the ignition. A yell from inside stopped him in the act of putting on his helmet.

"Don't forget the drinks, Pedro, you dipshit!"

He hung the helmet on the handlebars and dashed inside. Ann snatched her chance. She leapt on the bike and jammed the helmet onto her head. The engine started first time and she wove the little vehicle into the traffic. Shouts behind her made her look around. Two men, one in chef's whites, gave chase. She opened the throttle and sped along the bus lane, dodging taxis and overtaking buses, but Pedro must have been training for a marathon. He pounded up the pavement, gaining on her every time she encountered an obstacle. Not only did he show no signs of slowing, but he had breath enough to call for others to stop her.

She made a rapid decision and swung the moped through the gates and zigzagged up the ramps to the Palácio da Justiça.

With a horsepower of 13, the bike going uphill could outrun the fittest human being. She skidded around the corners and forced the engine to a whine on the straight sections. When she got to the terrace, she could see a clear run to the other end of the property. The only things in the way were people, strolling through the grounds and taking pictures. With a glance over her shoulder and a sigh of satisfaction, she leaned on the horn and drove right along the path, forcing everyone to jump out of her way. At the other end, a security guard came pounding in her direction, his hand on his weapon. Ann yanked the bike hard left to avoid him and with a shower of gravel, found herself back on Rua 10 de Julho, the main stretch to the theatre. Her instincts said north-east, so she wove her way through the city until she saw a sign. Aeroporto Internacional AM Eduardo Gomes and the familiar icon of an aircraft. Now to find Rocco and Gil.

The airport layout confused her and she circled the terminals until she understood her mistake. Charter planes had a smaller set of buildings nearer the entrance. She retraced her route and with a momentary hiatus in her panic, spotted the hangar where Rocco had dented the tool cabinet in frustration. An airport security barrier blocked her path but when the uniform in the cabin saw the pizza bike, he lifted it without question.

Just when she thought she'd made it, the man stepped into her path.

"I didn't think you delivered out here," he said, his eyes on the pannier.

She gave him a friendly smile. "We deliver everywhere, chief. Next time you place an order, ask for Fátima and I'll bring it to you personally. Have a great festival!"

He stood back and waved her on with a bright-eyed grin. She waved back, buzzed past towards the hangar, eased off the throttle and booted the kickstand into place. Yanking off her helmet, she looked around the vast concrete space. The plane was parked outside now, blocking the view of the interior. Only the legs of the pilot and two mechanics were visible on the other side of the aircraft. She pressed herself against the hangar wall and risked a glance inside. Rocco paced up and down, waving his arms and shouting. Gil was leaning against a wall.

Ann returned to the bike and scooped up the two rapidly cooling pizza boxes. The marker on the outside ticked the box saying Quattro Stagione. *Something for everyone.* She wiped the sweat from her forehead and took them to the doorway of the hangar.

"... who she really is, do you? We have to get out while we can. Now O Cabrito has got hold of her, she won't slip away easily. You and me, we have a job to do. Gil, *pà*, listen to me. Whoever she is, she'll bring you nothing but trouble."

Ann scrunched up her face in amusement. Not only did she get to make another dramatic entrance, but Rocco had given her the perfect cue.

"That's not true. This time I brought you pizza."

Both men stared at her, both managing their reactions. Rocco exaggerated his incredulity while Gil masked his relief.

"Right, lady, I want to know who you are and how you know so much." Rocco's eyes dropped to the pizza box and she knew he was equally curious about its contents.

She placed the boxes on the oily table and yanked a tissue from the dispenser to wipe her hands. The trouble with having so many disguises was remembering which one applied where. Poet, journalist, runaway, she had no authentic identity in these men's eyes. She opted to fudge the issue.

"It was a bluff. I know enough about O Cabrito's business to understand the value of information. That's all."

"That's all? How do you know?" demanded Rocco.

She told a half-truth. "I got close to a similar network a while ago. But then I decided that line of work didn't really suit me."

"BULLSHIT! Enough of this slimy, snaky double-speak. Who are you and what did you do? You were either a cop or a gangster's girl, that much is clear."

"A gangster's *girl*? Because women don't have the guts to manage an operation, right? You know where you would be if I hadn't got the guts to walk in there this morning? Down some alley lying in a pool of your own blood with a silk bag over your head. Don't insult my intelligence, Rocco."

He rounded on her, his gaze blazing. Maybe bringing up her rescue was poorly timed. "Don't you insult mine! Journalist? You are nothing better than a shitty spy. Yeah, fine, you got us out this morning but now O Cabrito has a price on my head. I ask you again, who are you? Who *were* you? You owe us that information!"

"She owes us nothing." Gil straightened. "It's none of our business. All Ann wanted was to hide from her past. It was me who invited her to join us and I invented the journalist cover story. She's not a spy and she has no agenda. Listen. O Cabrito dismissed us and took Ann as his hostage. I don't know how she escaped and I doubt he does either, but it was his mistake, not yours. When they can't find her in the city, the first place they'll come looking is here. We have to go."

Rocco strode out of the hangar to the plane. "Paolo! How soon can we leave? You sure? Yeah, twenty minutes is fine. Just enough time to eat a pizza." He came to stand one pace away from Ann and pointed to the boxes on the ground. "If there's pineapple on there, you're dead."

She folded her arms and jutted her jaw. "No one puts pineapple on a Quattro Stagione."

"*Que mulher!*" He laughed and grabbed her in a bear hug. "I'll give these to the guys. They deserve it for fixing this machine and I'm still digesting that *feijoada*." He took the boxes around the aircraft and was greeted with voluble enthusiasm.

Ann risked a look at Gil. His eyes were dark as he walked towards her. "Thank you for saving our hides this morning. I'm glad you managed to escape and get here in one piece. There are still a whole lot of things I don't understand."

"Yeah, I know and I'll tell you as much as I can without compromising myself."

Rocco reappeared and clapped his hands together. "Time to get onboard. For once I met a woman who's smarter than me and I'm big enough to stop sulking. Ann Sheldon, you've got a lot of explaining to do. But now, let's get out of here."

12

The plane Rocco had chartered was not the smallest aircraft Ann had ever flown in, but a hot-air balloon didn't count. Other than the two seats up front for the pilot, and if there had been one, a co-pilot, there were was simply a hold of a similar size to Ann's beach cabin. Along the sides, two ledges had four safety belts attached to the fuselage. Strapped to the floor were several packages the size of a bale of hay wrapped in sacking, and two polystyrene containers lashed to the pilot's seat.

They clambered up the metal steps and into the aircraft. Ann chose to sit on the left, close enough to the pilot to see the view. The guy took off his earphones and grinned over his shoulder.

"*Boa tarde*! First time upriver?"

She nodded, shouting over the noise of the engines. "Yes! I live on the coast. I've never been this far into the rainforest."

"My name is Paolo. Do you want to sit up here? You'll get the bird's-eye view." He patted the co-pilot's seat.

Ann always snatched an opportunity when she saw it, even if it might incense her travelling companions. She strapped her backpack into a safety belt and scrambled into the cockpit, leaving Gil and Rocco behind. The pilot gave her a pair of earphones. She put them on and belted up. Over her shoulder, Rocco leaned over to tap Gil's knee and indicated the earphones dangling behind his head. They both donned headsets.

"Everybody ready?" Paolo's voice was tinny in her ears.

They all replied in the affirmative and Paolo taxied away from the hangar towards the runway. He spoke to Air Traffic Control, confirming the number of passengers, flight path and destination. Ann kept her face blank but puzzled over his words. He told Manaus ATC that his destination was Barcelos, a 400-kilometre flight, when Ann knew their destination was at least 500 kilometres away. Perhaps pilots transmitted only as far as the next area of ATC control, where Manaus would hand over to the local air traffic managers. Paolo appeared to be a friendly kind of bloke, so she decided to ask after he'd finished his official business.

The plane trundled along to a quieter runway and when he received permission from the control tower, Paolo revved up the engines and accelerated into the heat haze. It was a dreadful cliché but the sense of liberty on leaving the ground filled Ann with euphoria. Manaus, its market, the festival, black silk hoods, hot city streets, O Cabrito and his goons left far below, they were flying into the unspoilt density of nature. Her face split into a smile as she gazed at the landscape below. The time would come when she would have to face the consequences – again – but now she relished the freedom of being airborne.

"We'll follow the course of the river," said Paolo. His voice in her ear triggered uncomfortable memories. At least here she could take the phones off, unlike her wire. That constant sense of being judged, guided and discussed like a chess piece had never really left her. Even now, when running, swimming, sleeping or eating, she still sensed a presence in her head. She directed her attention to their pilot.

"Rio Negro? How far are we going? Right to the source?"

"No, nowhere near that far. This river begins in Venezuela. Only a few hundred kilometres into the rainforest for us today. Our flight path is pretty low so you should get both the big picture and the detail. If anyone gets thirsty, there's a cool box behind the co-pilot's seat. All OK in the back there?"

Rocco grunted. "Today has been shitty and will probably get worse. I'm going to take a nap. No acrobatics to impress the lady, you hear me? And if there's any danger of a storm, wake me up." The big man took off his headset and lay flat out on the ledge, his arms forming a pillow behind his neck.

Because Gil was sitting directly behind her seat, Ann couldn't judge his mood. Instead she asked, "I guess you've been here before, Gil?"

"Many times, but it never loses its wonder." His chin rested on her seat, just above her left shoulder, looking out at the enormous expanse of green jungle and black water. "I don't think it ever will."

Where the edge of the city met the jungle was the most extraordinary sight. Grids and lines and man-made patterns imposed on nature gave way to the wilderness. Gil and the pilot were discussing the plane and the problems that kept it grounded the last two days. Their conversation was technical and dull, plus Ann was more interested in the vast scale of the Amazon jungle. She tuned out of their chat to feast her eyes on what she could see. Hundreds, perhaps thousands of square kilometres of lush, dense green rainforest reached away to the horizon. Maybe it was the relief of an only-just escape but the scale of the panorama made Ann emotional. The higher they rose, the stranger the jungle became. An undulating expanse of shifting greenery, like algae on the surface of a pond, it concealed a host of deadly creatures lurking beneath. Clouds cast shadows, ominous ghosts floating and haunting the souls below. The Rio Negro flowed wide, so wide it seemed like the sea, around tree-covered islands edged with sandy beaches.

"Anavilhanas," said Paolo, pointing at the islands. "So many animals, birds and fish, it's a conservation area. That's one of the places you can see the pink dolphins."

Ann gazed down at the designs created by the archipelago. It reminded her of Haida Gwaii artwork, all curves and arcs outlined in black. Pink dolphins in a black river swimming around islands designed by indigenous Canadians; it was all a bit *Alice in Wonderland*. At the same time, absolutely wonderful.

She adjusted her cans to ease the pressure on her ears and tuned into the conversation between the two men. Gil Maduro had a surprising amount of knowledge when it came to small planes. He should have been in the co-pilot's seat, not her, but she was enjoying the scenery too much to offer to switch places. One of his comments about the flight plan nudged her to ask Paolo a question.

"You told ATC in Manaus that we were flying to Barcelos. But we're going farther than that, aren't we? Don't you have to file a full flight plan from the point of take-off? Or are we stopping halfway?"

"No, we're not stopping anywhere. As it is, we'll be lucky to land in daylight. Barcelos is an officially recognised landing strip; the closest to where we plan to land, give or take a hundred kilometres. Flight plans must have a proper destination or I can't take off."

"So you file a fake plan?" Ann sensed Gil's head turn towards her and recalled his words. *Just remember, keep your judgement to yourself. You're an outsider.*

"We have no choice," Paolo replied. "There's no other way in or out. Except the boats, I suppose, but they take weeks. Our ways must be strange for you, living on the coast, right in the middle of the action."

Ann thought about her shack at the end of the beach, as far away as she could get from any kind of action. Branca dozing on the veranda, the heron's cry from the roof and the constant soothing swell of the surf, lulling her to sleep. A wave of homesickness took her by surprise. The first time she'd been homesick for anywhere other than the place she used to call home.

"It's different," she said, with a quick smile at Paolo. "But I wouldn't have missed this for the world. It's a privilege to see the lungs of the planet," she breathed, in genuine awe.

They flew above the river, passing occasional towns and settlements, absorbing the endless rolling vistas of green. After a while, Ann's eyelids began to droop and she shook herself awake. Too much feijoada, red wine and aguardente before a fear-filled departure had worn her out. She yawned and focused on the horizon, now cloudy with a sooty-looking smudge up ahead.

Gil's voice came through her headphones. "Is that ...?"

Paolo's eyes narrowed. "Looks like it."

"Shit. I'll wake Rocco."

"Yeah, and both of you belt up. I'm going as low as I can or I'll be flying blind." He gave Ann an unconvincing smile. "There's a storm up ahead. Hold tight and let's hope it's not a bad one."

Rocco swore when Gil woke him, swore louder when he saw the approaching storm and uttered no other words than profanities for the next twenty minutes. Paolo took the plane into a dive. The angle was steep to the extent that Ann thought he was planning a crash landing on the river itself. The storm was upon them in a matter of seconds, converting day to night and hammering the tiny aircraft with torrential rain. Paolo fought with the controls, battling gusts of wind and sudden pockets of stillness, his silent concentration more terrifying than Rocco's stream of blasphemous curses. From Gil Maduro, not a single word. Sheet lightning illuminated the jungle like a camera flash, leaving Ann blinking in its aftermath. The plane veered sideways and for a heart-stopping instant Ann could no longer hear the engines. Thunder cracked so close, the vibrations seemed to shake their fragile metal box. *Not here*, she whispered, *not like this*. Plunged into a piranha-infested river, thousands of kilometres from any hope of rescue would be an ignominious end.

A horn sounded and Paolo moved the steering column forward. Ann had no idea what was going on but was sure Maduro did. His face was between the pilots' seats, watching Paolo intently. He wore his usual expression of tension but Ann got the impression he wasn't unduly afraid. The horn began to blare again and Paolo reacted the same way, speeding up until it stopped. The aircraft steadied and Ann looked at Gil for reassurance, unwilling to bother the pilot.

He removed his cans and motioned for her to do the same, leaning close to her ear. "That's a stall warning. It's just an alert to tell you to speed up or you'll have a serious problem." He placed a hand on her shoulder. "Nothing to worry about."

Ann nodded her understanding although his words only exacerbated her feeling of helplessness. *Warning, alert, serious problem?* Below, the myriad of greens that previously reminded her of a rippling pond turned black, lashing back and forth, more like a maelstrom. It wasn't difficult to imagine the storm as the wrath of the gods. What else possessed such force to wrench and yank those massive trees as if to tear them from the earth?

The plane dipped and ducked, the windscreen blurred with so much water they might have been facing the mother of all fire hoses. Her hands clutched the edges of her seat, gripping harder every time the fuselage shook. So powerful and impressive on the ground, the little Cessna now seemed like a child's toy at the mercy of the elements. And these elements were merciless.

Ann glanced at Paolo. She had no idea how he could see where he was going. She must have appeared doubtful because he gave her a concerned look. Of course. All he needed now was a panicky passenger. She attempted a smile and replaced her earphones, just in time to hear Rocco swear. Again.

The plane shot upwards, leaving her stomach behind as if they were in a high-speed elevator. The troubling fact was that the aircraft was not ascending with its nose, guided by Paolo, but more sucked into a vacuum by forces she could not name. Gil's reassuring hand became a tight grip and Paolo's physical efforts to regain control caused him to break into a sweat.

Her immediate terror of crashing was underlined by the recognition of Paolo's predicament. Responsible for three lives as well as his own, he and his skills were all that stood between them and a horrible death. She knew that feeling and hoped never to experience it again.

The engines whined to a pitch which made Ann want to close her eyes but she didn't dare. In an instant, the elevator motion stopped and the plane jerked forwards, once more led by its nose. The left wing dipped. There, far below, flowed Rio Negro. As fast as it had descended, the storm was over. The rain lessened, and the sky returned to a palette of violet swirls and peacock greens on grey, as if someone had spilt petrol on asphalt. Paolo steered a steady course down to their previous cruising altitude.

Gil clapped Paolo on the shoulder. "Well done. That was some excellent flying. You are a real pro."

"Yeah, you got us through it," grumbled Rocco. "Next time, just go round the goddamned thing. How far away are we?"

Paolo swiped a hand over his damp forehead and checked his instruments. "That was a beast. You OK, Ann? The noise is the worst, but it's completely fine to let her blow her horn now and then. Twenty minutes till we land at base camp. We're out of the frying pan, people! Are we ready for the fire?"

Ann gave him a shaky thumbs-up and stared down at the jungle canopy, seeking the reassurance of the ground. Something had changed. One section of the rainforest bore a series of marks resembling the skeleton of a fish, and between the bones, the forest was grey and ashen, devoid of trees.

It took her several minutes to work out what she was seeing and when she did, the scale of the damage robbed her of speech. Far below, logging trucks crawled along those fishbone tracks, the size of beetles from this distance, but Ann knew each articulated lorry must be carrying several tonnes of dead wood. Hectares of jungle destroyed.

She regained her voice. "Is this the timber camp?"

Paolo followed her sightline. "No, that belongs to another company. A few different ones operate in this area and more have muscled in every time I fly over. That's new." He pointed away to his left, where smoke drifted into the air, obscuring whatever was beneath, "*Garimpeiros*. They're mining for gold. It's not legal, but the last time the government sent a team to investigate, they didn't come back. No wonder they call this the Wild West, right?"

Ann said nothing, enveloped by a profound sadness. It was one thing to read about deforestation but another to see the damage wrought by invaders in person.

"Looks like we'll touch down just before dark," said Paolo, with an optimistic note in his voice. "Starting our descent now."

The sky changed once more, post-storm steel wool giving way to a peaceful dusky indigo. While relieved the journey was over, Ann dreaded what was to come. Paolo manoeuvred the Cessna towards a few scattered lights which passed for a landing strip. The wheels hit the ground and the plane bounced along bumpy earth before coming to a halt in front of a Quonset hut, like a giant rounded greenhouse.

Rocco yanked open the hold door for him and Gil to clamber out. A man hurried across the rough terrain and greeted Paolo with a wave. He introduced himself to Rocco and Gil as Dr Telmo Carreira and enquired anxiously if they had brought his packages.

"They're all there, Telmo," said Paolo, leaping down from the cockpit. "Sorry about the delay. This old bird wasn't airworthy until this afternoon." The two men shook hands. "How's everything here?"

"Shittier than last time I saw you, if that's possible. Oh!" The doctor caught sight of Ann coming around the aircraft and seemed dumbstruck.

"Ann Sheldon, freelance journalist. Pleased to meet you, doctor."

He shook her hand, his face creased with concern. "This is no place for a woman, my dear. No place for any decent human being, to be honest. Can I please get my medication into a cool space? Officers, your unwelcoming committee is waiting. You'd better deal with them first."

At the mouth of the Quonset hut stood around a dozen men, standing in a variety of confrontational poses.

Rocco groaned. "Terrific. As if I haven't had enough macho arseholes today. Paolo, Gil, come and back me up, but I'll do the talking. Ann, you help the doc unload his packages." He strode in the direction of the hut.

Ann watched them go, wondering what the hell she was doing in another aggressive and potentially deadly place. She assessed the doctor, whose wrinkles and stooped gait made him seem older than she had first assumed.

"Are we expecting trouble?" she asked.

"Sabre-rattling is all. The boss and the priest are away, so these meatheads think they are in charge. It's all snarls and barks, at least for now. If Bruno was here, I would be seriously worried. Can you untie the packages and slide them across to the door?"

"Sure." Ann heaved herself up and into the hold, releasing the cables binding the polystyrene to the pilot's seat. She couldn't help checking the standoff, backlit from the mouth of the hut, as cinematic as the gunfight at the OK Corral. But her exhaustion and fear drained all beauty from the scene. These situations, all too familiar from her previous work, were what she'd run away from. To think she could be drinking a Cuba Libre on her veranda right now if it wasn't for Gil Maduro.

The package she released was far lighter than she'd expected and it slid towards the doctor after one sharp shove. "Who's Bruno?" she asked, starting work on the second set of ties.

"A mad dog who should have been destroyed a long time ago. The only person with any control over that maniac is the priest and even he loses his grip from time to time. Why the hell would a person like you voluntarily come to a place like this?"

Ann dragged the heavier package to the hold door. "I could ask you the same question. Aren't doctors better paid in the cities?"

"Those with a licence to practise, most definitely. Those without have less of a choice. I did one year at medical school and dropped out. But I can dress and sew up wounds, pull teeth and prescribe pills when I have them and sometimes when I don't. All the skills you need when working with loggers. Take the lighter of these two and I can manage this."

As she hopped down to help, a figure walked in their direction. Gil Maduro. Ann couldn't see his expression in the dark.

"*Tá bem?*" she asked.

"*Tá bem.* Just a bit of dick waving. Rocco handled it pretty well. Told them to keep out of our way and we'll do them the same favour. Let me carry that for you."

Ann shouldered her backpack and followed the two men towards the lights from the hut and other flimsy buildings which constituted the camp. Night had fallen and visibility was poor.

"This is not going to be easy," Gil said, his voice discreet. "The loggers sleep in bunkhouses and there's no such thing as a guest room. Rocco and I are going to sleep in the boss's cabin. Ann, you can have the priest's quarters. We'll do interviews tomorrow morning, talk to the boss when he returns, then fly out in the afternoon. Never walk around this place alone, you understand? Stick with one of us at all times."

The doctor nodded with some vigour. "Very good advice. Once we drop these packages at my practice, why don't we have dinner together? You have no idea how starved I am of civilised conversation. The food is rough but reasonable for such a basic camp. There's the canteen or two different bars. One of them even has music."

Paolo passed them on his way to the aircraft. "Where are you going to sleep?" Ann asked him.

"In the plane. I have to keep an eye on it because of the stowaways. Someone's always trying to escape. Don't blame them, to be honest, but I can't take the risk of having an undeclared person aboard. That's why I'm going to lock it up now. See you in the music bar."

They stepped into the Quonset hut, filled with vicious-looking diggers, chainsaws and lifting machinery. Everything seemed to have teeth and sharp edges. At the other end, the hut opened onto a torn-up rectangle of earth, with pyramids of logs along one side, broken foliage and wood chippings littering the ground. To the right, the sound of the river. To the left, lights glinted from two lines of temporary buildings.

The doctor hitched his package higher under his arm and

made a sweeping gesture with his left hand. "Welcome to Rio Negro's very own Sad Hill."

The scent of tree-sap, smoke and scorched earth pervaded the air. Her instincts detected a malevolence about the place and alarms shot through Ann's whole body. Even though she'd only just arrived, she couldn't wait to leave.

13

"This is what we call Main Street," said the doctor, leading the way alongside two parallel lines of earthmover tread marks. He pointed to the right. "Over that side is the office, the boss's cabin and the canteen-cum-church which also serves as a meeting hall when the management makes announcements. Behind them, those lights are the loggers' accommodation. Four men to a unit, sleeping in bunk beds, and a communal wash-house at the end."

To Ann, it looked the set of a Western, with unconvincing façades, one rutted road and an air of hostility to strangers. She chided herself. She was tired, hungry and unsettled, prone to negative impressions. Tomorrow would be a better time to form an opinion. Although she doubted it would change much.

"And this is the entertainment quarter?" asked Gil, indicating the barn-like structure on their left. It had only three walls and a corrugated tin roof, with around a dozen tables and a rough wooden bar. Contemporary pop played from a speaker unequal to the task, and several resentful faces stared in their direction.

"Downtown, indeed. That's Bar Musica, next door is the

shop and that little shed at the end is another bar, but for those who want to watch TV. Soap operas, or telenovelas, are an obsession here. We'll take a left at this corner and mind your step because you never know what you might tread in. Behind Bar Musica is the priest's place. I don't know how he stands it, but he swears by earplugs." He went ahead of them through the deepening dusk. "Come this way. My quarters are two doors down, so if you need anything, you know where to find me," he said to Ann.

She wished it was light enough to see where she was treading.

"Here we are. This is my surgery. It's not easy to keep things hygienic in these conditions, but I do my best."

To Ann's surprise, his cabin was padlocked. From around his neck, he withdrew a chain to open the door. They trooped inside and placed the packages on the ground. It looked like a GP's consulting room with metal medicine cabinets, a desk, two chairs and an examining table.

"You sleep in here?" asked Ann, trying to minimise the incredulity in her voice.

"No, no. There's another section at the rear. Further from the music bar, because at the weekends, that can go on till two am. Unfortunately, my sleeping quarters are right next door to the brothel." He pointed at the two-storey building they had just passed. "That gets pretty noisy at all hours. Do you want to drop your pack at the priest's cabin and then we can eat?"

Ann tore her eyes away from the brothel, the place Alexandra Lemos had fled in the middle of the night. "Oh, no thanks, my pack comes everywhere with me. Yes, I'd love to get something to eat and then I need some sleep. It's been a trying day."

"Let's go to Bar Musica. In the TV place they hiss at you for talking. If we go now, we can eat and leave before the loggers come over from the canteen. It's Saturday night. That's when things sometimes get messy."

Ann glanced at Gil and noted the shadows under his eyes. His expression told her he'd had more than enough of messy for one day. "Lead the way, doc," she said, resisting the urge to squeeze Gil's arm.

When they entered Bar Musica, a needle didn't actually slip off a record, nor did everyone stop talking and turn to stare, but there was no mistaking the fact they were being watched. Rocco was already leaning on the bar with Paolo, and to Ann's relief, a blonde woman.

"Where the hell have you been? I ordered beers for everyone but told them not to pour yours until you finally drag your sorry arses in here. The gods are smiling on us, my friends, the chef is Mexican and tonight's menu is fish tacos! Oh, this is Veronique. She's a TV person, filming animals having sex and all that weird shit. Veronique, Gil's another cop and Ann's a journalist."

Veronique broke into a wide grin and she opened her arms for an embrace. "I can't tell you how happy I am to see another woman in this joint! Pleased to meet you, Ann!" Her accent was French and her smile sincere.

In spite of her reservations, Ann leaned into the hug, placing her faith in female solidarity. Veronique was short, around five foot three, with close-cropped hair. Her body was muscular and her clothes looked military grade. She smelt of citrus fruit.

"Same here. This place feels very masculine," Ann replied, wondering what Veronique would make of her own sweaty, dirty appearance.

"It's a shithole. There are worse places in the world for women but the devil himself couldn't drag me there. You're a journalist? What kind of things do you write? Ah, sorry, Gil, I'm being rude. Pleased to meet you too. I'm not a 'TV person', as Rocco puts it. I'm a documentary maker for a natural history channel. Only part of my job is filming animals having sex."

The barman cracked open three more beers and after an outraged exclamation from Rocco, a fourth. "Find a seat. Tacos take twenty minutes. I call you when ready."

Rocco lifted his phone and took a picture of the man in his dirty grey vest.

"What's that for?" the chef asked, his expression halfway between anger and concern.

"I'm a cop, *amigo*. I record everything. Thanks for the beer and if the service is good, a healthy tip is coming your way. *Obrigado*."

They pushed two tables together and Ann sat between Gil and Veronique, her backpack between her feet. "How on earth do you cope here alone?" she asked the Frenchwoman.

Veronique switched to English. "I'm not alone, actually. My cameraman is with me. Not right now because he's gone with the priest and the camp boss to get some aerial footage of the region. It's tough, no kidding, but we're coming to the end of our stint and flying out next week. That can't come fast enough. *Santé*!"

Ann raised her glass and joined the others in a toast. She drank deeply. The beer was welcome, cold and delicious. She reminded herself she was still dehydrated and too much alcohol could be dangerous. "*Santé*. Good to meet you. What's your documentary about?"

"Biodiversity. The range of animal, bird and fish species in this region is outstanding. We've also got footage of extremely rare flora we'd never have known about but for the local people. Look out, natural history world, we're going to blow your minds!" She mimed an explosion from both her temples.

"That's something I'd love to see." Her enthusiasm for the beauty of the area struck Ann as incongruous. "Isn't it odd, recording the richness of the rainforest while living amongst the people who are tearing it down?"

Veronique lowered her voice. "That's the elephant in the room. It's one of those cognitive dissonance things. We just don't talk about it. People can be very sensitive." She gave a cautious glance around the busy bar.

"Sorry. I was warned not to judge what I don't understand. How long have you been working up here?"

Rocco interrupted. "How about speaking a language I can understand? More beers?"

"Not for me, thanks," Ann answered in Portuguese. "I've only just started this one."

He shook his head as if disappointed and fetched three more bottles. Two for himself and one for Paolo.

Veronique followed Ann's lead and reverted to Portuguese, as they were on a blander topic. "Six weeks at this camp, but we've been up and down Rio Negro these last three months. Is this your first time?"

Ann's gut feeling told her the documentary producer was trustworthy, but she stuck to her story nevertheless. They talked about their experiences of Brazil because Veronique had also spent some time on Ilha do Marajó. Gil joined in the conversation and the subject turned to wildlife reservations.

The tacos arrived; little fishcakes with tortillas, chopped vegetables and some spiced coconut milk. They were messy to assemble, but a refreshing blend of flavours and Ann found that even after *feijoada* and all the trimmings, she could muster quite an appetite. In her experience, fear often burnt a lot of calories.

She bought a round of beers and noticed the bar was filling up. Their table attracted a lot of attention. A couple of men came over to greet Paolo, staring unselfconsciously at Ann. But the majority of loggers eyed them with suspicion from a distance. Dr Carreira started to get fidgety as the conversations grew louder and the arrival of one hefty guy seemed to bother him more than most. The big man went straight to the bar, ordered a beer and turned to drink it, leaning his elbows on the bar. He fixed Rocco with an intense stare, but the Manaus cop didn't acknowledge the obvious aggression. Presumably he was used to it.

"Ann, are you ready to leave? I can show you the priest's cabin now, if you like?"

"Thank you, doctor, yes, please. I'm worn out. Thanks for dinner, Rocco. Goodnight, everyone, see you in the morning."

Gil got to his feet. "I'm going to turn in as well. Is there a bathroom here?"

The doctor indicated the rear of the building. "There's a pretty basic toilet back there although most of these guys piss in the alley. Come this way, Ann, and will you please call me Telmo? You're not one of my patients."

The walk to the priest's hut took all of five minutes. Unlike the doctor's, it wasn't locked. Ann expressed some concern about security and the doctor showed her how to slide a wooden plank through two interior handles to bar unwanted entry. It didn't match the safety level of her own beach shack, but it offered the minimum of reassurance. She said goodnight to Telmo, lit the lamp and looked around the rudimentary facilities. The priest had a single bed, a plastic bowl with a water jug, and behind a palm-leaf screen, a chemical toilet.

She stripped down to her bra and pants, preparing to wash and brush her teeth when someone tried the door handle. Ann snatched up her knife.

"*Quem é?*"

A low male voice spoke. "*Abre a porta.*"

"Forget it. There's no way I'm opening this door. Get out of here and leave me in peace."

"Come on, lady, I only want to talk."

"I said no." She pulled back the taped up fabric which

substituted for a curtain just a couple of centimetres and dropped it immediately. Outside stood the huge man from the bar who so disturbed the doctor.

He rattled the door handle again. "That's not very friendly. Open the door." The plank barring the door suddenly seemed very flimsy, a baffle against a bear.

"Didn't you hear me? I told you to go away. You picked the wrong woman, *pá*."

"What's your name, lady? Let me in and we can get acquainted. I have a thing for ..."

A male voice interrupted. "What the hell do you think you're doing?" Ann recognised Gil's tones, loud and authoritative.

"Piss off and mind your own business. The lady and I are having a chat."

"I don't think so. You leave her alone and go back to the bar."

"Who the hell are you to tell me what to do?"

"Inspector Gil Maduro of the Soure police force. That woman is my colleague and I'm telling you to leave her alone."

"Of course. Cops!" He spat the word. "You and that big ugly bastard fly in here to throw your weight around and stick your noses where they're not wanted. Watch your back, inspector. People like you have a habit of meeting with unfortunate accidents in the jungle."

"Just let us do our jobs and we'll do the same for you. Goodnight."

There was a tense silence before heavy steps crunched away. "Go to hell."

Ann pulled the curtain again to see the huge lump walk away. When he'd returned to Bar Musica, Gil tapped on the door.

"Ann?" he called. "Everything OK?"

She pulled on her T-shirt and slid the plank from its fastenings. The door swung open and her lamp illuminated Gil's face. Her knife was still clutched tightly in her right hand. "I'm fine. But I had been alone for all of three minutes before he turned up, so what next? Maybe I should go back to the plane. At least Paolo can lock those doors."

"You have no lock?"

Ann shook her head. "Just a wooden plank to hold the door shut and that's none too sturdy. Why are you here? I thought the boss's hut was on the other side?"

"It is. The way that guy in the bar looked at you, I had a bad feeling. When I came out of the bathroom, he'd gone and I had a pretty good idea where. Get your pack and come with me. Rocco can sleep here so if that ape comes back, he'll get a nasty shock. You and I will share the boss's hut. It's OK, there are two beds."

She didn't need asking twice. She dressed, grabbed her rucksack and shut the priest's hut behind her. Gil led the way back to the bar, where he told Rocco of the change of plan. With much back-slapping and ribald laughter, Rocco gave her the thumbs-up. Ann gave him a weary smile. She didn't care what Rocco or anyone else thought. All she wanted was a safe place to sleep.

The boss's hut was made of breeze blocks, sturdier and much larger than the others, similar to the brothel. As Gil unlocked the door, Ann spotted a smaller Quonset hut to their left, just visible in the limited light, which had to be the canteen/church/meeting hall. It looked like a cattle shed.

Inside the management's accommodation was far more luxurious than the basic huts she'd seen thus far. The first section was a cosy seating area with a decent-sized TV and side table filled with bottles of liquor. In the kitchen corner, complete with sink and stove, there was an electric cool box, similar to hers at Praia do Pesqueiro. This place, like the doctor's, evidently had its own generator.

Gil opened the dividing door to reveal a double bed, shower unit and a large, modern wardrobe. The boss clearly took pains over his appearance. "You're in here. I'm on the sofa. Can I take a shower and clean up before bed? Maybe there are some cold drinks in the kitchen. I could use another beer."

"You rescued me, Gil, so I'll sleep on the sofa."

He sighed, rubbing his face. "Shut up. Tonight, we're not operatives, but watching each other's backs. No discussion. Get us a drink and I'll be five minutes."

From the selection in the little fridge, Ann chose a bottle of Bohemia beer for him and a still water for her. She sat on the sofa, closer to relaxed she had been for the previous twenty-four hours. She was with Gil Maduro, the safest place she knew. Tomorrow they would fly out of this lawless, violent and unpredictable camp, back to Soure, the ocean and Branca. She let out a short laugh through her nostrils. Homesick for her home-from-home. The laugh was about to morph into tears so she drowned them with a long draught of cold water.

The door slid open and Gil emerged wearing a blue T-shirt and cargo pants, his feet bare. He came to sit beside her and clasped his beer bottle. "Thanks. I only packed for a couple of days and after all this bullshit, everything is dirty. I washed my clothes, left them to dry over the shower and borrowed some things from our host. I hope you don't mind," He slugged some of the golden liquid and closed his eyes.

"I don't mind. Will he?"

Without opening his eyes, Gil replied, "He can shove it up his ass." He released a long sigh. "Today seems like it lasted at least a week."

"Yeah. Sometime in my life I must have been this tired before, but my memory blocked it out. Thank you for looking out for me. With you in the next room, I might be able to sleep."

He smoothed damp hair from his forehead, his eyes still closed. "Just returning the favour."

Ann considered that comment and chose not to delve deeper into its meaning. "What happens tomorrow?"

He was silent for so long Ann thought he had nodded off.

"Tomorrow?" he asked, those deep brown eyes blinking open to meet hers. "We get out of this shithole. But first we have to interview the boss, the madam, the priest and some of the loggers. Let's pray to God one of them is not that arsehole who just hassled you. Rocco and I will work as a team but there is one thing you could do."

She shifted to face him. "Tell me."

His expression softened. "You can't help yourself, can you? Leaping into the action, no matter what the cost. OK, listen. Rocco and I want to interview the woman who runs the brothel. She's a cynical old bitch, according to the doctor, and I can understand why he hates her so much. The one thing we can't do is interview the girls. In the face of authority, they'll shut down and we'd be wasting our time. If you could chat to them, sympathise, invite confidences, that sort of thing? I'm not holding out much hope, but we have to go through the motions."

Attempting any kind of subterfuge tomorrow seemed like swimming up the Rio Negro. "I'll try," she said, allowing her neck to rest on the sofa. "I promise I'll try. Unless I have a shower and a long, uninterrupted sleep, I'll be good for nothing in the morning. Goodnight, Gil, and thank you for keeping me safe."

He closed his eyes again. "A conversation for another time. Sleep well."

14

I n her beach hut on Praia do Pesqueiro, it was impossible to sleep through the natural alarm call of the jungle awakening. Here, in the depths of the rainforest, her surroundings were eerily silent. Ann slept till seven, which for her was a lie-in. Considering her emotional state the evening before, she was surprised to sleep long and deeply, free of nightmares and waking with a more positive outlook on the day ahead. She washed and dressed rapidly, aware that access to the bathroom was awkward until she got up. Voices reached her as she packed her rucksack and when she opened the door, Rocco and Gil were drinking coffee in the kitchen corner.

"Good morning!" Rocco beamed. "How did you sleep?"

"Very well, but after yesterday, who wouldn't? How about you?"

"Pretty good in the end. I had a visitor at two in the morning. Apparently he'd seen me in the bar, liked the look of my face and wanted to get friendly. When I opened the door, he changed his mind. I don't think he was expecting the beard." He roared with laughter, his eyes dancing with glee.

Ann tried to join in with his amusement, but could only

imagine what might have happened if she'd been alone. Her reticence didn't bother Rocco.

"You know, I've seen that guy before somewhere."

Gil picked up a fresh cup. "He was staring at you in the bar."

"Yeah, I know that, but I know his face from somewhere else. It'll come back to me. *Ai*, my back is stiff. That priest must be a right short arse. A man of my size was never going to fit in that bed and I ended up putting the mattress on the floor. I could have slept on this sofa if you two would just get it on. What a waste!"

Ann wasn't sure if he was referring to the sofa or the opportunity. She risked a glance at Gil, who shrugged and offered her a cup of coffee. "If you're ready, I'll use the bathroom and then we can get to work. The boss's plane is due around ten this morning. I think the best place to start is the brothel."

Rocco's face fell. "The brothel! Before breakfast?"

Cynical was one word to describe Dona Candida. The woman had the sharpest eyes and a thin mouth curled in a permanent expression of disapproval. Her rail-thin body was clad in widow's weeds and a roll-up cigarette smouldered between her yellowing fingers. She insisted on seeing ID for all three of them before allowing entrance to the premises. On learning Ann was a journalist, she refused point blank to let her in and kept up a string of insults throughout the entire negotiation.

Ann kept her mouth shut, reining in all her urges to tell this hateful hag to go to hell.

Reluctant to leave her outside alone, the two inspectors debated with the madam until the door of a nearby hut opened. Veronique stuck her head out, probably alerted by all the noise.

"Hey, Ann! Why don't you come over? We've made fresh juice."

With a nod to Gil, Ann made her way over the damp morning earth only to be halted by Dona Candida's screech.

"Marguerite, Ruth, you give that woman nothing! Nothing, do you hear me! Especially not your real names. *E tu, francesinha, cala-te a boca!*"

Ann feigned confusion while processing what the brothel owner had given away. The girls obviously used aliases and by saying 'And you, Frenchwoman, shut your mouth', the old bat had revealed that Veronique was in possession of some useful knowledge.

The older woman hurried the police officers indoors and slammed the door of her establishment, built of similar materials to those of the management buildings. Outside Veronique's hut, a couple of plastic chairs sat on a wooden stoop, decorated with jungle vines. She invited Ann to take one and handed her a beaker of pinkish liquid. She spoke in Portuguese. "Açai and cupuaçu – as fresh as it gets. Girls, I know what that *bruxa* said, but you can come and say hello. This is a friend of mine. Her name is Ann."

Two young women came to stand in the doorway, both holding similar beakers. They looked from Veronique to Ann, wary as wildcats.

Ann chose not to make any overtures and leave it up to them. "Thanks, Veronique. At least some people around here are friendly."

"That's the way Candida operates. She attacks first and asks questions later. No bird or animal I've ever encountered has a louder screech. I'd love to say her harsh manner hides a soft heart, but to be honest, I don't think she has one." Both girls tried to suppress a guilty snigger. "What do you think of the juice?"

Ann took a sip of the thick liquid and relished the sensations in her mouth. "Mmm, wow! It's a bit like blueberry and banana but there's something almost chocolately ... what is that taste?" She took another sip.

The smaller of the two girls answered. "That's cupuaçu. It's a fruit that tastes of chocolate. Good for your skin, too."

"I've never had it before. Maybe it doesn't grow where I live." She let the statement hang in the air, trusting in their natural curiosity.

"Do you come from France, like Veronique?" It was the same girl who spoke. What she lacked in height, she made up for in confidence.

"No. I come from Britain but these days I live on Ilha do Marajó." She took another sip of juice, registering the exchange of glances between the young women. "Right on the beach, in fact, not far from Soure."

"That's where she lives!" exclaimed the short one, pointing to her friend. "Juliana's house is next to Praia de Barra Velha." Instantly she clapped a hand over her mouth. "I meant Marguerite."

Ann didn't react to the girl's slip. "I don't know Praia de Barra Velha. I'm a bit farther up the coast, on Praia do Pesqueiro."

Marguerite/Juliana nodded with enthusiasm. "I know it. It's where my friends and I go surfing. It's my favourite beach."

"Oh, yeah? If you surf there, you probably know Serena, the blonde super surfer." Ann adjusted her ponytail, affecting a casual disinterest. "I'm teaching her English."

"Serena's amazing! You know she surfed the Pororoca? She's the best, far braver than any of the boys." The girl came a little closer.

"She really is. Are you also a surfer, Ruth?" Ann used the name the harridan had yelled, sticking to the script.

"No, I can't swim. But I do like beaches and surfer boys."

Both girls giggled and Ann was struck by how young they were. "I miss the beaches in the summertime."

"Me too," said Marguerite/Juliana, her expression wistful. "Especially Praia do Pesqueiro."

Ann saw an opportunity to expand the conversation. "If you know Serena, you probably know Alexandra, the girl who went missing, no?"

In an instant, the girls' faces closed down and they shook their heads.

"No, we don't," said Ruth. "Let's go in, Marguerite, and I'll do your hair." They retreated into the hut and closed the door. Ann clenched her fist, furious with herself for being so clumsy.

"You can't blame them," Veronique murmured in English. "Yet another elephant in the room." She glanced at her watch. "There's usually a church service at ten on a Sunday, but seeing as the priest isn't here yet, they've moved it to midday. The men attend, at least the majority, but the girls don't. That might be a good time for you to have a relaxed chat. I'm going down to the landing strip to meet the plane and my camera-man. Do you want to wait here for your friends or come with me?"

"I'll come with you, please. Thank you for the juice, and also for the advice. I'll try to talk to the girls again later." She handed over her empty beaker and swung her rucksack over her shoulder. As they walked between the huts, Ann considered the timescale. If Veronique had been in this camp six weeks, she had probably encountered Alexandra herself. She ventured a question, hoping not to alienate her only ally.

"I understand the missing girl is a sensitive topic with her colleagues. But how about you? Is it something you can talk about?"

Veronique blew air through her lips. "I share a cabin with two of the girls, but I don't hang out with the others. Everyone was shaken when Alexandra disappeared because we all know there's nowhere to go. Alexandra and Juliana, otherwise known as Marguerite, were very close. The loss hit her hard, poor kid. Sometimes, the friendships between these girls are the only thing that keeps them going. Juliana has around two weeks more to serve and she believes she'll find Alexandra waiting when she gets home. We all know how it feels to hold on to a dream, right? *Mon Dieu*, they're early!"

The sound of a small aircraft buzzed above their heads, flying so low it was almost brushing the trees. The two women picked up their pace and arrived at the landing strip just as the little Cessna hit the ground. By the time it taxied to a halt behind Paolo's plane, there was a small crowd waiting to greet the passengers. The second Ann clapped eyes on the camp boss, she detested him. She knew who he was, without a doubt, as the five men who emerged from the aircraft were easily identifiable: the priest by his dog collar, the cameraman by his equipment, and the pilot by his uniform. That left a man in a short-sleeved shirt and tie as the figure of authority and his minder, a squat, chunky lump of meat. The boss stalked across the rough ground and his 'returning hero' wave turned Ann's stomach.

"What's that guy's name?" she asked Veronique. "The one who thinks he's a movie star."

"Juan-Carlos Ablos."

When Ann looked blank, she tried again in her French-accented English. "He's the camp manager and his name's Juan-Carlos Ablos. My cameraman is a Brit, like you. He refers to him as 'Wanker Up Yours'. I think you two will have a lot in common. Damien!" She waved at the ponytailed man, who was wearing all his bags across his body, like a packhorse.

He looked up with a broad grin, giving them a triumphant fist-pump. An argument broke out amongst the waiting men, impressing upon Ablos their displeasure at having two police officers and a journalist in the camp. Fingers pointed in her direction and the atmosphere made Ann uneasy.

Then the priest's voice rose above the others. His tone was one of offended outrage that such unfriendly and belligerent attitudes, not to mention foul language, should disturb the Lord's Day. He reminded them of the service at twelve and suggested they might use the intervening time to consider their behaviour.

Slack-jawed, Ann watched the men apologise and accept his criticisms. In his own gesture of appeasement, Ablos offered to hold a meeting immediately after the service to hear their grievances. That seemed to suffice. They dispersed in grumbling groups of twos and threes.

Damien the cameraman had reached Ann and Veronique, but just like them, he was eavesdropping on the drama. Only when his fellow passengers had entered the Quonset hut did he turn his attention to the two women in front of him.

"See, that's the difference between them and me. The priest threatens them with the wrath of God whereas I'm attracted to the angels. Good morning." He gave Ann a warm smile.

Hearing another London accent speaking English evoked a whole spectrum of feelings in Ann, from familiarity to discomfort. He was nothing special to look at; medium height, curly brown hair with eyes the colour of a muddy stream. Yet something about him engendered trust and reassurance.

Veronique made the introductions. "Damien, this is Ann, a journalist accompanying the police. Ann, this is the other half of our production unit, Damien. He's a brilliant cameraman and fearless explorer, but on account of having an Irish grandfather, he believes he has kissed the Blarney Stone. I'll let you decide."

Damien put down his holdall and held out his hand. "Pleased to meet you, Anna. What do you think of Butlin's?"

"It's Ann, not Anna, and I had more fun at Disneyland."

"Damn!" He grimaced. "That's on page 3 of the Boys' Handbook of Girls. Get their names right! Sorry. Anyway, I've had nothing to eat other than a bowl of rice since yesterday and I'm starving. Shall we get some breakfast, Dorothy?"

Veronique turned to Ann with an 'I told you so' look. "Yeah, I want to hear about the trip, but let's go to the bar, not the canteen. Too much testosterone puts me off my pancakes."

She relieved him of two black equipment bags and led the way along the main drag. They stopped to watch the little plane take off again and Damien waved goodbye to the pilot. As they turned the corner to Bar Musica, they came face to face with Rocco, Gil and Paolo. In a second, Ann noticed two things: first, Rocco's eyes lighting up on seeing Veronique, and throwing a suspicious glance at Damien. Ann could think of better locations for a holiday romance than a timber camp in a rainforest, but she supposed Rocco was good at spotting opportunities. Second, Gil's tense expression relaxing into warmth as he caught sight of Ann.

Their eyes locked and she gave him a confident smile. That guy was becoming increasingly hard to resist.

"Perfect timing," said Veronique, in Portuguese. "We are just going to have some breakfast." She made the introductions and Damien said how pleased he was to meet the police officers in polite, humble language. His non-confrontational attitude evidently pleased Rocco, who asked blunt but enthusiastic questions about his trip.

The bar was quiet and the only offerings were *huevos rancheros* or cassava pancakes. Ann opted for the eggs and vegetables. As they ate, she was content to absorb the atmosphere and listen. Damien went into detail about the flight inland and its purpose. His Brazilian Portuguese was fluent and as far as Ann could detect, unaccented. She was impressed, as were Rocco and Gil.

A local pilot from Barcelos had flown them 200 kilometres north into the Parco Nacional do Pico da Neblina. There they had arranged a meeting with leaders of the indigenous people. Juan-Carlos Ablos was on a mission to persuade the leaders to grant permission for an initial exploration of the land. The priest was supposed to act as an official reassurance although it hadn't panned out that way. A Catholic priest and his dog collar had no more significance to them than a badger. The people had listened patiently to Damien's explanations then asked them to leave.

Even though things hadn't worked out for the logging company, it proved an extremely valuable exercise for the documentary maker. He had some incredible footage of both the region and its inhabitants, both human and otherwise.

"How did you communicate with these people?" asked Gil. "I know some speak Portuguese but the more remote areas have their own languages. Rocco and I have been on a couple of cases together when neither of us could speak to the locals. Did you have an interpreter?"

For a few seconds, Damien couldn't answer as he was still swallowing a mouthful of pancake. Veronique replied in his stead.

"He studied Amazonian dialects and languages just so he could get closer to the indigenous inhabitants. Not all of them welcome observers like us, but some are willing to share their stories. This is why Damien is such a useful partner. I mean, a documentary-making partner. We work together, nothing more." She grinned at her cameraman and squeezed his forearm, but Ann knew that remark was aimed directly at Rocco.

"Which means I'm still single. Form an orderly queue, ladies." Damien waggled his eyebrows at Ann. She recognised the move. *I'm only joking. Unless you're interested?*

She smiled but kept her attention on the yellow yolk spilling over her veggies, ignoring his enquiring gaze. She sensed the cameraman's interest in her as a woman and it made her want to retreat from human interaction. A warm body and gentle caress would break the protective eggshell she'd hardened around her vulnerability. *Keep away and I can stay alive.*

Damien seemed unfazed. "And you guys? Two cops and a journo in town at once? That's unheard of in this seething metropolis. What's the story?"

Again, Veronique spoke first. "The runaway. Remember the hue and cry when one of Dona Candida's girls ran off? This is the official investigation."

"Oh, right. That was over three weeks ago, wasn't it? But I guess Manaus cops have all kinds of other issues to deal with." Damien didn't look up from his breakfast.

"I'm the Manaus cop and yeah, we had some delays." Rocco shrugged. "Gil's connection to the case is because the girl was from his patch and Ann is a sort-of local journalist. It's not likely we'll find anything but we have to go through the motions. Talking of motions, I need the toilet. Gil, when you're ready, we should get these interviews done."

"Sure. Ready when you are. I'll pay the bill." Gil went to the bar. Veronique leaned closer to Damien and started speaking in fast French. Reluctant to eavesdrop, Ann turned to Paolo.

"You fly up here every week?"

He had an easy-going expression and a ready grin. "Sometimes twice a week. Yesterday's flight wasn't typical, you know. That was one of the worst storms I've seen and I've been flying this route for nine years. My wife wants me to do more training and fly the big birds to Miami and Rio, but my heart is in the jungle. No one else knows this place like I do."

Damien and Veronique had broken off their conversation and were listening.

"My respect for pilots knows no bounds," said Damien. "Without you guys..."

Veronique jumped in. "There's an incredible perspective from the air, you're right. But there's an 'ole other world on the ground. The big picture is only part of the story because it's made of details. Thousands of tiny details." Veronique's eyes were intense, conveying her passion.

As she spoke, Gil took his seat and Rocco returned from the bathroom to stand with his hands on his hips.

"Ready to go?" asked Rocco.

"Hang on a sec." Damien placed his cutlery on his plate. "Veronique's absolutely right. By flying into a logging camp and out again, you haven't really seen the rainforest. There's more beauty in these jungles than you would believe. Animals, birds, trees as old as this earth and waterfalls to take your breath away. For example, there's a village a boat ride away from here. Totally traditional and home to a tribe that goes back centuries. They tell stories you'll never forget. If you like, I can take you. It's a once-in-lifetime experience." Damien addressed the party as a whole but his eyes came to rest on Ann.

Rocco belched and shook his head. "We have to fly out this afternoon. Paolo has to get back to Manaus and so do I. Thanks for the offer though. Damn, that chef is good. I could eat that all over again."

"That's a shame. I think you would have found it very interesting." This time, Damien addressed Gil in particular, his gaze meaningful. There was no obvious reason for the intensity of his stare and Gil looked as puzzled as Ann felt.

"How far is it from here?" Gil asked.

"About an hour and a half upriver but only forty-five minutes downstream on the return journey. There's no other way of getting there; only they know the route through the jungle. What time do you have to leave?"

Paolo looked at his watch and then at Rocco and Gil. "I'd

like to be in the air by two o'clock, latest. How much more do you have to do here?"

"Talk to the boss, speak to the priest and we're finished."

"Father Mendoza is holding a service at midday and Juan-Carlos is meeting some of the men directly afterwards. I'd advise you to speak to both of them before twelve," said Veronique.

"Maybe while you're conducting your interviews, I could take Ann to the village? You can learn a lot from such people." He seemed to be communicating something other than his words, but Ann couldn't work out what he was trying to say.

Paolo waved a pancake in no particular direction. "There's another possibility. I'm coming back on Tuesday to collect these two." He jerked his thumb at Damien and Veronique. "So you could stay on a couple of days and come back to Manaus with them. You said you wanted to keep your head down for a while," he reminded Rocco.

"Now that's a terrific idea," said Veronique. Her voice was almost a purr. "Take advantage of your time here to go exploring. You never know what you'll find in the jungle."

Her suggestive tone implied she and Damien had some kind of information they wanted to impart. Ann's confusion centred on why they wouldn't simply spit it out. Not only that, but the Frenchwoman evidently had every intention of seducing Rocco. By the look of things, she wouldn't have to work too hard.

"Gil? You have two more days to spare?" asked Rocco. "What about you, Ann?"

She looked out at the miserable scattering of buildings, constant smell of diesel and permanent sense of threat. Her thoughts strayed to Branca and the beach. "It's not the most inspiring place I've ever stayed. And now the boss and priest have returned, where would we sleep?"

Rocco clapped his hands together with a sound like a

gunshot. "We'll work something out. Paolo, swear to me on anything you hold holy that you will be here on Tuesday. If you let me down again, I'll chop you up and feed you to the piranhas."

"Wait a minute," said Gil. "Ann doesn't want to stay here and unless we get something useful from Ablos or the priest, this whole trip has been a waste of time."

Ann opened her mouth and the words came out before she decided to speak. "Ann doesn't want to stay here, that's true, but I would like to see that village. If everyone else is prepared to stay till Tuesday, so am I."

Everyone looked at Gil. He studied each face around the table. "In that case, you can leave now, Paolo. But I second Rocco. You'd better be here first thing on Tuesday morning or the piranhas are the least of your worries."

"Yeah, you hear that?" Rocco pointed at Paolo. "Don't mess us about. Gil, can you give me ten minutes? I need to use the plane's radio before he leaves. *Vamos!*"

A look of triumph flashed between Damien and Veronique. "Great!" she said. "I'll go and make arrangements for your accommodation. Why don't we meet at the jetty after lunch and then whoever wants to take the boat trip can sail up the river? Ann, don't forget a hat!"

Everyone had somewhere to be on a Sunday morning, except Ann. The sound of the plane taking off told her Paolo had departed. Rocco and Gil left Ann and the documentary makers in the bar in order to pin down the boss and the priest for an interview. Damien wanted to show Veronique his latest footage so they left for his cabin. Ann didn't fancy hanging around the bar on her own but wandering around the camp was an even worse idea. This rootless, unsheltered feeling should have been familiar, yet she had always managed to find refuge, even in the most inhospitable circumstances. One way of doing that was by attaching herself to some kind of protector. She finished her coffee and left the bar, ducking through the gap between buildings until she found the doctor's hut.

The padlock was no longer present, so she assumed he was home and rapped politely on the door. It took over a minute before he yanked back the curtain and scowled. He opened the door a fraction.

"Do you mind? I'm with a patient."

"Oh, I'm sorry. I didn't think you'd be working on a Sunday."

His scowl deepened. "I work whenever people need me, Ann. What do you want?"

"A place of safety, actually. I've got nowhere else to go."

The puff seemed to go out of him and he nodded to a bench beside his hut. "Take a seat. I may be a little while." He went inside without a backward glance.

The sun was already brutally hot so Ann accepted his offer and sat in the shade. This, she supposed, was his waiting room. A plank rested on some logs under a sheet of tarpaulin serving as a makeshift awning. Basic, but it did the job. The second she sat on the bench, a lizard raced out past her feet, hotly pursued by another. Whether they had romance or murder in mind, Ann could only guess. She cast her mind over the conversation at breakfast, trying to read between the lines. Were Damien and Veronique trying to tell them something or laying a trap? It couldn't be as crude as sexual attraction, she was reasonably sure of that.

Flies landed on a pile of something indistinguishable near the opposite construction. Ann tried to recall which building was which and identified it as the shop. She'd not yet had the pleasure of sampling its range and wondered if it would be safe to do so while the doctor was occupied. Just as she was debating, the door opened and Dr Telmo Carreira came out, carrying a plastic bucket covered with a lid.

"You can go inside now. Please lock the door and stay here until I return. That will be in around one hour. The patient needs to rest but whenever she's ready, she can leave." He hurried away towards 'Main Street', his twitchy demeanour reminiscent of the White Rabbit with his fob-watch. *Alice in Wonderland* again. Perhaps she should spend some time paying attention to her subconscious. Or maybe the disorientation and unfamiliarity was reminiscent of a bizarre dream.

She entered the hut to see the girl she'd met earlier, Juliana alias Marguerite. The teenager was wrapped in a blanket, lying on her side on the examination table with her eyes closed. In this environment, she appeared younger than ever, her hair braided into a French pleat and without make-up. Although she seemed groggy and disorientated, when she opened her eyes and registered Ann's presence, she radiated hostility.

"Hello, Marguerite," said Ann, with a smile. She stuck to her official name for fear of giving offence.

There was no response. Ann locked the door as the doctor had asked, dumped her backpack, eased herself to the floor and sat cross-legged looking out of the window, giving the girl time to collect herself.

It took five minutes before soft rustling sounds told Ann the patient was moving. She looked over her shoulder and saw the young woman had eased herself into a hunched sitting position. She offered another smile which was not reciprocated. Instead, the girl spoke, her voice hoarse and tight. "You want to find Alexandra Lemos. But you're looking in the wrong place. You won't find her here."

Ann swivelled on her bum to face the bed. She kept her tone soft and understanding. "Marguerite, are you in pain?"

The teenager gave Ann an emotionless stare.

"I don't want to interfere. I'm just wondering if I can do anything to help."

Marguerite shook her head, a slow, definitive gesture.

"OK. Thanks for telling me about Alexandra. Veronique mentioned the fact you two were friends. Is that true?"

"Don't speak about her as if she's dead. Alexandra and I *are* best friends. Anyway, Marguerite is what they call me at work. I'm not working right now and my name is Juliana."

Ann noted the flinty tone and began to admire this young woman. "Juliana it is. Please call me Ann. Yes, I'm trying to find out what happened to Alexandra. Her family are very worried."

"As if they give a shit! They forced her into this, same as my family forced me. The only thing they care about is the greasy roll of reais we earn on our backs. They have no idea." Her voice cracked and she shook her head, eyes squeezed shut. "Alexandra got out. Good luck to her."

"Good luck to her," Ann echoed. She gave it a moment, conscious of time ticking away. "The one thing I can't understand is *how* she got out. The river is far too dangerous, even if she had access to a boat. There's only one plane a week. She wouldn't survive in the jungle more than one night and in this camp, there's nowhere to hide."

Juliana opened her eyes, pressing her fingers in a bridge over her nose. "One plane a week and in sixteen days, I'll be on it. Alexandra and I used to dream of escaping." Her expression grew gentle. "We had a hiding place we used to go, nothing special, just a pond in the jungle. That's where we'd go to talk about running away. We planned it, every detail and we knew we could pull it off. The only thing stopping us ..." She trailed off.

Ann waited, gazing at this eighteen- or nineteen-year-old beauty, whose spark was dampened but not extinguished. "The only thing stopping you?" she prompted, her voice as gentle as a lullaby.

"Where to go? We dreamed of going home, surfing, dancing, drinking beer on the beach, and just being young again. It's nothing special, I know that, but it's all we wanted. That's impossible. Even if we could go home, our families would sell us to another Dona Candida to service another camp. We have nowhere to go."

With a growing awareness of how little she knew about these girls' world, Ann ventured another question. "How did you and Alexandra plan to get out? I mean, she's gone and you're leaving in two weeks. I can't imagine you're giving too much away by telling me her plan."

Juliana's eyes flashed with anger. "I get to leave in sixteen days. That's two weeks plus two days, lady. You just don't understand! I shouldn't even be talking to you. If Dona Candida hears about this, she won't let me on the plane. I can't spend another month here, I'd rather die."

Her body became rigid and her eyes black.

"Is that why Alexandra escaped? She could bear it no longer?"

"No." Juliana wrapped her arms around herself as if she were cold. "Alexandra was due out the month before me but she couldn't wait another day because the puking had started."

"Puking? You mean morning sickness?"

"Yeah. It happens sometimes. Dona Candida can spot the signs before you even know yourself. If one of us falls pregnant, she makes us get rid of it. Dr Carreira knows what to do."

The skin on Ann's body turned to ice. She couldn't form the question but Juliana's body language gave her the answer she needed.

"Don't look at me like that! And anyway, it's done now." The girl's voice was raw and her tension electrified the air.

"No judgement, I swear." Ann bowed her head and waited for Juliana to speak.

When she did, her voice was soft, as if telling a bedtime story. "When Alexandra knew she was having a baby, she wanted to keep it. You can't do that here. The only way was to get out. So she did." Juliana let out a bitter little laugh. "The funny thing is she used to call me the brave one."

Seconds ticked by as Ann absorbed what both girls had suffered. She could not afford an emotional response to this revelation or Juliana would crack. Ann knew how vital it could be to hold things together when you were hurting.

"You two have more courage than I can imagine. Truly. Can you tell me how she got out?"

The young woman struggled to get her emotions under control. "Yeah. Alexandra waited under the priest's hut until the plane came in. While the pilot was at the canteen, she got inside and hid. He flew off without even realising she was there."

Ann recalled Paolo's words about the need for security around the aircraft. "Did you see her get in the plane?"

"No, but I know that's what she did. We'd planned it together, but only she had the guts to actually do it."

"I see. Juliana, why are you telling me this?"

"Because you and me, we come from the same place. When you go home to Soure, keep your eyes open for a pregnant teenager with a butterfly tattoo like this." She slipped off the blanket and pointed to the design on her left shoulder. "Then you've found Alexandra. Just don't make her go home to her family. Look, I have to go now or that old bitch will get suspicious. You stay here till the doc comes back. *Tchau.*"

"*Tchau* and thank you. I appreciate your trust."

The girl unlocked the door, peered outside and hobbled out into the heat. The surgery was cooler than most of the camp dwellings, but held a smell of blood and antiseptic Ann found upsetting. Instead of sitting in this grim little room, she waited outside until the doctor returned. She refused to think about what had been in that bucket or what he'd done with it.

Juliana was telling the truth, Ann was sure. The girl genuinely believed her friend had achieved the impossible. But Ann was equally certain Paolo had not unwittingly flown off with a stowaway on board. If Alexandra's intention was to board the plane and found it locked, what had happened next?

15

"Not exactly a luxury yacht, but it's the fastest way to get where we're going," said Damien, pouring diesel into the outboard motor.

The vessel was made of wood, around ten metres long and painted in green and red stripes. There were four rows of planks to sit on and no shade. Ann now understood Veronique's insistence on a hat. Of the petite Frenchwoman, there was no sign. Only she, Gil and Damien stood on the little jetty upstream from the main dock reserved for huge timber boats. Ann put two and two together. In all likelihood, Rocco would be enjoying some company that afternoon. She asked no questions and climbed into the boat to sit near the bow, the best place for unimpeded views. Gil stayed at the rear, taking instructions from Damien about steering the canoe. The cameraman had brought his kit and intended to film anything of interest while Gil guided them upstream.

Ann's concern about heat and mosquitoes seemed justified, as the boat attracted a small cloud of the bloodsuckers. Her long-sleeved shirt and bug-spray were a feeble deterrent. Then

Damien yanked the starter cable, the motor burst into life and the boat peeled off into the current.

Instantly, the insects vanished and the breeze acted as a natural coolant. With its red-brown water, the hue of strong tea, this river had far more depth and nuance than mere blackness. The colour reminded Ann of her shower stall when she rinsed off her henna. Either side, the banks were a riot of greenery, tendrils of foliage trailing into the water, with a broad stretch of china-blue sky reflecting off the surface. Trees grew out of the river, their trunks twisted and misshapen into a strange kind of beauty. Damien sped up, the bow of the boat carved a line through ripples and the engine settled into a background buzz.

For the next forty minutes, Ann relaxed into a rare feeling of complete freedom. She released her hair to blow in the wind, lifted her face to the sun and took in the serenity of water. Apart from the sound of the motor, everything was peaceful, green and as it should be. This was the rainforest she had dreamed of; a cloud of tiny multi-coloured parrots flashing like precious gems as they relocated from one tree to the next, a solitary alligator basking on an island barely the size of its body, two pink dolphins bobbing alongside the boat until they gave up on them as a food source and sank into the depths like teabags. In her previous life, she'd be making inane utterances, such as, 'Look at that! Wow! Isn't this amazing?' or trying to preserve the moment on camera. Those days were gone. Here, she immersed herself in the moment, trusting her mind to remember and her soul to heal.

Damien called out to draw her attention to the left bank, where a waterfall tumbled from a cliff, an endless cascade of white water refracting rainbows in the sunshine. Even at this distance, the spray was fresh and invigorating on her skin. Voices indicated the presence of a small village on the riverbank. Two women waved and half a dozen kids leapt into little boats, attempting to chase them. Damien put down his camera and yelled some words. Whatever he said stopped the children's frantic paddling and with downcast faces and drooping shoulders, they turned their tiny crafts towards home.

After another ten minutes chugging up the wide expanse of Rio Negro, the boat slowed. Damien took over the controls and nudged the boat towards the right bank. No jetty or landing stage was visible, just thick overhanging branches and vines. Gil came to sit beside Ann.

"We're going up one of the tributaries. It's overgrown and not much wider than this boat, so we have to watch out for spiders or snakes in the trees. The most essential thing is to keep quiet. We're the intruders here." He unfolded a length of tarpaulin. "You hold one side and I hold the other. It acts as protection. Damien has his own version."

Ann glanced over her shoulder to see the cameraman with all his equipment sheltering under a beach umbrella. He made a crouching motion, as if advising them to huddle. They huddled, shoulder to shoulder. It was overgrown, humid and hard to believe the boat could penetrate this far into the rainforest.

The engine's buzzing slowed to the sputtering of a hairdryer as they inched their way into this swampy, dark and dense corner of the world. Whenever something hit their fragile tarpaulin, Gil's body tensed, pressing closer to Ann. Leaves, jungle fruit and dead branches all seemed like deadly predators until they fell at their feet. Just as claustrophobia was causing Ann to clench her fists and curl her toes, the river opened up to a lake-like shape with a jetty, a few houses festooned with washing-lines, an array of canoes and the smell of cooking fish.

Damien spoke as he secured their boat among the others.

"Here's the thing. These people have their own language and behaviours, so don't impose your attitudes on them. Not as a Portuguese cop or a British backpacker. Just be aware that while they may seem unsophisticated to your eyes, they are incredibly knowledgeable about their environment. Many of the younger ones can also speak Portuguese so be careful what you say."

A man and three kids came to greet their visitors, all clearly familiar with Damien. One of the kids wore a Little Mix T-shirt, at odds with Ann's sense of remoteness, while the other two wore nothing other than a pair of shorts. They stared at Ann and Gil with the mistrustful curiosity of wild birds. The man wore a form of sarong, with earrings and jewellery made from fish bones. His extensively tattooed skin was the colour of a conker and his face, painted with white stripes, sagged with age.

Damien and Gil each offered him a paper bag, which he accepted and looked inside. He cracked a gleeful smile. He took out three small pieces of dried meat from Gil's bag and handed one each to the boys. They ran off into different houses, all chattering with excitement. The man opened Damien's bag, which contained a six-pack of beer. His smile spilt wider. Two teeth in his lower set were missing.

He and Damien spoke in low tones, with frequent gestures at her and Gil, a form of introduction, she assumed. Eventually, he led the way to a clearing and a circle of stones, with a burned-out fire in the middle.

"The village elder would like to tell you about this tribe and the area belonging to these people. But first he offers you a drink. This is a tribal speciality. It may seem strange but please don't refuse."

"Is it ..." Gil began.

"Delicious? Yes. It's also very strong. Just take one small sip from the bowl when we pass it around."

From the houses the boys had run into, some women began to emerge, their eyes bright with interest. Although Ann hadn't been sure what to expect, the women were not bare-breasted, wearing paint or painful-looking piercings. Most wore shorts and T-shirts or a sarong. One girl had on a denim mini-skirt. The chief spoke to a pair who might have been twins and they ran off across the compound. The rest came to take their places in the circle, smiling at these visitors who turned up unannounced. Ann smiled and said '*Olá*', but other than nods, no one responded. As they sat down on the flat stones, it was obvious three of them were pregnant.

Damien listened to the wiry man's voice once more and relayed his message. "The chief apologises. The village is half empty because the men have gone to trade with another tribe. Their journey takes several days. He asks why you have come so far." He directed his question at Gil.

Addressing the male and ignoring the female was to be expected. Ann had picked up on the patriarchal vibe from the outset. Time to let go of her cultural outlook. She was the guest and would do things their way.

"A father came to me in great distress." Gil spoke deliberately and addressed the chief, leaving pauses for Damien to translate. "His daughter was working at a timber camp and due home this month. She did not return with the others. We," he tilted his head in Ann's direction, "are here to find out what happened to her."

The chief said nothing, his gaze over their heads. The twins returned, carefully carrying a large vessel similar to a half a gourd and handed it to him. He made a brief speech and drank. Then he passed it to Damien, who did the same. He transferred the bowl of liquid to Gil and now Ann got a look at the contents. The consistency of soup, it was the colour of a winter sky and looked as appetising as a puddle.

"Say a few words of thanks and express gratitude for their

hospitality. Then drink." Damien's voice had an uncompro-
mising note.

Gil made a polite speech and took a small sip. Ann knew
him well enough to see it cost him quite an effort. He handed
the gourd to her and attempted a reassuring grin but Ann
could see his eyes were watering. She hesitated, a random
conspiracy theory flashing across her mind. What if Damien
had lured her and Gil here to poison or drug them as some
kind of example to culture vulture tourists?

She uttered a few polite platitudes, then bent her head over
the liquid and took a mouthful. The taste sent alarm bells
through her nervous system, saying 'bad, gone off, spit it out!'
but she could not be so pathetic. She swallowed and the liquor
hit her throat, making her own eyes tear up. She passed the
swampy stuff to the next woman who accepted with as much
delight as if it was her birthday cake.

The gourd travelled from one pair of hands to another
until the two young women who had brought it took their turn.
They then returned it to where it came from. Ann almost
moaned with relief. If that stuff had come round again, she
couldn't have done it. It had the fermented, bubbly, sour taste
of something turning rotten, and its potency was worrying.

The chief began so speak, his voice melodic and almost a
chant. At certain points, the women joined in or added an
echo. Kids emerged from the huts but simply squatted or sat at
a distance. The song or story went on, making a few of the
older women visibly emotional. The voice and its cadences
affected Ann too, although she had no idea of the content, but
somehow she knew it was a lament. Damien made no attempt
to translate, resting his chin on his hands and looking at the
ground.

When the chief ended his recital, there was no applause or
cheering, just a collective hush. To Ann, the village seemed

darker and sadder, as if remembering an ancient grief. The jungle sighed and the sky began to cry. Huge fat raindrops fell at their feet, trees swayed like mourners and the heat of the afternoon turned clammy on her skin.

As one, the villagers rose and ran to their homes, shouting incomprehensible instructions. Damien said something Ann couldn't hear and everywhere she looked there were rainbows. It occurred to her she was either tripping or drunk. Someone dragged her upright and she stumbled alongside Gil towards a shelter. It had no walls but a thatched palm roof. The ferocity of the downpour drenched them both on the short run from the stone circle and they stood gasping at the curtain of needle-like rain pounding the camp.

"My backpack!" she cried, staring up at Gil.

"I've got it. It's right here. I brought Damien's gear and your pack. Are you OK? Your eyes are completely black."

"Where is it? Oh, thank God. That drink! They drugged us. What the hell was in ... where's Damien?"

"He and some of the kids have gone to secure the boats. These storms can cause a flash flood and we cannot afford to lose our only means of transport. Ann, listen to me. That stuff is fermented manioc sometimes mixed with hallucinogens. They make it ... well, that doesn't matter, but it can have a powerful effect on the uninitiated. I want to keep an eye on you until you come down."

Ann's head was reeling and she knew she had something profound to say but the rain drowned out her thoughts. Logic made a fleeting reappearance. "How come you're not stoned? You drank it too!"

He shook his head, looking past her. "Here they come. No, I didn't drink any of it, just put it to my lips. I know well enough to avoid that stuff. Hey, Damien, how was the boat?"

Damien dashed out of the deluge, puffing as if he'd run a

marathon. He couldn't speak but gave two thumbs-up. Three young boys ran past and shot into the open doors of their houses. Their feet threw up splashes as they crossed the compound, the ground was already so waterlogged.

"It's fine," heaved Damien. "We lashed all of them to the trees in case the jetty gets ripped away. Thanks for taking care of my gear." He wiped a hand over his face and wrung out his ponytail. "The storms don't usually last long, but they can change the river currents. Thankfully, we've got a motor. I wouldn't chance it in a rowing boat."

Drips of rainwater began to penetrate the shelter and Damien took his equipment to the other end, where there was a low wooden table between two long benches. He helped himself to a pile of firewood and made a criss-cross structure beneath the table where he could place his black camera bags above the ground. Gil and Ann joined him to sit on the benches and watch the forces of nature. In her state of heightened awareness, Ann sensed the jungle was trying to tell them something, demonstrating its power and omnipotence. She was the only one who could hear its story.

Gradually the cracks of thunder receded and the rain, almost imperceptibly, began to abate. Threatening clouds in shades of slate billowed and rolled across the sky, as if the storm hadn't finished with them yet. The rainforest was aptly named.

Gil checked his watch and looked across the table at Damien. "It will be dark in a couple of hours. If we're going to get back to camp tonight ..."

"I want to talk to the chiefs." Damien stood up and stretched, rolling his shoulders. "They know these rivers better than anyone. If they think it's dangerous, we stay overnight, no question. I wish I'd bought more food. These people live a hand-to-mouth existence and don't exactly have a wine cellar stocked for visitors. If we stay, they are obliged to feed us. Eat tiny portions, no matter how hungry you are. Don't drink any more *masato* either – it's precious to them." He ran off into the rain.

The sublime connection binding Ann to the jungle and the universe narrowed back to a feeling of normality. Staying in a remote village seemed even more alarming than sleeping overnight at the timber camp. Then again, getting into a narrow wooden boat to navigate a swollen, raging river was even less of an attraction. The euphoria she had experienced earlier that afternoon evaporated into a maudlin desperation. She shouldn't be here. She should be at the beach with no more significant decisions to make than what she would have for dinner. In an attempt to connect to reality, she turned her face to Gil. He looked bedraggled and tired, but still dignified.

"OK, so what is *masato*?"

Gil studied her face. "Basically, it's a kind of hooch made from roots or fruits, like American moonshine or Chilean *chicha*. There's no single recipe because this drink exists across the Amazonian basin in various guises. I suspect this particular batch also contains hallucinogens judging by the size of your pupils."

It was one of the rare occasions Ann actually wished she had a mirror to see what he was talking about. But she had given up those long ago. "So why were you so weird about drinking it?"

He shook his head and looked out the dark skies. "It's not to my taste. I really hope we can get back to the camp tonight. From start to finish, this trip has been full of delays and transport problems."

"Gil, I know you well enough to recognise when you're withholding information. I'm going to ask you again. What is *masato*? And how is it made?"

Gil pulled at his shirt, billowing air between his chest and the fabric to dry it. "As I said, the base is fermented manioc root. Each tribe adds its own extra ingredient, very often local herbs or plants to make drinkers trip and have visions. What makes it unusual is that the women of the village chew the root to break down the starch and spit it into a container. There it ferments and becomes alcoholic. In most cases, the alcohol destroys any possibility of spreading infection and disease. But I am a little bit choosy about whose saliva I want in my mouth."

Ann closed her eyes and rested her spinning head on her hands.

Within half an hour of the storm blowing out, the sun returned, raising the temperature to the point where the village became steamy and humid once more. The chief, Damien, Gil and Ann, accompanied by the boys, walked down to the jetty to examine the damage and assess the chances of a safe passage downriver. Ann watched an elegant crane launch itself into the air, covering kilometres with a few flaps of its wings. She longed to be able to do the same. Just take off and fly all the way to the coast and her little shack on stilts.

The boats were undamaged, but the tributary to the Rio Negro was more of a torrent than the quiet stream they had navigated a little over two hours earlier. Three of the boys walked down the bank and returned with solemn expressions. The answer was undeniably negative.

The chief made another speech, gave orders to the boys who scattered in all directions, then led the way back to the village. Damien explained that he had sent them to gather food for a village feast because in his view, the river was deadly. "Forget what I said earlier. Hosting guests is regarded as great good luck and they want to celebrate. They won't allow us to help in the preparations, so we will have to show our appreciation in some other way. Have either of you got anything we could give as a present? Not money, they have little use for that. Something decorative or practical?"

Ann mentally scanned the contents of her backpack and thought about what she could afford to lose. "I have a Swiss Army knife," she offered. Her precious flick knife was essential to her sense of well-being, but she could trade her multi-purpose device. That was replaceable.

"Ladies and gentlemen, we have a winner!" Damien said in English then returned to Portuguese. "What about you, Gil?"

"I don't have much with me. I need my police equipment and anyway, that isn't mine to offer. All I have are personal items, like clothes and toiletries."

"What about your bracelet?"

Gil fingered the plaited black leather band around his right wrist. "This? You think they'd like it? Sure, I'll take it off."

"Perfect. Your bracelet, Ann's knife and I'll play them a film of the celebration. I think they'll be happy with that. OK, let's go party. By the way, he's offered us a choice of where to sleep. We can sling hammocks in the main shelter or use one of the houses left empty by the men. I like being in the open air, so I'm going to swing in the breeze. You?"

An impulse seized Ann. "We'll take the house. Probably not as luxurious as the boss's cabin we slept in last night, but at least I won't lie awake afraid of being eaten by a rampaging jaguar."

In two sentences, she had claimed Gil, intimated they were a couple and chosen to spend another night under the same roof as the inspector. But this time, there would be no separate rooms. Gil made no protest but was silent as they entered the village and Ann wondered if she'd been presumptuous. The women were preparing a fire and readying fruits, fish in banana leaves, rice and plantains on the communal table.

"This looks incredible!" Gil exclaimed. "Yeah, Ann's right. Hammocks are bad for my back. You'll understand when you get to my age."

"Ha!" Damien laughed. "You're what, two years older than me! Although you have got a lot of grey hairs."

"No wonder, in my job. If all did was spend my days filming monkeys, I'd look ten years younger."

"Monkeys?!"

Ann listened to them teasing one another and smiled, wondering what surprises the night would bring.

Forbidden from helping with preparations, Gil, Damien and Ann sat on a palm-leaf mat at a distance from the communal areas and watched the activity as darkness fell. Gil asked Damien about his experiences in Brazil and the Brit was only too happy to share his enthusiasm.

To Ann's ears, he sounded extremely knowledgeable about the indigenous tribes for a cameraman on a nature documentary.

"What was that song about?" she asked. "Maybe it was a poem rather than a song, but after we drank that *masato*, the chief recited something. I couldn't understand a word and I might have been slightly inebriated, but I got the feeling it was sad."

"The saddest. He was telling their story, the story of this tribe. Older generations tell it to the younger ones and it's repeated often so that no one forgets."

"What happened?" asked Gil.

"What happened? We happened. European colonialists came over the sea and 'discovered Brazil'. You know your country's history better than I do, Gil. The song or poem, whatever you want to call it, talks about the white man's arrival, bringing diseases, violence and slavery. He was not just talking about the 16th century but also the 1980s on. Goldminers, wood-loggers and ranchers invaded their land, treating it as nothing more than a source of profit. That's the essence of the story. We don't understand their view of the world."

"What is their view of the world?" asked Ann, her voice soft.

Damien sighed and threw up his hands. "It's incredibly simple and at the same time, impossible for people like us to appreciate. The fundament is that everything has a spirit. You, me, the jaguar, the peccary, the lizard, the fish, the river, the banana plant, the jungle canopy and the forest floor all have a spirit. From the ant to the antelope, everything is connected and they respect that. What's key to this outlook is they are not superior. They work with nature, but don't seek to dominate. These people are nomads in the sense they build a village, fish, plant crops and hunt, but appreciate when they have taken enough. Then they move on so that nature can recover. This tribe and many others in this region consider themselves defenders or protectors of this system. As far as they're concerned, this *is* the world."

His words contained a passion lit by a furious fire. They sat on the palm mat, watching a naked toddler wobble after his mother.

"Something tells me you're a bit more than a natural history cameraman," said Ann.

"Something tells me you're a bit more than a journalist," he replied, but with nothing more than amusement in his tone. "No camera, no notebook, only a pair of sharp eyes. Actually, I am a natural history cameraman but the world of nature is also the world of humanity. Yeah, the hunting habits of the tapirs are intriguing. So is the fact that some tribes consume the ashes of their dead by eating them in soup. Their concept of organic is a long way from pesticides and supermarket packaging. People are and have always been a part of this forest, not trying to be master, but surviving as one element in a functioning system. Until we came along."

Gil leaned forward, his shoulder brushing against Ann's. "That's true. We came along, like invaders of another planet. Bringing sicknesses against which they have no immunity. Prostituting the women and giving them venereal disease. Pillaging their homeland for anything of worth and leaving devastation behind. You don't need to tell me. I'm aware of what's happening."

"Oh, really? So what are you doing about it? I've been here a short time and don't have the whole picture but it seems to me the only effective activity comes from the NGOs. Sure, the government makes all kinds of official promises, but unless they're upheld and transgressors prosecuted, those cynical mining and logging bastards continue to devastate protected regions. You're a cop from the coast, Gil, I know that, and I'm not laying all this on your shoulders. But everyone who knows what's actually going on must spread the word. You've seen this with your own eyes. You too, Ann, whether you're a journalist or not. This doesn't just affect this village, this tribe or even the Amazonian basin. What they're doing will affect the entire planet. Ah, your lecture is over because it looks like dinner's ready."

The twins from earlier in the afternoon were adorned with feathers and a multitude of necklaces, beaded anklets and stripes of colours on their arms. They beckoned to the trio seated on the mat and drew them towards the fire. Small glows of light burned in wide-brimmed vessels like upturned sombreros between the stone circle and the shelter. Ann took her place between Gil and Damien, and the chief made a speech. For some reason, he did not sit on his central stone, but paced around the fire, addressing each upturned face. When he'd finished, he threw out an arm and all eyes followed his gesture.

Out of the shadows and into the light came two figures, both moving slowly.

"What's this?" Ann whispered to Damien.

"Wait and see."

The taller woman was wearing a head-dress made of reeds or vines, her face painted and her long skirt swaying as she approached. Her hands rested on the shoulders of a girl, who shuffled reluctantly into the firelight. Gil Maduro's words echoed in Ann's mind. 'They're sending me to investigate a missing person case. One I cannot solve.'

Ann's lips parted in amazement. *Looks like you just did.*

The girl who stepped into the circle was easily recognisable as Alexandra Lemos. The next jaw-dropper was the woman behind her. She sat on the chief's stone and in fluent Brazilian Portuguese, announced herself as the village chief, thanked the saggy-faced man for standing in for her and stated the order of events. Alexandra would speak. If they wished, the police could answer. Then the celebrations would begin. Her name was not important and neither were theirs.

One milligram of that woman's authority could command a stadium. Here, in a group of fewer than thirty individuals in the semi-darkness, she was a goddess. In comparison, the young woman who stepped forward to speak, her hands folded over the barely-there bump, visibly quailed at addressing such a large group.

"My name is Alexandra Lemos. I ran away from the camp to save my baby. These people found me in the jungle and brought me here to a place where I can be happy. They are good and kind and never make me do anything horrible. I will not return to the camp. I will not return to my family. I am nineteen years old and able to make my own choices. My choice is to stay here. If you try to remove me from this place, that is a crime according to Brazilian law. It is my right to stay here and give birth to my child. I want to stay."

Her delivery invited applause but not a single person moved. All eyes turned to Gil Maduro.

He stood and cleared his throat. "Alexandra, I am very pleased to find you well."

Beside Ann, Damien translated for the rest of the village.

"My mission was to find out what happened to you. I believed that was an impossibility and assumed you were already dead. Seeing you alive and carrying a new life fills me with joy. I see you have great friends in this place. I did my job and have no desire to relocate you to anywhere you do not wish to go. My friends and I will leave you tomorrow and I give you sincere congratulations."

It took a few seconds, but when Damien finished his translations, the group stamped their feet and ululated to the skies. That, Ann gathered, was a standing ovation.

The chief's smile gleamed and she swept an arm towards the shelter. "The dispute is resolved. In good faith, we eat, drink and dance together."

Eat, drink and dance they did. Ann stuck to guava juice and cachaça, avoiding the *masato* altogether. She ate grilled fish and fruit with spiced rice, and tried to keep up with the stomping, shouting movements around the central blaze. Damien made a speech in the tribe's language and presented Ann's knife and Gil's bracelet and showed them the footage of the previous few hours on his laptop. Ann's laughter at her own useless rhythm chimed with their hosts'. The film was the highlight of the evening and everyone began packing away soon after. Their assistance was gently rebuffed, so Gil and Ann sought out the chief and thanked her in Portuguese.

"We do not appreciate foreigners. We trust Damien. On this occasion, he was right. I ask you to please leave here first thing in the morning. You people disrupt our lives. Sleep well and *boa noite*." She sallied off into the darkness.

Gil reached for Ann's arm to guide her away from the stone circle. "The cabin is the last on the left. I've got a torch. You got your backpack?"

She clasped his fingers between hers. "Yes, it's here and I'm ready for bed. What a night!"

16

With the help of the tiny light produced by Gil's phone, he and Ann made their way across the compound and into the cabin. Like all the other constructions, it had no door, just an open entrance. Inside, there was a raised platform on the right and another at the rear, while on the left, two hammocks hung limply. Ann tested one of the communal beds and found a mattress filled with dried grasses. It was surprisingly comfortable. Gil flicked the torch around the rest of the small wooden house. It was clearly used for sleeping and nothing else. Life in this village was lived outside. There was a rough piece of sacking tied up over the door. Gil pulled at the ties and it fell across the doorway, blocking out the moonlight.

"Or would you prefer to leave it open?" he asked, shining the torch at her face.

"No, let's have the minimum of privacy." Ann kicked off her shoes and began to undress. Her skin goose-pimpled in the night air, much cooler since the storm at sunset. She pulled her T-shirt over her head and saw the torch beam heading in the direction of the other platform. She cleared her throat. "It's colder than I thought and as there's no lock on this door, well, no actual door to speak of, I'd prefer it if we slept in the same bed. If you wouldn't mind?"

The torch beam stopped and there was a charged pause. "No, I wouldn't mind." The light approached and went out.

Zips and the soft sound of fabric told Ann he was taking off his clothes. She reached for one of the thin bedcovers and drew it over herself, her skin hyper-sensitive. He lay on his back beside her in the darkness and she caught the scent of his sweat, a trace of his aftershave and the aroma of wood smoke in his hair. She knew she was unwashed and probably smelt less than fragrant, but that didn't seem to matter much here and now. She turned to face in his direction.

"You found Alexandra," she murmured. The couple of inches between their bodies crackled with so much electricity, Ann could almost visualise it.

"We found her. This wouldn't have happened without you." His voice was low and throaty.

Ann wished she could see his eyes, but shining a torch in his face at this juncture might kill the moment. Last time he had made a move, she rejected him. Expecting him to try again was unfair. If she'd changed her mind, it was up to her to say so. This wasn't a Jane Austen novel.

She snaked out a hand until her fingertips made contact with his arm and stroked his skin. His breathing was shallow as her hand continued its journey over his chest and up towards his jaw. To her embarrassment, a tremble ran through her body, her nervousness betraying her. What kind of a seductress was she, shivering with fear? She turned his face towards her and pulled him closer. The second the warmth of his lips met hers, all nerves vanished. He rolled onto his side with a moan and pressed her against him.

In an instant, her body came alive and made its needs known. Dispensing with butterfly kisses and delicate caresses, the shivery seductress stood down, replaced by a ravenous feral cat. She writhed, arched her back and dug in her claws, enfolding him and abandoning herself to a craven, selfish desire. Everything about him was a banquet to a starved wretch: his stubble against her cheek, the muscles of his torso, his weight, his tongue, his fingers, his scent and the feeling of being filled, completed and satisfied made her release a single cry to the heavens. For as much as passion suffused their hut with fireworks, they had stayed as silent as mice.

Mice? Ann smiled to herself as she curled into Gil's side, her head on his shoulder, his arm wrapped around her. *More like rabbits.* His lips pressed against her forehead and her eyes closed.

Sex in total darkness is an exceptional experience, especially if it's the first time. Without visuals, four other senses come to the fore, calling on the sixth – imagination. Yet without seeing what happens, it's harder to commit to memory. Which is exactly why Ann wanted to wake at dawn and make some more beautiful memories.

The village had other ideas. Kids were running around outside their hut before daybreak, and twice someone lifted the curtain to peek in. Gil was asleep on his side, his hair wild and his lips parted. Ann shuffled down the bed and wrapped one of the bedcovers around herself. She drew back the curtain to see a brilliant rainforest sunrise with steam rising from the jungle like autumn mist. People were moving around the compound, lighting the fire, pounding cassava and making something that smelt very much like coffee.

From where she stood, Ann saw Damien in conversation with the deputy chief and at one point they both looked in her direction. She waved and shouted, "Just coming!"

Inside, Gil sat up with a start. The sheet had slipped,

revealing the puckered skin of the burn down the right side of his torso. Ann took a second to appreciate the man but parked her lust. One day, very soon, she would enjoy Gil Maduro in broad daylight and at her leisure.

"Everyone's awake and waiting for us. I'll get dressed and try to do a basic toilette. Then I think it's coffee and back down the river. You OK?"

He blinked and stared at her. "I had the most amazing dream."

In two paces she was beside him and caught his face in her hands for a kiss. "You know what? I have a feeling that might be one of those recurring dreams. But not now, Gil. We have to go. Get your pants on."

The villagers were not ones for a big send-off. After drinking something coffee-ish, they were asked to leave. The female chief and Alexandra did not emerge, but the chief's stand-in, this time without his paint, escorted them to their boat. No one could miss the message: You. Go. Now.

Damien placed his camera equipment in the rear and started the motor. Gil sat beside Ann and all three waved their farewells as the boat curved around and set off downstream. The waters were higher than the previous day and even the little tributary hurried them away, much like the villagers. Once they hit Rio Negro, it was a different proposition. The deep brown currents pounded and surged to such an extent, Ann's courage failed her. The speed of the water was merciless.

Gil seemed to have the same thought. "Damien!" he yelled behind him. "No way can this boat cope with these conditions. It's lethal, look at it! If we capsize, we're dead!"

"I'm not taking us into the current! We'll crawl along the shallows, hugging the left bank. But I need you to look out and warn me about dangers up ahead. After yesterday's storm, there'll be tree trunks, smashed canoes and dead animals washed against the banks. I'll keep the speed to an absolute minimum and you sit in the bow. Shout and raise your hand to tell me where to go; right, left or straight up if I need to stop."

Gil scrambled over the benches to sit on a bench directly in the prow, his posture erect and his head surveying their route. Even with the engine in its lowest gear, the speed unsettled Ann. Trailing vines and branches brushed their heads as Damien steered the boat as far away from the maelstrom as possible. Twice, huge roots blocked their path and Gil indicated right. The closer they got to the main current, its pull increased and Ann found herself clenching the flimsy wooden bench until they reached calmer water.

A bloated deer bumped against the hull as they turned a bend and its lifeless eyes chilled Ann's heart. Her fears almost overwhelmed her until Gil glanced over his shoulder, with a secretive smile. That had the opposite effect. The beautiful waterfall they had passed yesterday was a furious stream of solid water, pounding into the river. Ann gave thanks it was on the other side.

"Another two kilometres, I estimate!" Damien called. "Oh, fuck!"

Directly ahead was a tangle of shattered timber, fishing nets and upturned hulls. Somewhere further upstream, a village had lost its jetty, its boats and means of survival. It protruded like an iceberg, blocking their path. Damien swung the boat right, out into the current, but couldn't quite avoid a glancing blow as the hull bounced off the knotted confusion. To Ann's horror, it broke loose and swirled into their wake. With no engine to slow its progress, it gained on them, a pile of destruction which would add their feeble craft to its mass.

Ann screamed a warning and scrambled over the benches to Damien. He yelled something incomprehensible and pointed to his gear. Whether he wanted her to lift it or hold it down she had no idea. She crabbed her limbs over the black equipment bags, her own backpack protecting her head. With a roar at Gil, Damien powered the boat to a terrifying speed, bouncing off the river surface, causing splashes to hit Ann's head, limbs and backside. The momentum made her sick and she dared not raise her head to check Gil was still clinging to the bow. It took three minutes before the boat slewed left towards the bank and the engine cut out.

Damien wiped river water from his face and looked down at her, his nostrils flaring. She nodded and got to her feet, her eyes searching for Gil. He emerged from under one of the benches, mopping his face with his shirt.

"Everyone all right?" he shouted.

"Fine! Ann, get the equipment out of the water as fast as you can. The camp is around the next bend but I want to be sure that shit is a long way out of our path before I start the engine."

She lifted all the black bags onto the bench behind the motor and waited. Two minutes later, the deadly detritus washed past, in the centre of the roiling river. Yesterday, that mass had been essential items for a community's survival. Today, it was a lethal snowball crushing everything in its path.

As their pulses returned to normal, Damien started the motor and Ann reached for Gil. Wet, stressed and exhausted by fighting the elements, they held each other until the boat drew up to the smaller of the two jetties. Gil and Damien leapt onto the boards, roping the vessels to its moorings. Stage one of the return journey was complete. Ann handed Damien's equipment to him, piece by piece, and accepted Gil's forearm to pull her onto dry land.

"Are you OK?" His eyes locked on to hers.

In that instant, Ann's armour melted away. Gil Maduro felt, smelt and tasted like home. She wanted to explore this man, regardless of the risks. Her legs were shaky and her hands unsteady, but she reached a hand behind his neck and drew his mouth to hers.

"Maduro!" Rocco roared from the ramp above. "Quit Romancing the Stone! We need to make an arrest!"

Gil took off at a run. Damien snatched up his equipment and struggled uphill. He called over his shoulder in English, "All hands on deck, mate! Let's go!"

Like a seasoned professional, Ann gathered her strength and her rucksack, chasing the cameraman up the incline, aware she had very few resources to draw upon. Rocco led the way to the management office where Juan-Carlos Ablos was standing outside, his arms folded and his permanent shadow of a bodyguard at his side.

"It makes no difference how many of you there are. You will still be outnumbered and I will have a riot on my hands."

"*Basta*! Listen to me! I am a police officer, a government agent with the authority of the law on my side." Rocco's stature and volume was intimidating. Even the minder wavered.

"I'm not prepared to discuss this here in the street. Let's go to the canteen." Ablos shook his head and locked his office.

The party of six walked the short distance to the near-empty Quonset hut. At the other end, two men were preparing the day's lunch. Ann caught the smell of frying onions and found herself salivating. The group settled themselves at a table near the entrance.

Rocco explained the situation. "Right, Gil, my professional and official colleague, here is what's going on. The night I spent in the priest's hut, some guy came knocking, thinking Ann was inside. I recognised him but couldn't place his face. Then I remembered seeing him on the police database. Before Paolo flew out, I used his radio to check if it was the same man. I was right. Bruno Diaz is a fugitive, wanted for various violent crimes in two countries. Yesterday afternoon the police force in Manaus radioed the camp office, confirming Bruno's status and ordering an immediate arrest. Ablos took the message. But for some reason, he decided not to tell me until this morning. And strangely enough, Bruno Diaz hasn't turned up for work today. That's an odd coincidence, don't you think?"

All eyes rested on the boss. His bodyguard placed his palms on the table as if ready for action. What kind of action, Ann couldn't tell.

"In that case," said Gil, "Juan-Carlos Ablos must be arrested for aiding and abetting a fugitive from the law. Rocco? Would you like to do the honours?"

Ablos held up his hands in a pacifying move. "I didn't tell you until today because you can't arrest him yet. There's no point in causing trouble until you can safely get him out. That means the plane needs to be here and ready to leave as soon as you have him in cuffs. If you try to arrest him today, the rest of the workers will attack you and probably me too. I sent Bruno on an errand last night to keep him out of the way until tomorrow morning. When he returns, I will ask him to report to me. You can arrest him and put him straight on the plane without his workmates knowing anything about it. I'm trying to help you, if you will only listen."

Rocco's eyes bored into him and then he switched his focus to Gil. "And what if Bruno does not turn up tomorrow morning?"

"Then we take Senhor Ablos to Manaus and charge him with obstruction of justice."

For several seconds, Ablos flicked his gaze between Gil and Rocco. The bodyguard's head rotated around the party like a dog waiting for a command. No one spoke.

The arrival of Veronique broke the tension. The French-woman hesitated in the entrance to the hut, apparently seeking permission to interrupt. Rocco looked up at her and gestured to the seat beside him. Veronique flashed a quick smile at Damien and Ann as she slid into her place beside Rocco.

Ablos addressed the two police officers. "Do it my way and save us all a lot of unnecessary trouble. I don't want my work-force disrupted and you don't want to lose your man. When the plane arrives tomorrow, I promise you Bruno will be back."

"He already is." To everyone's surprise, it was Veronique who spoke. "I just saw him get off one of the trucks. He went straight into the bar. He's there right now, drinking a beer."

Rocco pushed back his chair but Ablos reached out an arm to stop him. "Don't do anything now! Please, Inspector Delgado, it's for the best. Leave it till tomorrow morning. What are you going to do with him if you arrest him now? Where can you hold him? Trust me! Play along as if everything's normal and take him when the plane arrives."

Rocco shook his head. "And risk losing him again? I don't think so. Gil, let's go."

"NO! Not in the bar, for the love of God. I'll get someone to send him to my office. You wait there and when he comes in, do what you have to do. Then take him in the back room. It's the only building with a secure section, because it contains the safe and the men's wages. All we can hope is the loggers don't find out. This is such a disaster." He rested his forehead in his palm for a second and then frowned in the direction of the two cooks. "Hey!" he shouted. "I need one of you to run an errand!"

The two men exchanged a glance and one walked down the length of the hut towards them. He wore a vest and running shorts. It made sense. Slaving over a hot stove in this heat was a thankless task. "*O que é?*" he asked.

"Go over to the bar and find Bruno. You know who Bruno is, right? Tell him I want to see him in my office immediately."

The man started to leave but Gil held up a hand, like a traffic cop. "No. Please wait a moment. Sorry, Ablos, but I don't trust you. He's not going over there alone. Ann, Veronique, I want you to follow this guy at a distance and make sure he delivers the message and only the message. Damien, will you come with us? We are armed, obviously, but Bruno is a big guy. We might need your help." He cast a disparaging glance in the direction of Ablos. "You had better cower in your cabin." He gave the cook a nod. "Thank you. Please deliver the message from the boss now."

The two women got to their feet and followed the young cook across the street and into the music bar. Exactly as Veronique had said, Bruno was leaning against the counter, beer in hand. As they entered, he turned around and gave them both a leer. He grabbed his crotch with his left hand and said, "OK, why not? I'm always ready for a threesome."

His expression changed from a lascivious grin to an irritable grimace as the cook came to stand in front of him. "Out of the way, you turd."

The man stood his ground and spoke in an apologetic tone but loudly enough for all to hear.

Bruno listened with a look of disbelief. "What, right now? I just got in and I'm thirsty. Oh, damn it all to hell. All right, I'm coming." He slugged his beer and slammed the bottle on the bar with such force Ann was surprised it didn't shatter. He barrelled out of the doorway, waited until a haulage truck rumbled past and crossed the street in the direction of the office. The cook followed at a respectful distance.

Veronique widened her eyes at Ann. "We've done our bit. Now why don't we stay out of the way and leave it to the professionals? God, I cannot wait to leave this place. How was your trip upriver?" She gave Ann a knowing smile. "Did you find anything … interesting?"

In the turbulence of the last twenty-four hours, Ann had almost forgotten the fact that they'd actually achieved their mission. "You could say that," she smiled back. "Veronique, I could do with a shower and something to eat. Do you have plans for lunch?"

"Nothing that can't be changed at short notice. But first I want to be sure they've nailed that bastard," said Veronique, her gaze fixed on the office building. Just then, the door opened and Damien emerged.

He lifted a hand in the air and raised a triumphant fist. Still carrying his camera equipment, he crossed the street to meet them. "One large ugly logger is now under arrest and judging by his language, none too happy about it. Gil and Rocco are going to take it in turns to guard him. I'm going to speak to Ablos. We need to radio Paolo to warn him he will have six passengers tomorrow, one heavier than most. God, I cannot wait to get out of this place."

Veronique laughed. "That's just what I said. Ann wants to clean up and then get something to eat. You want to join us?"

"Is the Pope Catholic? Let me lock this stuff away and I'll meet you in the bar." He lowered his voice to a whisper. "Just remember to say nothing about what's going on in the office. It's vital the men don't know Bruno's been arrested."

Veronique suggested the safest place for a shower was the brothel. Unused during the day, the building had two shower stalls and guaranteed privacy. Dona Candida allowed Veronique access to the facilities for a small fee. "She charges extra if you use the mirror," she laughed.

Ann made up her mind to buy both members of the film crew lunch as a thank-you and stepped into the bathroom. The system was much like her own shack – rainwater collected on the roof and a lever allowed some of it to spill onto the bather below. She cleaned herself, aware of her body in an entirely new way. Her mind flew back to the previous night and her hunger for Gil Maduro. She hadn't finished with him yet.

Once washed and dressed in fresh clothes, Ann became aware of another kind of hunger. Poor Gil must be as exhausted, dirty and empty as herself. Probably worse, after arresting Bruno. She decided to take him and Rocco some food before she ate, already picturing his slow smile.

Veronique was waiting outside the building, chatting to a couple of the girls. The three of them sat in plastic chairs under a tarpaulin, drinking juice. The sun shone on the dirty yellow awning transforming the scene into something more innocent, as if three young women were just enjoying the breeze on the stoop. One of the girls was Juliana, the one who'd spilled the beans about Alexandra's pregnancy. Ann had an urge to reassure her, but Juliana already believed that her best friend was absolutely fine, and there was no reason to give Alexandra's secret away.

"Hi there," Ann said. "Did you guys get thrashed by that storm yesterday afternoon?"

Juliana looked up with a smile. "Yeah, the storm hit us. Everything feels fresher today. I guess it washed away a lot of the shit."

"I know how that feels," said Ann. "Veronique? You ready?"

The Frenchwoman got to her feet. "See you later, *meninas.*"

They walked through the scrubby alleyways towards the music bar. Ann spoke. "I'm buying lunch, to show my gratitude to you and Damien. But before we eat, I want to take something to Rocco and Gil. What time do the men come down to the canteen?"

"Between twelve and two. They eat in shifts so the work can continue. You don't need to worry about the cops. Damien took some tacos and water over there just now. Oh, dammit, I just gave away the menu. It's fish tacos again."

"I love fish tacos. To be honest, right now there's very little I wouldn't eat."

"Or drink? Damien mentioned you tried the *masato.*" She laughed, lifting her face to the sky. Ann laughed with her and noticed a slight redness around Veronique's jaw line. She touched her fingers to her own chin, aware of the tell-tale beard rash. So both women had got their man.

"They didn't tell me what was in it and I only had a sip, but it messed with my head. Gil and Damien only touched it to their lips, apparently. I wish they had warned me."

They entered the bar which was almost empty apart from the priest and doctor conversing at a table near the back. They acknowledged the newcomers with a nod but made no other friendly overtures. That suited Ann just fine. She ordered at the counter and Veronique selected a table as far away as possible from the professionals.

"I've tried *masato* twice and it took me days to recover. Damien would have drunk it. He's developed some kind of immunity, I believe, and that's one of the things that make people trust him. He dives right into their world. What did you think?"

"Of the alcohol, the camp or the situation?" Ann didn't need an answer. "I think that girl got lucky. She seems content and they are happy to have her. Alexandra and Juliana and probably many other girls have a stoicism I can hardly imagine. They're tough because they have to be. Why didn't you just tell us where she was?"

"We had no right to tell you. It wasn't our decision. All we could do was take you there and let her choose if she wanted to show herself. I'm glad she did. It's a happy ending." Veronique grinned as Damien entered the bar. "I ordered tacos for you. I hope that's OK? Because if not, tough shit."

"Tacos again? But I wanted the veal with Marsala mushroom sauce and duchesse potatoes! Where's my glass of Beaujolais Nouveau?"

"Your bottle of beer is behind the bar, keeping cold. What's going on over there?" Veronique jerked her head in the direction of the office.

"You're not getting a word out of me until I had a drink." He bounced out of his chair and raised a hand in salute towards the doctor and priest. Once he'd claimed his bottle, he sat opposite them, his young, tanned face showing no signs of the day's stress or dangers. He raised his beer for a toast and spontaneously burst into song. "One Day More!"

"Shut up, big mouth. Is Rocco OK? What happened? What about Gil?" Veronique's concern for the other officer came a second too late.

"The cops are in control. They had him at gunpoint the moment he opened the door. He cursed them and Ablos and me to hell and back, but there was nothing he could do. Yay, tacos! It's been too long!"

Even though they'd eaten it before, the food was a delicious blend of chilli heat, the sweetness of mango and sour lime juice wrapped up with the freshest of fish. They ate in silence, devoting their attention to their meal. Finally, Veronique asked another question.

"Did you get through to Paolo?"

Damien nodded and took a swig of his beer. "The plane is ready and the forecast is fine, so barring unforeseen circumstances, it will be here tomorrow morning." He wiped his mouth with the back of his hand. "That's the only thing I'm going to miss about this hellhole – Guido's cooking. Those were the best tacos I've ever had."

"What did he say about the extra passenger?" asked Veronique.

"Who?"

Veronique tutted in exasperation. "Paolo! You did tell him there would be six of us plus our equipment?"

"Yeah, I did. It won't be Paolo, though."

Ann frowned. "Why not?"

"Dunno. The guy I spoke to said we'll have a different

pilot. Can't remember his name. Who wants another beer? OK, that's two. Ann, what about you? Ann?"

"Oh, sorry, I was miles away. No, thanks, I'm done."

The sound of male voices and the crunching of vehicles announced the first wave of loggers returning for their midday meal. Ann tried to shake the sense of foreboding that bothered her, but couldn't help feeling the change of pilot was bad news.

17

Most of the loggers opted for the canteen, so only five sweaty workmen entered Bar Musica for Guido's fish tacos. Three out of the five had a moustache and all of them were shouting rather than speaking their conversation. Perhaps the habit of spending most of the day yelling at each other over loud machinery was hard to switch off. Whatever the reason, it was enough to drive the doctor and priest from their table.

Damien downed his beer and prodded Veronique. "You and I have some editing to do. What I filmed yesterday will definitely add value. Want to see? Ann, you're welcome to hang out at my place. It's not exactly the Ritz. Oh, no, it's far more sophisticated. Think Claridge's."

Ann twisted her face into a smile. "No, you two go ahead. I'm fine. I'd like a chat with Guido and then I'll go over to see how the guys are managing their prisoner. Hey, I didn't say thank you for taking us to the village and getting us out again. Thank you. You are one hell of a guy."

Damien prodded Veronique again. "Hear that? I'm one

hell of a guy. I'm getting that printed on a T-shirt in case you forget."

"You never let me forget. *On y va*! See you later, Ann."

Ann watched them leave and took the dirty plates to the bar. Guido worked the place alone, so if he was out back cooking, you either waited or banged on the bar for his attention. Patience was a skill Ann had honed for years. She sat at the bar and waited. Guido came out twice, bearing two trays of tacos, shooting her a 'what-do-you-want?' look. She just smiled and shook her head.

Footsteps came up behind her and just as she was about to snap around, Rocco announced himself in classic Rocco style. "Ha! So I'm not the only one who's still hungry. Guido, my man, another two portions over here and I'm in dire need of some tequila." He heaved his backside onto a stool and gave Ann a knowing look. "Don't worry about your boyfriend. He's taking the first shift and we'll switch every three hours. From midnight onwards, we're working together. Have you seen Veronique?"

Guido removed the dirty plates, greeting Rocco with a salute. He grabbed a bottle of Jose Cuervo by the neck and two shot glasses.

"Just one portion of tacos and the tequila is for him, Guido," said Ann. "I'll stick to beer, thank you. Yes, Veronique and Damien are working on their film. Is Gil safe in there with that psycho?"

Rocco accepted the shot from the barman and threw it down in one. "Now that's what the doctor ordered. One more of those with a plate of tacos and I award Guido the title of Best Chef and Barman in the whole of Rio Negro."

The chef laughed, cracked open a beer for Ann and returned to the kitchen to start cooking.

Ann pushed her point. "Rocco? How about Gil?"

"You know what? I knew it, the second I saw the pair of

you. Rocco, I said to myself, these two are going to make a perfect couple. Of course, that was before I learned you were on the wrong side of the law."

"Thank you, Oprah, but I asked you a question, not your opinion on my moral fibre or the odds of our having a successful relationship. Is Gil safe?"

Rocco gave a hearty laugh, but Ann couldn't be sure how much of it was genuine. "Gil is perfectly safe. Listen to me, Ann Sheldon." He dropped his voice, faced forward to stare at the wall and clasped his hands together. "We're pretty similar, no? We both broke the rules. Maybe you're the smarter one because you got out. My future in the police force is shaky. I've made compromises, turned a blind eye and taken bribes from organised criminals. Not that I'm the only corrupt cop on my force, but the one with the highest profile. But, and it's a big but, if I can deliver that nasty bastard Diaz into the hands of the Manaus police and tie up the case of the missing prostitute, I get all the gold stars. Previous indiscretions overlooked and a likely promotion. This is my chance to wipe the slate clean. That's why I can't risk that ugly brute taking flight. I don't trust Juan-Carlos Ablos or his knuckle-dragging bodyguard to keep Bruno Diaz under lock and key. In this hellhole, the only person I trust is Gil Maduro."

They sat side by side, staring at a poster depicting brewery logos as sponsors of the 2014 World Cup. Guido delivered a plate of tacos and poured Rocco another shot of tequila, then came out from behind the bar to collect dirty plates and empty glasses. While Rocco eagerly wrapped up pockets of food to stuff into his mouth, Ann's temper raged to a white-hot fury. She could not accept everyday police corruption any more than she would tolerate assumptions about her past.

She kept her tone low and acidic. If it gave him indigestion, so be it. "Right, you listen to me, Rocco Delgado. You've got it all wrong. We're not similar in any way. Comparing our roles is like comparing Rio Negro and the Solimões. We're formed by different backgrounds and nothing, and I mean nothing, about us is any way alike. You broke the rules and relinquished your integrity. Corruption paid off and now all you need to do is to skip out of town once in a while then reap the rewards."

Rocco stopped eating, his expression thunderous. "Don't you dare judge me. You don't understand what it's like here and now."

"No, I don't understand what it's like here and now. Neither do you understand what it was like there and then. Look at me! I'm the original Miss Goody Two-Shoes! I stuck to the letter of the law, obeyed orders, put myself at risk and never once spoke up. I did everything right, Rocco! They want to use unethical practices, fine. They ask me to delude nice guys and collude with violent scumbags, not a problem. I sucked it all up and bore the consequences, but only ever on behalf of the authorities. Not for personal gain. That's the difference between you and me. The only reason I'm on the run is because they were planning to throw me to the wolves. After all I've sacrificed, I refuse to be the fall guy."

Rocco scooped some fish into his tortilla and chewed, his face thoughtful. The loggers finished their meals and laid down their cutlery, heading out to work, still talking at a volume as if they were on opposite sides of the street. Ann noted they all wore a kind of tabard, marking them as supervisors or foremen. Perhaps that explained why they wanted to eat apart from the workforce. Guido switched off the crappy music and started clearing their tables, humming an unrecognisable tune.

"Yeah, that makes a lot of sense." Rocco helped himself to a swig of her beer, nodding. "An undercover cop who bolted. No wonder you've got a bunch of people hunting you down. Does Gil know about all of this?"

She exhaled all the tension in her shoulders. "I haven't spelt it out but I think he has a pretty good idea. The thing is, much as I like the guy, I can't hide behind him. Until I met you and O Cabrito, my disappearing act had worked reasonably well. Now I have to take off again and find somewhere new to conceal myself."

"Hmm."

The bar was now empty and quiet, other than the sounds of dishwashing from the kitchen.

"Tell me your real name." Rocco's tone was seductive and his smile charming apart from the fact he had chilli stuck in his teeth.

Ann reclaimed her beer bottle. "See this? Shove it up your arse."

"Wait, don't be like that." Rocco clasped her wrist until she shot him a murderous look and he released her. "Sorry, I wasn't trying to play macho. What I mean is there's another way. Not everything is black and white. You can tread the middle ground by playing a clever game. Work with the winners, you know what I mean? Ann, or whatever your real name is, you're smart, not bad looking and well trained. It's just a question of adapting to your circumstances."

She swallowed the rest of her beer in three gulps and placed the empty bottle on the bar.

"All I've heard since this trip began is 'don't judge what you don't understand'. There's a lot I don't understand, Rocco, but if I let go of my moral compass, I might as well give up. Thanks, but no thanks. I'm on my own."

She expected a kickback to her rejection, but Rocco nodded and went back to squeezing limes over his food. "I was right."

In the act of shouldering her rucksack, she stopped. "About what?"

"You and Gil would make the perfect couple." He scratched his beard. "You're not the prettiest girl he's dated, but you've got all the qualities he loves. Integrity, fire and you don't take any bullshit. With a bit of creativity, you could make this work."

Ann raised her eyebrows. "Like you and Veronique?"

For the first time, he had the grace to look embarrassed.

"*Tchau*, Rocco, *até logo*." She left the bar, checked both ways for trucks and crossed the street to the office and Gil Maduro. *Not the prettiest girl he's dated?*

She was approaching the office when she saw Juan-Carlos Ablos emerge from his cabin, wearing a striped shirt and cream-coloured trousers. Her first thought was what kind of ridiculous popinjay would wear cream trousers at a timber camp. She decided to be friendly.

"Hi, Juan-Carlos! Are you heading over for one of Guido's specials?"

"Oh, hi." His face was the opposite of pleased-to-see-you. "No, I'm going to do some on-site supervision regarding goals in comparison to management targets."

The concept of a double-speak bullshitter crossed her mind one second before the siren sounded, blasting through the camp at such a volume Ann clamped her hands over her ears. Juan-Carlos's complexion paled to the colour of his chinos. The minder ran to the Ford Troller beside the cabin, grabbed two hard hats and jumped into the driver's seat.

The door of the office opened. Gil Maduro stuck his head out and shouted a question. Ann couldn't hear a word. Across the road, Dr Telmo Carreira ran towards them, carrying a holdall. The siren stopped.

The echo reverberated in Ann's ears until she registered Gil's voice demanding a reply. "Ablos, what the hell does that mean?"

The doctor answered. "It means there's been a serious accident. Medical personnel *and* management are required on site."

He gave the boss a chilling look, alerting Ann to a full-scale emergency. Ablos did not move.

The medic heaved himself into the Troller beside Ablos's bodyguard. "Anyone with medical training? I could use another pair of ..."

The siren sounded again. Telmo Carreira's expression shifted from concern to horror. When the hellish row stopped, the doctor crossed himself and appealed to Gil. "Two emergencies. We need another truck. God help us."

Gil cupped his hands around his mouth and bellowed. "ROCCO DELGADO!!!"

In less than thirty seconds, Rocco pelted out of Bar Musica, his weapon trained on Ablos.

"No, the problem's not here!" Gil shouted. "Accidents at the camp. Take one of those vehicles and follow the doctor! I've got the prisoner under control. Ablos, what kind of manager are you? Go with my colleague and support your men."

The Troller sped away, soon followed by an ancient, rusting Chevrolet with Rocco leaning forwards over the steering wheel and Juan-Carlos pressed as far into the passenger seat as he could go.

"I should go with them," said Ann. "First aid in the field is not my speciality but I'm not squeamish and can handle ..." The siren cut her off.

Gil didn't hesitate. He ducked inside, grabbed a first aid pack and as he was locking the door, the siren stopped. "Ann, go to the shop and requisition any emergency equipment they've got. I'll find us a vehicle."

By the time she'd collected the measly supply of plasters, dressings, gloves and antiseptic wipes available, Gil was outside on a trail bike. She jumped on behind him and clung on one-handed.

The journey lasted around fifteen minutes, fourteen

minutes too long, in Ann's opinion. It was like driving through a war zone. The track was treacherous and Gil almost lost control when the back wheel slid into a rut. He wrestled the machine onto the central section, while Ann clamped her thighs as tightly to the seat as she was able. Smoke rose from smouldering tracts of land, punctuated by the occasional surviving palm tree. Nothing but ruined, blackened acres either side of the uneven wood-chipped road that passed for a track. Beside the dirt road, Ann counted a dead anteater, two flattened macaque monkeys, one rotting carcass she could not identify and several snakes contorted into odd shapes after their death throes. Every kilometre they travelled dragged her spirits lower.

Around one corner a logging truck thundered in their direction. Gil lurched the bike off the edge of the track, out of harm's way. Ann winced as the massive lorry rolled closer, cringing at its ability to crush them like any other jungle creature. A cab with two trailers, each laden with a pyramid of wood, was a terrifying threat of massive wheels, machinery and stacks of tree trunks. In spite of the grim circumstances, the driver saluted them with a cheerful wave. Working here, like any other battlefield, must require a level of desensitisation, Ann acknowledged. Not that the loggers had any choice.

They powered on until eventually the road spread out into a compound made for huge articulated transporters and loading machinery. It was bigger than the entire camp Ann had just left. At the far end, two skidders dragged felled trees into the clearing where a gang of men used chainsaws to cut them into logs. Obviously work didn't stop because of an accident.

Ann spotted the Troller and Chevrolet parked beside a Portakabin and a crowd of people standing in a circle. They rode closer and when Gil came to a halt, Ann slid off the bike, her legs less than steady.

The doctor was kneeling beside a prone body while Rocco

tended to another man sitting upright with a bloodied shirt. The inspector looked up as they approached. "Whiplash!" he yelled. "A sapling knocked three of them into a gully. Can you deal with that one?" He pointed to where two of the foremen were bent over a logger in the recovery position.

Gil performed a cautious examination of the unconscious victim as the assembly watched in respectful silence. A quick scan of the faces told Ann that neither Juan-Carlos Ablos or his bodyguard were part of the crowd. She crouched beside Gil. "What can I do?"

"Get some gloves on and clean him up, as gently as you can. Looks like he was hit across the head. He's got an injury to his eye, a dislocated shoulder and a serious head wound, but no broken bones that I can see."

"Can I get some water?" Ann asked the foremen. The balding one nodded and fetched a litre bottle from the Portakabin. As he closed the door behind him, Ann caught sight of a pair of crossed legs inside, wearing cream chinos. She soaked a cotton pad and swabbed the blood and dirt from the injured man's face. His lips were a pale shade of blue but one brown eye fluttered open. Gil covered the other with a dressing.

"Bring that stretcher over here," called Telmo Carreira. "Two of these men need surgery. Put Edu and Simon in the back of these vehicles and take them back to camp. I need to set Edu's leg and stitch Simon's head," said the doctor. "

The two foremen stretchered the unconscious Edu into the rear seat of the Troller and crossed themselves. The angle of the victim's leg disturbed Ann. That was a serious break.

With great care, Gil and Rocco lifted Simon and laid him on the back seat of the Chevy. Simon groaned in pain despite their gentleness.

The doctor was standing by the Troller. "Where's that idiot driver?"

Ann ran over to the Portakabin and opened the door. Ablos

was sitting at a trestle table, filling in some forms. His minder was drinking a coffee. "We have to get these men to Telmo's surgery fast. Let's go." She beckoned the minder. "Drive very carefully. You have a badly injured man in the rear."

The bodyguard downed his coffee and hurried out the door.

"Wait!" Ablos got to his feet and followed.

Ann took a second to look around the room and saw a map indicating the forest felled thus far and the intended expansion of the project in two circles highlighted in yellow. Voices outside jerked her into leaving.

"Come on!" shouted the doctor at Ablos. "What are you waiting for?"

The minder jumped into the Troller and started the engine. Telmo called across to Gil and Rocco. "Can you two take the Chevrolet? I'll need your help to carry Simon out at the other end."

"No!" Ablos's protest came out like a squeal. "I have to get back to camp. Caring for the workforce is part of my responsibility and takes top priority."

The balding foreman came to stand in front of his superior, his expression contemptuous. "Right. We all know how seriously you take that role. You don't deserve to be called a boss. In fact, you don't deserve to be called a man. I'm going to radio the camp to stop any trucks coming up." He waved a hand to signal the vehicles could go. "Let's get these men out."

It was painfully evident Juan-Carlos Ablos had neither respect nor admiration from his workforce. No wonder he needed a bodyguard. The camp manager was weak, vain and out of his league. The foreman was the only one who knew what he was doing.

"My personal security operative must stay with me at all times." Ablos was panicking, his face red and posture uptight. No one paid him any attention.

"Ann, can you handle the bike?" asked Gil, preparing to toss the keys in her direction.

"Sure!" She wasn't sure at all but could snatch an opportunity when she saw one. She caught the keys and turned to Ablos, who watched the two off-roaders driving slowly away.

"Would you like a lift, Juan-Carlos?"

Ann straddled the bike and started the engine. Her fear of riding the vehicle through this terrain was realistic. Gil had struggled to keep them upright and his upper body strength was far superior to hers. But if she could stay in the centre and avoid the wheel ruts, she might be able to manage. She sparked the ignition and looked over her shoulder. "So? Staying here or coming with me?"

His face was the picture of affront but one glance at the two foremen behind him, their arms folded, made up his mind. He swung his leg over the saddle and gripped the seat. Ann twisted the throttle gently but the bike surged forward. She wasn't expecting quite so much power. Ablos jerked backward with a gasp and grabbed her by the waist. She took off after the two vehicles, her concentration intense on steering the bike between the two deep grooves made by the logging trucks. After a few minutes she spotted the intermittent brake lights of the Chevrolet and eased off on the throttle. The central section was muddy and covered with wood chips, leaves and broken branches, which made it difficult to assess the ground beneath. It also covered her and her passenger with dirt. *What a shame for his lovely cream chinos.* Only imagining the pain of the injured men in the trucks up ahead stopped Ann from feeling pure schadenfreude. Every rut and gully triggered a sympathetic jolt of agony for the broken loggers, especially as this rough road was a bone-shaker for the healthiest among them. She balanced speed with caution, assessing the terrain with hyper-alert eyes.

On first sight of the camp, she released a sigh of relief. Ablos spoke. "I need to get out here. Stop the vehicle and let me off, please."

"Senhor Ablos, don't you want to go straight to the surgery and check on the health of your workers? I appreciate this is not the most dignified arrival, but certain things are more important than your reputation."

"I said, stop the vehicle please." His voice was imperious.

She resisted the temptation to do a wheelie and tip the irritating little tit off the back, but only because she wasn't sure with a bike this heavy that she could pull it off. She slowed and came to a halt a hundred metres before Main Street. When he let go of her waist and got off, dusting down his trousers, Ann skewered him with a piercing stare.

"That guy at the site was right. You don't deserve to be called a man."

She drove forward a metre, grasped the brakes and twisted the throttle, spinning wood mulch and mud all over Senhor Ablos and his pastel outfit. *Not everything learned as a wild child was wasted.* She rode away with a bland smile as if she'd just dropped her granny at a tea party.

She parked the bike beside the shop and made her way to the surgery. Rocco and the minder stretchered the first injured man onto the doctor's collapsible trolley and manoeuvred him inside. He was still breathing but not conscious. The second Rocco had fulfilled his obligations to the wounded, he sprinted across the street to the office. Ann remembered the prisoner and sent a silent prayer that Bruno was still locked in.

The second logger was sitting upright but clutching his shoulder. Gil and the minder helped him to his feet and into the doctor's little clinic.

"Thank you, thank you, now please leave them to me." The doctor closed and locked the door behind them.

"Your boss is down the street," she told the bodyguard.

He nodded but lit a cigarette, apparently in no hurry to get back to work.

To Ann's enormous relief, Rocco was standing outside the office, both thumbs in the air. "He's asleep! I think we all deserve a beer!"

"Thank God." Gil's voice was almost a groan as they crossed the street. "If he'd escaped, Rocco would never have forgiven me."

Rocco's attention was drawn to something over their shoulders and his smile of triumph stretched into a huge grin. They turned to see Juan-Carlos Ablos walking down Main Street, as filthy as if he had been caught behind a muck-spreader.

"What happened to him?" asked Gil.

Ann shrugged. "Dunno. Maybe the shit hit the fan."

18

Later that night, the shit really did hit the fan.

After cleaning herself up at the brothel, she spent an hour talking to Veronique in her cabin. Half a dozen of the girls joined them, keen to hear details of what happened after the sirens frightened the life out of everyone. Ann shared the little she knew, agreed that logging was one of the most dangerous professions in the world and even knelt with them to say a prayer for Edu and Simon. When they left to report for work, Ann took her pack and sought out Gil Maduro.

He was neither in the bar nor the canteen and none of those she considered 'friendly' cabins. She didn't dare try the doctor's surgery. Finally she returned to the office.

Rocco opened the door to her light rap. He waggled his eyebrows, pointed to the desk on the left and pressed a finger to his lips. Ann saw the hunched bundle under the table. His light snores filled her with relief and Rocco stood beside her, the pair of them smiling fondly as if they were parents of a newborn.

In an unsubtle mime, Rocco communicated that she should

lock the door and only wake Gil in an emergency. She pointed at him and raised her eyebrows in enquiry. With a gesture less subtle still, Rocco gave her to understand he needed the toilet.

She rolled her eyes, waved him out and locked the door behind him. She lay on the floor, rested her head on her pack and closed her eyes.

When she awoke, night had fallen and the only light came from an anglepoise lamp on Ablos's desk. She sat up with a start to see Gil sitting in the boss's chair, watching her with a wry smile.

"Good sleep?"

She sat up and rubbed her face. "I've had worse." Her voice sounded creaky. "Is there any water?"

He came to crouch beside her, holding a bottle.

She took it and slaked her thirst, draining at least half. "Thank you. I needed that."

"My pleasure. Thank you for keeping me company. How do you feel?" He reached out a hand to help her up.

Something about being observed while she slept rankled. "Give me a second. What time is it?" She unfurled herself and loosened all the stiffness in her joints with an expansive stretch. Then she got to her feet, without his assistance.

"Almost ten. In half an hour, Veronique is going to bring us some enchiladas and beer, if you're hungry."

"May angels bless that sainted _française_. Hungry is an understatement. What about ...?" She jerked her head at the back room.

Gil dropped his voice. "I fed and watered him earlier. When Rocco turns up, we'll take him out to do his ... necessaries. Shall we?"

He waved an arm at the desk. "Not exactly what I planned for our first date, but we can improvise." His manner was tentative, as if unsure of her reaction.

"This is not our first date." Ann leant her pack against the desk and slid into a chair. "That would need the right atmosphere, a table for two and a pair of pretty earrings. When we get back to the coast, maybe you can take me to that classy bar just outside Soure."

His expression relaxed. "Pousada Figueira. Yes, we can drink cocktails by the pool like we did last time. As far as I remember, you chose a Bucks Fizz and looked beautiful." He reached out a hand, fingers splayed and Ann clasped it, weaving her fingers between his. The urge to kiss him was over-powering but it was neither time nor place.

Instead she voiced her concerns. "Gil, something bothers me. When we were at the airport, having problems with the plane, I remember Paolo saying he was the only pilot who knew this route. So why would the charter company change personnel now? I asked Veronique and the girls and they don't recall seeing any pilot from Manaus other than Paolo since they've been here. It feels suspicious."

He frowned. "That can't be right. What about the guy who flew Ablos, the priest and the others to the National Park?"

"He was a pilot from Barcelos who operates solo, Damien told us that. I'm talking about the weekly run from Manaus to this camp by the same charter company used by the police and all the logging firms. Paolo is the only person who flies the Manaus to camp route on a regular basis. Why would they switch?"

"Hey, don't get stressed about it." He ran the back of his fingers down her cheek. "Paolo tends to exaggerate. He's *one* of the few pilots who flies this route. Maybe he's sick or working another job. The most important thing is the plane will be here tomorrow. The minute we land in Manaus, I'm going to pull out all the stops to get us on a flight to Soure as fast as possible. We don't want to head-butt with The Goat again. If everything works out, tomorrow night we will be in our own beds."

Ann raised an eyebrow. "Beds, plural?"

He grinned and squeezed her hand. "Well, maybe if you were to invite me …"

Loud voices outside wiped the smile from his face and he looked out the window. Outside the management accommodation where they had spent their first night, an argument was getting heated. Gil went to the window, followed by Ann.

Ablos and his bodyguard were on the stoop, facing around half a dozen men. The leader of the group was the balding foreman she'd seen earlier. He was shouting and pointing an aggressive finger at the boss. The bodyguard took a step forward with a pacifying gesture but the men did not retreat.

"I don't like the look of this," muttered Gil.

At that moment, a hammering came at the door. Gil checked the window and unlocked it for Rocco to rush in.

"Shit, damnation and hellfire! I thought this place was too small to keep a secret and I was right."

"What's going on, Rocco?"

The big man locked the door and peered out the curtains. "The men thought Bruno was on a job for Ablos so accepted his absence without question. But that goddamned trucker with a big mouth let slip he brought Bruno back this morning. They're not stupid. There's only one reason he's gone AWOL and that's because we arrested him for the murder of the missing girl. The only thing they don't know is where he is being held, but that will take them all of sixty seconds to figure out. Prepare for trouble. I told Veronique to get Damien and bring him over here. I'm gonna try and calm these guys down. That won't be easy after all they've been drinking. Ablos, that dickless waste of space, can take care of himself."

With that, there was a knock at the door. Rocco stood with his hand on the door handle.

"Who is it?"

"It's Damien and Veronique. Can we come in?"

Rocco opened the door and the documentary crew came into the room, complete with their backpacks and all the camera equipment. Both looked worried and for once Damien had no witty quip to lighten the moment.

"A group of them have gone to the brothel. They think he might be hidden there. They're in a nasty mood," said Veronique, her face pale.

Rocco agreed. "No surprise. They know that *fraco* would throw them all ..." He broke off as a thumping sound came from the back room. "Fantastic! Exactly what we need. That stupid horse's ass broadcasting his location. Gil, go and shut him up."

"Too late," said Gil, his attention on the men outside. "They're coming over."

"Damien, lock the door behind us, but stand by to open it if things get ugly. Gil, come with me." Rocco checked his gun and replaced it in his holster.

The two police inspectors stepped outside, bracing themselves with their hands on their hips. Just before Damien closed the door and turned the key, Ann caught sight of a crowd of angry faces. The group of six had swelled to around twenty men.

Rocco's voice boomed out, causing the mob to fall silent. "You have no business here. Go back to the bar or home to bed. This has nothing to do with you."

"You've got the wrong man! Bruno is innocent! You release him immediately or you'll have us to deal with."

Above the murmurs of agreement and growling threats, Ann could hear Ablos's whiny voice. "I warned you this would happen! I told you they would riot."

"Shut up, Ablos. Nobody is going to riot. We're all going to calm down and get on with our jobs. Inspector Maduro and I have arrested Bruno Diaz for a list of crimes committed here in Brazil and also in Venezuela."

"He didn't do anything to that girl! She ran away! Let him go and you will have no more trouble from us. If you don't, we will break him out of there."

"Are you threatening two armed police officers, employees of the government? Are you telling me I should release a man wanted for rape, assault and even murder? Listen, I'm here to do a job. My orders are to arrest Bruno Diaz and take him to Manaus. That is what I'm going to do and anyone attempting to stop me will feel the full force of the law."

Some incomprehensible shouting followed until one voice made itself heard above the others. "Two of you against thirty of us? You don't stand a chance."

"Yeah, you're not the only ones with weapons, you know."

"Let him out! Let him out now!"

"We're going to kick your arse!"

Ann was clenching her fists so hard her knuckles were white. She glanced at Veronique and Damien, whose jaws were set and brows furrowed. From somewhere, a bell started ringing and the threatening shouts subsided. Ann strained to hear what was happening. A voice was speaking but she could make out none of the words.

"It's Father Mendoza," whispered Damien. "He's trying to make them disperse. God help the old fella."

A slow hand clap began, joined by stomping feet and grew faster and faster, drowning out the priest. Not even a man of the cloth could muster enough authority over this drunken mob.

Something struck the cabin, making everyone inside jump.

"ENOUGH! Throw another stone and I will shut this camp down, marking every last one of you as a troublemaker for police intelligence!" Rocco's roar echoed from the buildings across the street.

"Not if you don't make it out of here." A hoarse male voice emerged from the silence. "You wouldn't be the first and you won't be the last uniforms to go missing. The jungle is a dangerous place for cops. We asked you nicely. Let him go."

"Let him go and we'll do the same for you." The man's words elicited a ripple of laughter as he mirrored Rocco's own words.

Another stone hit the cabin, followed by several more. One shattered the window and glass shards burst inwards like a firework. Ann, Damien and Veronique backed up to the rear wall, dragging their bags in retreat. The thuds grew faster, rocks hitting the roof, the door and judging by the angry yells, Rocco and Gil. A shot rang out over the crowd, pausing the assault for a second until it resumed with renewed energy. A sense of duty propelled Ann to act and she grabbed her knife, determined to do what was necessary. She whirled to Damien and shouted at the top of her lungs. "Film this! Someone must record what's happening!" She mimed a film camera motion in case her voice was inaudible over the thunderous battery on the walls, roof and doors. She flicked open her knife, unlocked the door and readied herself for physical combat.

On seeing the ugly mob, rocks in hands, fear and a sense for self-preservation paralysed her limbs. To go out there was to offer herself as a sacrifice. To cower inside would only prolong the agony. A stone hit Rocco's shoulder with a nasty crunch and just as he raised his weapon, an unearthly scream pierced the air. The barrage of stones slowed to a few random thumps. The shriek came again and Ann recognised the shrill voice of Dona Candida.

"Get out of my way, you stinking louts! Move, I said! Put that down, Rodrigo, or you'll regret it. All of you! Drop whatever you have in your hands right now! Aren't you ashamed of yourselves, acting like a bunch of Neanderthals? Now stand back and listen to me. If you don't leave this place immediately and go back to whatever you were doing, I will take my girls, every last one of them, out of here on tomorrow morning's plane."

Her words seemed to subdue the men and the prevailing sound was Shakira's tinny tones coming from Bar Musica. No one moved.

Candida hadn't finished. "What's more, we won't come back. Yes, I'm serious. Ask yourself what's more important. You want to break that ugly brute out of jail tonight and spend the next month with only each other for company? Or you let him face justice for what he has done and you keep your lady friends? Think about it, you idiots. What happens next time you get drunk on cachaça and fancy some action? Who are you going to cuddle up with? Bruno? Ha! Just go back to the bar and stop interfering with things that don't concern you. Otherwise, I'm closing up shop tonight and I swear to the Virgin Mary, tomorrow we'll be gone for good. Do you understand me?"

There was a hostile silence for several seconds. Then a conciliatory voice spoke.

"It's a question of loyalty, Dona Candida. We have to look after our own."

"Shut your big mouth, Carlos. Look after your own? Ha! What about Ruth? You've been 'looking after' her the last few weeks, no? No wonder she's sweet on you. It would be a shame to say goodbye so soon."

The hoarse voice spoke up. "We owe Bruno. He's one of us."

Candida's voice was like a whiplash. "You know who else is one of you? Edu. When he got hit by a tree today, which one of you brought him to the clinic? Tell me that, you drunken assholes!"

Not a single man attempted to answer.

"It wasn't the boss, the foreman or any of Edu's apparently loyal colleagues. You know who got him here for medical attention? These cops. Let me tell you something else. Edu is going to lose his leg. His life as a logger is over, even if he survives the amputation. But rather than respecting your injured brothers, you get drunk and want to start a fight on behalf of the biggest bully this camp has ever known." Candida spat onto the dirt. "I am ashamed and disgusted by every last one of you. I pity the poor priest when he hears your confessions. Get over the road to the bar, raise a glass to Edu and take a minute to think about the true meaning of brotherhood."

Ann held her breath, but the sound of shuffling feet told her the crowd was breaking up. Bruno seemed to sense the same thing and started banging against the wall with such force Ann feared for the integrity of the building. She ducked inside and locked the door, meeting a pair of shocked eyes and a camera lens. Damien's brows rose but before Ann could answer, someone tapped on the door.

"You can let us in now. The doctor is here." Gil's voice sounded calm and unruffled.

Gil led Dr Telmo Carreira inside, followed by Rocco who tapped her arm. "Keep an eye outside and warn us if they come back. Damien, we need your help to hold Bruno down. The doc is going to inject him with a sedative."

Ann went out into the darkness, surprised to see Dona Candida still standing there. The madam had one arm wrapped across her chest and the other hand clutching her pendant, glaring across the road at the noise from the bar. Under the camp lights, her face looked harsh, mean and yellow, rather like a preserved corpse. Still frowning, she reached into her pocket and pulled out her cigarettes. She took one for herself and offered the packet to Ann.

"I don't smoke, but thank you."

Dona Candida shrugged and lit up, taking a long drag.

"That was very brave of you, to tackle the men like that."

The woman didn't respond for a moment. "They're like

dogs," she rasped. "Got to show them who's the boss. The only person they respect is their mother." Her glare strafed Ablos's cabin and her nose wrinkled into a sneer. "Some people never understand the meaning of authority." She turned her focus on Ann. "Did you find her?"

The question was so unexpected, Ann could think of no way to answer. From inside the office came the sounds of a struggle and an enraged yell. She tensed until she heard Rocco say, "Well done, doc!"

Dona Candida continued. "I guessed what must have happened. She's the only one, you know, in all my years of servicing these camps. Nearly thirty years and not a single girl got away. Except her. Well, good luck, I say. Time to go. Something tells me we'll be busy tonight." She stubbed out her cigarette and set off across the road.

"Goodnight," Ann called after her. Without turning, the older woman lifted a hand. Whether it was a wave or a dismissal, Ann couldn't tell.

Gil emerged from the office. "Bruno is out cold and the doctor will watch him for a while, just to make sure he can breathe. Rocco and I are going to sit out here until around one o'clock. The lights go out at midnight and if they try anything, it will be then. We're all going to sleep here in the office for safety. You, me, Rocco and the film people. Not that we'll get much sleep. Another thing, on tomorrow's flight we have to take the guy with the busted leg. Telmo says he needs a hospital."

"Edu? On the same flight as Bruno?"

"We have no choice. His injuries are life-threatening. I know it's not going to be easy but it's the right thing to do."

Ann smiled up at him and reached out to touch him. He took a step away from her.

"Don't. Not here. Those drunks are still watching and if they think you're important to me, they'll make use of that information. I'm going next door to get some blankets and stuff from that *alfaceiro*."

The rejection stung a little, but he was right. She watched him go, amused by his description of Ablos as 'that *alfaceiro*'. Lettuce-eater. It suited him.

The night was interminable. Ann and Veronique each created themselves a nest of cushions and blankets behind one of the desks, Ann on the left and Veronique on the right. Since Bruno was incapacitated, Damien offered to sleep in the back room to keep an eye on him. Meanwhile, Rocco and Gil sat in plastic seats at the front of the building, with guns and torches at the ready. They spoke too softly for anyone to make out what they said, but conversed sporadically.

Ann was wide awake, attuned to the sounds of the camp winding down for the night. The jukebox finally fell silent, male voices grew fewer and quieter, someone pulled down a metal grille over the counter at the music bar and the string of lights guiding loggers to their bunkhouses went out. This was crunch time.

The silence would have been complete other than a synchronous duet of snores from the room behind. Ann closed her eyes, knowing it was hopeless. Until Rocco and Gil were safely inside the building, sleep would evade her. She couldn't see Veronique but sensed the other woman was equally alert. At one point, the door opened and Rocco's huge frame blocked out the moonlight. He came inside and lay down beside Veronique. His whispers were audible as he told the French-woman he would get two hours rest and relieve Gil.

It made no sense to lie there restless, so Ann got up, wrapped herself in a blanket and went outside to keep him company. There was no question of conversation, even in pillow-talk whispers. The last thing she wanted to do was distract him while he was trying to keep them safe. Instead, she took Rocco's chair and sat quietly, peering out at the shadowy outlines of the camp and staring up at the stars. At this distance, she couldn't make out Gil's expression but she heard him murmur, "*Obrigado.*"

The clarity of the night was a blessing. The air was chilly but visibility under the moon reassured her that anyone creeping up to the office would have a hard time staying out of sight. The second benefit of a cloudless sky was the familiarity of the patterns above her head. This was the same sky she stared at when lying on the beach, listening to Branca squeak in her dreams or the buzz of mosquitoes. This time tomorrow or the day after, she would be there with the dog, with the heron on the roof, with her tomato plant and hopefully, with Gil Maduro. Parts of her body she'd voluntarily retired had awoken and demanded sustenance. Ann craved him like a drug.

She risked a look at the man and his upright bearing as he surveyed their surroundings. It was a strange kind of limbo after last night's intense cleaving to one another but in a way their silent proximity brought them closer still. A crack from the lumberyard caused both to stare into the gloom until a shape no bigger than a fox scurried away behind the Quonset hut. Overnight vigils were nothing new so Ann drew on some of her favourite techniques, such as remembering every capital city of Europe and trying to spell them backwards. Reykjavik beat her every time. Even so, she dozed off twice, the weight of her drooping head jerking her awake.

When Rocco opened the door of the office to take over guard duty, there was still no hint of light on the horizon. She and Gil crept into the space behind the desk and covered themselves in blankets. Ann spooned herself around his body. "Sleep now," she whispered. And they did.

. . .

Daylight woke her and even though she tried to move out of Gil's embrace as gently as possible, his eyes flew open. He looked at his watch. "Six-thirty?" He scrambled to his feet and looked around the room. "Rocco?"

"He went next door to use the radio," said Veronique. "Damien took over the watch at five. I was just going over to Bar Musica to get some of Guido's coffee for us all."

Gil blinked and smoothed his hands over his hair. He shook himself, looked down at Ann and his face softened. "Good morning."

"Good morning." She smiled at him and her stomach flipped.

The door banged open, jangling everyone's nerves, and Rocco marched in like a tank. "We are on! The plane left just after six so should be landing here around eight. Damien says Sleeping Beauty is awake and needs a piss." He jerked his head in the direction of the back room.

Ann stretched and stood up. "How about Veronique and I leave you to deal with Bruno while we get some breakfast? What time do the men go to work?"

"Eight." Rocco consulted his watch. "They get up around seven, eat something and drive the equipment up to the felling site. That works out very nicely for us. Yes, go get some coffee and bread. Don't forget something for the prisoner. We will deal with him while you're gone and when the men have left the camp, we can get down to the landing strip."

After last night's showdown, Ann was more than usually jumpy when approaching the music bar. Guido served them a jug of coffee and a dozen *pãezinhos*, with a curious expression. When Ann paid him, he met her eyes.

"You take Bruno away?"

"Yes. On this morning's plane."

"Good." He shook his head with an expression of disgust. "That man is a devil."

Veronique shot Ann a sideways glance. They returned to the office to find Gil and Rocco arguing. Damien, Veronique and Ann ate their bread rolls and drank strong coffee while listening to the debate. It seemed the bone of contention revolved around Bruno's handcuffs. The police officers had cuffed his hands in front of his body in order for him to urinate. Rocco was adamant the cuffs should be returned to the original position. Gil was of the opinion the big man was still doped and therefore less dangerous. He could also use his hands to feed himself.

"It's exactly because he's doped we should do it now! If we wait until he's wide awake, it will take three of us to hold him down again. Don't be such a bleeding heart, Gil! Let's make sure that violent bastard can't do any more harm."

A knock came at the door and Ablos, complete with body-guard, entered the room. The boss, fragrant and crisp in his IT-manager short-sleeved shirt, wrinkled his nose as he took in the smell of five unwashed bodies. It amused Ann to see that today he was wearing brown trousers.

"Good morning. I trust you had no problems overnight. We will escort you to the landing strip and see you onto the plane."

Rocco noticed the food and coffee for the first time. He poured one cup for himself and another for Gil, then tore a bite out of a bread roll. He addressed Ablos and his security man. "Nice of you to step up at last. You were useless yesterday."

Ablos coloured. "I did warn you. Now all we want is to make sure you get safely out of our camp."

Rocco snorted, spitting breadcrumbs over the nearest table. "Listen, *amigo*, nothing on God's earth could make me stay in this shit pit one minute longer. I pray God I never see it and especially you ever again. Now shut the goddamned door."

It made sense. The workers were trudging down the road towards the equipment, ready to start their working day, casting resentful looks at the office and Juan-Carlos Ablos in particular. For a wild second Ann wondered if the workers might use the tree-moving machinery to tear the roof off the office and release Bruno. Or kill them all in the process.

Gil's voice, calm and relaxed, soothed Ann's nerves. "Senhor Ablos, why don't you have a coffee and a *pãezinho*? We'll wait here until your employees are in the forest and then relocate to the landing strip." He looked at the bodyguard. "Do you have a gun?"

The chunky man waggled his head from side to side.

Gil rolled his eyes. "I didn't ask if you have a legal firearm. Do you have a gun?"

The bodyguard nodded, with a guilty look at Ablos.

"Right. Then you can make yourself useful for once."

19

Veronique was the best person to act as a scout. A familiar figure around the camp, unthreatening and unarmed, she would arouse no suspicions. The Frenchwoman returned the coffee pot to Guido and when she came back, announced the coast was clear. The men had gone to work.

Rocco fetched Bruno from the back room. The big man looked every bit as ebullient and confrontational as usual, and Ann wondered if cuffing his hands in front was one of Gil's better ideas. The man had an air of unpredictable violence even as he helped himself to the remaining rolls. Everyone in the room stepped away. Out of reach and away from the stench of body odour. No one apart from Ablos had showered that morning, but Bruno stank. There was a collective sigh of relief when Rocco gave the order to leave.

With his gun pressed in the small of Bruno's back, Rocco marched his prisoner down the street and into the Quonset hut. The remainder of the party followed with their packs and bags, while Gil and the bodyguard brought up the rear, ready to defend the group against any have-a-go heroes. Other than the Mexican chef watching them pass, no one was visible.

They sat in a ragged group at the end of the hut, facing the runway. Rocco locked Bruno's cuffs to a chain in the wall and instructed Gil to act as warder. He stationed the bodyguard at the opposite entrance to be on the alert for any kind of rescue committee. Then he paced all the way round the structure, his weapon at the ready. Before he had even completed his circuit, the sound of a light aircraft engine reached Ann's ears.

She crouched in a frog-like squat as the Cessna wobbled towards the scrubby runway. It landed with a couple of bounces, a less professional arrival than Paolo would have delivered, taxied to the Quonset hut and the engine cut out. Ann strained to see the pilot through the glass but he was wearing some kind of helmet and she could not make out his face.

"*Hoi!*" yelled Rocco. "Turn this thing around! We need to access the hold."

The pilot ignored him, took off his headgear and opened the door to the cockpit. The second the sun hit his bald pate, Ann knew who it was. Adrenalin shot through her like a lightning bolt and she acted without a second thought, shouldering her rucksack and breaking into a run. A shot rang out and Rocco hit the ground with a grunt. Ann covered the length of the hut in seconds. She raced past the gormless bodyguard and instantly doubled back, running down the other side of the hut. If she guessed right, the man hunting her would do the opposite, hoping to hit his target as she fled the hut for the camp.

Her mind, in total contrast to her body, calmly assessed the facts. O Cabrito had repaid her betrayal, releasing details of her location to the highest bidder. Whoever won the auction must have been a heavyweight if they could afford to send Uncle Jack. The man was relentless. Ann had heard all the stories and taken them with a pinch of salt, until she'd seen Jack in action. After that, she believed every word.

She stopped, poised on the balls of her feet, at the south end of the hut. On the other side of the wall must be Gil Maduro, presumably still guarding the prisoner. She edged her face around the galvanised steel to see Damien and Veronique bent over the prone form of Rocco. There was no time to check if he was alive or even to reassure Gil. In a darting, jagged run, Ann bolted from the shelter of the hut, cut behind the aircraft and sprinted into the jungle. It occurred to her as she reached the cover of the trees, her urgent, desperate flight was the exact opposite of Alexandra's plan of escape.

No negotiations, no compromises. This was the endgame. Either Uncle Jack bagged his trophy or Ann killed him first. Armed with nothing other than a flick knife, she wouldn't bet on her odds. She ran between the trees, stopping every few paces to assess her next move and listen for any sounds of pursuit. She had to find somewhere to hide. A crashing noise to her left made her drop into a defensive posture but it was only a brown brocket deer, leaping away in fright. The deeper into the jungle she went, the harder it would be for him to find her. At the same time, with every step the risks of the rainforest increased.

She waited a few seconds, her pulse in her ears louder than all the birdsong and clatter of monkeys in the canopy. Behind her was nothing but forest. Two metres or so ahead, a path was visible. Ann's sense of direction told her that following it to the right would lead her back to the camp, so she turned left. Still no thundering footsteps hot on her heels, but a professional like Uncle Jack could move as stealthily as a panther.

After a few minutes, the path opened out to a small pond. Juliana's words came back to her. *We had a hiding place we used to go to ... a pond in the jungle.* Ann scrambled across a rock and found a gap, not much more than a metre square. She dropped into it and tried to quieten her mind enough to apply logical thought. Uncle Jack couldn't possibly intend to take her home to face the consequences. How would he keep her subdued enough to fly to Manaus? To London? Even as she thought it, she knew he would have ways. But how did he intend to handle the police? Rocco's body on the runway answered that question. Her stomach twisted as she thought of Gil. All those people thrown into jeopardy due to her. Because Uncle Jack's mission was to find her and kill her, that much she knew. Every obstacle in his path would be crushed.

Her only route out of there was via the Rio Negro. This little pond was fed by a trickling stream. Common sense told her it must flow out the other side and into the river. All she needed to do was follow it and she would come out on the riverbank. From there, she could make her way to the jetty, take the boat they'd used to visit the village and sail downstream to the next pocket of civilisation. Her rucksack contained enough emergency rations to help her survive for ... A rustling of leaves made her sit upright. Her intuition told her this was no jungle creature but a human being stalking his prey. She held her breath, waiting to hear any indication of his intention. Only the sounds of the jungle filled her ears.

Then a rock hit the water with a sudden splash and her intake of breath was audible. Ripples spread across the pond. The swoosh of someone wading into the water preceded a shadow crossing her vision. Less than two metres away, Uncle Jack stood in the water up to his knees, his gun aimed at her head. She clenched her hand around her knife although she knew it was useless.

He grinned, ridges forming across his forehead as he lifted his brows. "Hello, kiddo. I've not seen you around for a while. Come to think of it, nor has anyone else."

Ann lifted her chin towards him, refusing to plead or

grovel. It would make no difference anyway. Not with Uncle Jack.

"Got a message for you. I'll bet you can guess who it's from. He was desperate to be the one to find you and O Cabrito knew it. That old goat charged top dollar for this information. Our mutual friend paid the price because he's still sweet on you, even after what you did. He wants you dead, of course he does, but that's all. If the others get their hands on you, well, let's not go there."

"No, let's not." She kept her tone sharp. "I'm aware of what they can do."

"You can't blame them. Bad enough when one mole gets away but two? They've been humiliated and they want revenge. On both ideally, but you don't have police protection, which makes you the easier target. At least for now. They'll get him in the end. Long story short, your ex is doing you a favour. Jack, he said to me, put a bullet in her head. Clean and tidy. Let that be an end to it. All I want, he said, is a picture to prove she's gone. Quite romantic, if you think about it. So that's what I gotta do."

Ann stared at the barrel of his gun, turning over his words in her mind. "That's the message? He wants me dead? Like I didn't know that already."

"Oh, no. That was me managing your expectations. No, his message is this. Wait now, he made me promise to get this right." He slid his phone from inside his jacket and thumbed the screen, his gun not wavering from its aim at her forehead.

He grinned and read from the screen. "Tell her I've taken care of her sister."

All the blood seemed to drain from Ann's body. Katie. Not Katie. She swallowed and found her voice, sticking to her story. "I haven't got a sister. So what the hell is that supposed to mean?"

Uncle Jack shrugged. "Don't shoot the messenger. Oh,

right, you can't." He laughed to himself. It was an unpleasant sound. "Nice knowing you, kiddo."

With one hand he pointed his weapon and with the other held up his phone. A shot blasted out and Uncle Jack recoiled, staggered and fell backwards with a huge splash. Before Ann could react, Gil jumped into the pond and at point-blank range, put another bullet into the man's chest. Blood swirled into the pool, transforming the limpid amber water to a rusty red ochre. Gil kept his gun pointed at the body for a full minute, then replaced it in its holster.

He looked over his shoulder at Ann, his face scratched and sweaty. "We can't exactly call it quits, but at least it evens the balance."

She stared at him, blinking, releasing a juddering, unsteady breath.

He reached out a hand. "Let's get out of here."

Ann let him pull her up and she followed him through the forest, still processing what had just happened. One sentence ricocheted through her head over and over again. *Tell her I've taken care of her sister.*

When they got to the landing strip, Veronique was emerging from the cockpit of the plane, carrying a first aid kit. She saw them and clasped a hand to her sternum.

"Oh, thank God! You found her! Gil, Bruno got away. He yanked the chain out of the wall. Damien tried to stop him, but Bruno punched him with both fists and ran off that way." She pointed to the camp.

"Shit! Is Damien hurt? How's Rocco?" asked Gil, his gaze focused in the direction she indicated, still clutching Ann's hand.

"I'm not sure. I need to clean them up to see the full extent of their injuries. Rocco's regained conscious and I've stopped the bleeding. He was lucky. What about ...?" She left the sentence hanging, flicking her eyes to the jungle. "We heard gunshots."

"The threat is neutralised. We'll talk about it later. Now let's see the damage."

Gil led the way into the hut where a white-faced Rocco lay against the wall and Damien sat with his head in his hands. When he looked up, both his face and palms were smeared with red. Ablos and his bodyguard had vanished. Veronique knelt to clean Damien's face, using her water bottle to wash away the blood. The sound of approaching feet made Gil reach for his weapon but he lowered it on seeing the new arrivals. Dr Telmo Carreira and Ablos's bodyguard carried a stretcher into the hut and rested the patient on the ground near Damien and Rocco.

"Here's the doc!" said the bodyguard, a redundant state-ment if ever Ann had heard one. She recognised Edu's face and remembered what Dona Candida had said. Her heart twisted in sympathy.

While the doctor tended to the wounded men and instructed Veronique as to their care, Gil addressed the minder. "Where did Bruno Diaz go?"

The bodyguard's gaze snapped to the place where Bruno had been chained and his mouth fell open. "He's gone!"

"Yes, I know that." Gil sounded as if he was grinding his teeth. "But *where* did he go?"

"I've got no idea! When that bald guy came out shooting, I rushed Ablos to the office. My job is to keep the boss out of danger. Then I went and fetched the doc for that cop who took a bullet but he wanted my help to carry the logger. I didn't seen Bruno, but he can't go far in handcuffs. Should I go and search for him?"

Gil glanced over his shoulder at the makeshift emergency

hospital. "No, no. Even handcuffed, he's too dangerous." He tapped his thumbnail against his lips.

"Inspector Maduro!" called the doctor.

Ann and the bodyguard hurried after Gil. Damien looked awful, his head taped and bandaged. Rocco, on the other hand, had regained some colour in his face.

"Inspector, take all three of these men to a hospital. Damien will need stitches in his face and dental treatment for two broken teeth. The police officer has a bullet wound in his upper left torso. It seems the gunshot caught him in the armpit and although it's not life-threatening, he has lost a lot of blood. You will have to take the injured logger as well, as I am not equipped to perform such an operation here. Veronique knows how to manage their pain until you get them into an ambulance. I suggest you fly to Manaus as soon as possible."

"How?" Gil's voice was deadened.

"What do you mean how?" The doctor gestured to the plane. "Take that and go. Look, I'm going back to my surgery. On the way I'll drop by the bar to kick Paolo's arse so you can leave immediately. Good luck and I'm sorry I can't be more help." He scooped up his kitbag and left.

"You heard the man," growled Rocco. "Take the plane and let's get out of here."

Gil was shaking his head. "We have no pilot. He's ... indisposed."

"There's a pilot standing right in front of me."

"Rocco, there's no way I will fly this thing. It's been years. We might as well go swimming with the piranhas. I don't suppose ...?" He turned to the bodyguard.

"What? Me fly a plane? Not a chance. But I've heard you can radio the control tower and someone tells you how to do it. I guess the bald guy isn't coming back, then?"

Even Ann quailed at Gil's contemptuous look.

"Maduro, you stubborn prick, there is no alternative. We

either stay here in this festering shithole to be picked off by that murderous felon Diaz, or you man up and get us out of here." The effort of roaring at his friend caused Rocco some pain. He curled over and when he opened his eyes, they rested on Ann. "Another thing. People are after her and they know where she is. The next plane that flies in will have another bald guy or five bald guys, intent on killing her and anyone else who gets in their way. So what's your plan? We sit here like poisoned rats up a drainpipe, waiting for the dogs to rout us? You are the only one who can fly a goddamned plane. So fly the fucking thing!"

All eyes rested on Gil, who massaged his chin. "We'll radio Manaus for another plane. Ask them to bring Paolo and another pilot. It shouldn't take too long."

This time it was Veronique who spoke. "While my colleague has broken teeth, your friend bleeds to death and this man is in agony? You have to try, Gil."

"Try?" His voice was raw and harsh. "It's not like running a marathon! If I fail at that, only I have to live with the humiliation. If I fail at this, we all die on the sword of my ego."

Ann stepped up to his side. She said nothing, simply adding her support. He looked down at her, his jaw set. "What do you think?"

"If you get us out of here, I think we can call it quits," she murmured.

He exhaled a snort and studied the plane. Then he stalked across the tarmac. Veronique, Rocco and Damien sent Ann enquiring looks but she shook her head. How the hell would she know what he was thinking? The only thing she could do was follow him to find out.

After flicking through a small folder in the cockpit, Maduro walked around the Cessna, slid his fingers over the edges of the propeller and round the front of the wings, moved the side rudders and elevators on the back and inspected the horizontal pipes mounted under the left wing. His body language had something of an animal tamer, exhibiting dominance and respect at the same time, an awareness of a deadly force slumbering in a presently peaceful creature. With no appearance of urgency, he dragged a small stepladder from the hut, dipped a metal meter into both tank openings on the roof and then disappeared into the cockpit, scribbling into a text book and studying maps.

Inside, Ann was screaming, her nails digging into her palms. *We have to get out of here!* Not once did he glance at the injured and desperate in the shade of the hut. Gil Maduro would do things his way or not at all.

Twenty minutes later, the Cessna sped across the runway and five pairs of lungs released a collective sigh as the aircraft left the ground.

The not-very-bright bodyguard had been right about one thing. Air Traffic Control towers didn't exactly teach you how to fly but they did tell you where, how and at what height. Ann sat beside Gil, attempting to understand the flight plan, ATC instructions and the significance of the instruments. A constant mantra ran through her mind. *No storms, please, no storms.* Having seen Paolo, who flew this kind of aircraft for a living, struggle with the vagaries of the weather, she knew the effect a squall would have on someone long out of practice and running on nerves. They flew over the green mass of the rainforest and at times Ann slid into blankness, forgetting all her worries, allowing the undulating landscape to hypnotise her into a state of relaxation.

Then she came back to the present, and her concerns threatened to overwhelm her: the danger of flying a plane with lapsed training, whether they would be able to avoid O Cabrito in Manaus, if Rocco would recover not only physically but also in terms of his arrangement with the gangster, and how her own future looked, now Uncle Jack had found her hundreds of kilometres up the jungle. The one question screamed louder than all the rest: what had happened to her sister?

Gil's concentration was intense and Ann so in tune with his perspective, she picked up on his rising tension as the huge conglomeration of Manaus loomed in the haze. For her, seeing the city was an enormous relief. For the first time since they had left the ground, she looked behind at the three injured men and poor Veronique trying to keep them all comfortable. Rocco seemed to be asleep and Damien's face was once more in his hands. Edu was motionless, strapped onto his stretcher.

She took off her earphones and yelled over the noise of the engines. "All OK?"

Veronique looked up and made a wobbling motion with her hand. Ann understood. *Comme ci, comme ça.* Maybe, maybe not.

She replaced her headphones and spoke to Gil. "How long before we're on the ground?"

He glanced at the gauge. "Fifteen minutes, I hope. This is the hard part."

"How do you mean?"

"Getting into the air is easy. A safe landing is another story."

The radio exchange with the tower was short and Gil confirmed their clearance for landing. He flew parallel to the airport above the river, his face stony with tension. They kept flying past the end of the runway until he reduced speed and extended the flaps. The plane made a small jump, and he tilted it to the left. Ann gazed down at the mainland, with all its industry buildings along the coast. Gil seemed to mumble values from a checklist repeatedly while rotating his gaze between the left window and an instrument panel. He extended the flaps once more and reduced speed, keeping one hand on the throttle, and flew another left curve, much softer this time. The runway appeared in front of them, far, far below.

An unstable rocking began, making Ann clench her fists and a sound escaped her nose, adding to the whine of the engines. The air played with the plane as if it were made of paper. Short bursts of the stall warning horn blared at erratic intervals, causing Gil each time to dip the plane's nose. Ann heard Paolo's voice in her head. *Completely fine to let her blow her horn now and then*. It didn't soothe her.

Once they were above the runway, Gil pulled the throttle completely, and the drop in sounds from the idling engine made way for the wind noises from propeller and wings. Ann stopped breathing for a moment and thought she could hear Gil's frantic heartbeat through the hiss. Her eyes were glued to the runway which was still one hell of a long distance below. The stall horn sounded again, this time longer. She looked at Gil who grimaced and eased the throttle up for a moment. Following some stabilising manoeuvres against the winds which buffeted the aircraft, he pressed the nose down again. It felt like a daddy longlegs trying to resist the force of a hairdryer. By now, Ann estimated, they had flown over half the entire runway, drastically shortening the distance left for landing. Gil pulled and pushed the nose up and down constantly, like a dancer one step behind, reacting to movements instead of flowing with them.

As the tarmac approached at great speed, he pressed the intercom.

"Hold tight. It's going to be bumpy."

He was right about that.

The two wheels hit the ground with an incredibly loud whack that catapulted the plane back up into the air. Ann stretched her arms up to the ceiling to steady herself and wasn't sure if the short scream had escaped from herself or one of the others. Gil pushed the handle forward and sent the plane into another hopper. The end of the runway raced close now but it was impossible to slow the plane down since the wheels touched the ground only for a moment before shooting up several metres. Her shoulders tensed as they hopped again, only metres from the end of the runway.

When the wheels finally stayed on the ground, Gil hit the brakes with brutal force so that all the passengers slid towards the cockpit. Only the seatbelts prevented them from crashing into Gil and Ann's seats. It must have been hell for Edu and Rocco and not exactly fun for Damien.

The Cessna came to a halt on the small levelled area behind the tract. An incredible physical lightness welled up inside Ann, her gratitude for terra firma forcing tears of relief.

Gil pressed the intercom and said, "God bless long runways built for much larger aircraft." The engine growled as he turned the plane around and taxied to the terminal.

20

Ann's legs were still wobbly as they crossed the tarmac after seeing the three men loaded into the waiting ambulance. Veronique insisted on accompanying the patients and Gil didn't argue. Once the vehicle departed, an enormous sense of exhaustion settled on Ann, making her backpack feel as heavy as if it was full of rocks.

"What now?" she asked.

Gil's face told her he felt exactly the same way. "What now?" he repeated. "Good question. Let's find out when the next flights are leaving for Soure or Belém. I have to wait until Rocco is fully conscious because we have to get our stories straight. But you could leave today, if that's what you want."

Ann was torn. Her desire to get far from O Cabrito territory was a desperate need, but at the same time, the thought of being parted from Gil wrenched at her gut. "I'm sticking with you for as long as it's safe."

He gave her a dry look. "If it's as safe as the rest of this trip, you should get out now."

They walked to the terminal, hand in hand, and booked two tickets on a charter flight to Soure at 18.35. *Nearly home*, she whispered. *Nearly home.* Veronique sent Gil a message to say Edu and Rocco were undergoing treatment and would stay in hospital, but as soon as his dental work was complete, Damien was free to go. She and her cameraman were planning to check into a nearby hotel.

A taxi drove Gil and Ann through downtown streets far less crowded than during the weekend celebrations. The driver filled them in on the news although his passengers showed minimal interest.

"Biggest ever! You wouldn't believe the crowds! The best festival I ever saw! Can't believe you people went on an excursion when the action was happening here. The fun lasted three days! Apart from those storms, people danced for seventy-two hours straight." He blasted the horn. "What's the matter with that loser in the Fiat, driving like a grandma? It was so cool, you know, I think I got around three hours sleep a night, doing my shifts then going out to party. Hey, did you hear there was a terrorist attack at the Opera House? It's OK, nobody got hurt. The Riverboat Crew weren't so lucky. Six members dead in the last two days. No one claimed responsibility but they each victim wore a black silk hood and we all know what that means. Look at the way that asshole is parked!" He wound down the window. "Asshole! Yeah, what a party. Guess who got to see two of the finest singers in the world perform live? Aline on Friday and Roberta on Sunday. Those ladies have the voices of angels. This is the hotel you wanted, right?"

Gil paid the most verbose man in Brazil, walked into the hotel and booked a double room for one night. "You don't mind?" he said, as he handed over his credit card.

Ann didn't know how to respond. Was he asking her to stay another night or whether she objected to the double room? She decided that conversation could wait. "I don't mind. As long as it has a shower and a bed, I could sleep on the roof."

It wasn't quite the roof, but the seventeenth floor

commanded pretty good views across the city. Gil sat at the desk to make some calls, offering Ann first use of the facilities. She accepted gratefully, taking her backpack into the bathroom. She stripped off and stepped under the shower, tilting her face to the water as if receiving a benediction. Once three days of dirt, sweat and stress had vanished down the plughole, she set about hand washing enough clothes to wear on the flight home. She wrapped herself and her hair in towels and took her underwear, T-shirt and linen trousers onto the balcony to dry in the sun.

Gil lay spread-eagled on the bed with his eyes closed. Ann scattered her clothes over the balcony chairs and table and came to lie beside him. He opened his eyes and focused on her face.

"Feel better?" he asked.

"100%." She reached out a hand, brushing her thumb over his lips. Now was the time. In daylight, safe from predators, in clean sheets and freshly showered, she wanted to devour Gil Maduro.

"Give me a minute. I stink. Not quite as bad as Bruno, but almost." His eyes raked her body and he jumped to his feet. "I'll be right back. Don't go anywhere."

She curled up on the pillows and closed her eyes, smiling in anticipation. In thirty seconds, she was fast asleep.

An electronic ringtone infiltrated her dreams. She opened her eyes to see Gil's bare back with a white towel around his waist, as he stretched to answer his phone. The pillow next to hers had a dent and when she reached out a hand, the sheet was warm, as if a body had recently been lying beside her. She cursed herself for missing an opportunity then tuned into Gil's voice.

"Veronique, hi! What's going on? OK, great news. I'll go in

to see him later today. Any update on Edu? No, I suppose they can't. How's Damien? What, now? Yeah, sure. Can you give us ten minutes? We were asleep. Perfect, see you then."

He relaxed onto the bed and rolled over to face Ann. "Rocco's out of surgery but under observation overnight. Veronique isn't family so the doctors won't tell her anything about Edu. Damien has been treated and they're coming over in ten minutes."

"That doesn't give us long."

His gaze switched between her eyes. "No, it doesn't. When savouring a feast I've anticipated this long, I'm not going to rush it." He cupped his hand beneath her chin and kissed her. The right amount of gentleness with just enough pressure to signal intent.

She released a frustrated groan. "What's the time?"

"Quarter to three. We slept for over two hours and if we want to catch that flight tonight, I have to get to the hospital by four. Let's get dressed, do what we have to do and go home. Ann?"

"What?"

"When we get home, can we spend the night together? I don't care where. Your place, mine, a hotel, it doesn't matter. I want you."

She kissed him, trying to balance passion and professionalism. "Yes. Maybe if we like it, we could try it more than once."

He broke the clinch with a wolfish grin. "Always best to give things a trial run. Now I'm hogging the bathroom while you pack your clothes. Let's go." He leapt off the bed and into the bathroom with an energy Ann could hardly believe. She sat up, rubbed her eyes and caught sight of herself in the wardrobe mirror. Red hair in wild patterns, a far stronger tan than she'd ever have allowed at the beach and a smile that reminded her of Fátima.

The sun and wind had performed their laundry functions, so while Gil was cleaning his teeth Ann dressed and repacked her rucksack. Then she made herself a coffee and sat on the balcony, calculating options versus risks. Her heart made an impassioned plea for the beach, the village, the dog and the dangerously desirable man in the next room. Her head flashed up images of O Cabrito, Uncle Jack and an information network she knew only too well. She had stuck her head above the parapet and she'd been spotted. Now they would hunt her down.

There had to be a way of living under the radar on her beach. From now on, no travelling, minimal contact and absolute anonymity. With Gil's help, this could still work.

A knock came at the door and she was on her feet so fast her coffee spilt over the table.

Gil was already peering through the spyhole. "It's Veronique and I assume that's Damien. What a mess!" He opened the door and the film-makers came inside. It was the first time Ann had seen Damien without three black bags wrapped across his frame.

His face was wreathed in bandages, but his sparkling eyes authenticated his personality. "What kind of a shithole is this place? They don't even serve fish tacos!" he mumbled, his speech unclear.

The urge to embrace him was strong but Ann had no idea how badly he was hurt. Still, it was a lift to see one and a half familiar faces. Veronique looked amazingly clean and fresh in a white cherry-patterned dress, her combat shorts a distant memory.

"He's not drunk, it's just his mouth is still numb from the anaesthetic. Temporary crowns on two teeth and sixteen stitches in his face. His career as a matinee idol is over."

"Some women like the rugged look," Damien replied. At least that's what it sounded like to Ann.

"And Rocco?" she asked, swinging her backpack onto her shoulders.

Veronique filled them in as they left the hotel room and made their way down to the lobby. Rocco had received a blood transfusion and would have to stay in hospital overnight. His wound was not life-threatening but serious enough to make the doctors concerned about infection.

"As for his personality?" She shrugged as they emerged into the sunlight. "Nothing changes there."

In their short acquaintance, Ann had seen Rocco face down imminent death four, if not five times. Each brush with his own mortality had not dented his confidence in the least. Bandaged up in the hospital, he took one look at Ann's topknot concealed by a baseball cap and informed her she looked prettier with her hair down. Then he proceeded to complain that no one had brought him any beer, before ranting for a good five minutes about Bruno's escape.

"What you don't understand is that bringing an international fugitive to justice would have meant a promotion for me. No more ducking the O Cabritos of this world, no more hacking my way through the jungle in search of dead prostitutes, just a nice comfy chair and my feet up on the desk. This is all your fault." He pointed at Gil. "Didn't I say we should have cuffed his hands behind him?"

Damien answered. "It wouldn't have made any difference. He was raging and would have torn that chain out somehow. True, he couldn't have punched me in the face with his hands behind him, but maybe I was naive to think I could stop a charging bull. He's gone, Rocco, and we should be grateful to Gil for getting us here in one piece."

"Only just. That landing was as dodgy as they come. Remind me not to go flying again with you any time soon."

"You're welcome," said Gil, dryly. "What concerns me is how we report what happened."

"I've been thinking about that." Rocco grimaced as he shifted himself a little higher up the bed on his elbows. "The guy who flew the plane in. A hitman, right?" he asked Ann.

"Right." She gave no more details, aware of the interest from Veronique and Damien.

"But no one needs to know who he was hunting. Here's how I remember it. On official orders, we arrested Bruno, defended ourselves from his angry co-workers and were waiting for the plane to ship him out. When it arrived, Bruno recognised the big bald guy as a hitman sent to kill him. He flipped out and attacked us, injuring the camera guy. Gil managed to save the ladies and I got shot in the confusion. Bruno ran into the jungle and Baldy gave chase. Due to our injuries, we made the decision not to go in pursuit but to fly back to Manaus for hospital treatment. We have no idea what happened in the jungle. Maybe Baldy took Bruno out, maybe the other way around. The chances of anyone going to check are about as remote as anyone getting a beer in this bed."

"That tallies with my recollection of events," agreed Gil. "No authority figure is likely to go poking around in the jungle anytime soon."

"We're ready and willing to corroborate that account. But as for official investigations into the camp, I wouldn't be too sure." Veronique opened her bag and withdrew her laptop. "I'd like to show you a rough cut of our 'nature documentary'. This is what we plan to air as soon as we can go live. Ann, could you close the blinds?"

She set her screen on Rocco's bedside table, positioned it so everyone could see and pressed play. Some frantic drumming accompanied the introductory titles. Four yellow words loomed out of the dark green background: Death of the Rainforest, and the voiceover began in Veronique's distinctive accent. She spoke in English as Portuguese subtitles rolled across the screen.

"The Amazon basin is often referred to as 'the lungs of the planet', due to its role of absorbing and converting large quantities of CO_2 in our atmosphere. But a cancer is creeping through Earth's lungs, killing an ecosystem upon which the whole planet is dependent."

The room was silent, all eyes fixed on the aerial footage of impenetrable greenery stretching for thousands of kilometres. A soundtrack of a beating heart over swooping classical music reinforced the message until it zoomed in on acre after acre of destruction. The camera angle switched to loggers chain-sawing down trees with the shrieks of monkeys and birds in the background.

The narrator switched to Damien, who detailed the statistics of how much land had been lost. Just as Ann began to feel overwhelmed, the scene changed again. The screen showed the view from the cockpit of a small aircraft, coming into land at the very same camp they'd fled that morning.

Veronique's reassuring tones explained the company had permission to cut timber from a section of the jungle but were prohibited from encroaching on the land of indigenous people. A neat graphic showed how the loggers had ignored that ban and were moving deeper into the forest. One shot showed Juan-Carlos in a hard hat, consulting a map with his foreman. The camera panned across the scene, taking in all the elements Ann had found so disturbing. She realised she was scrunching her toes, half in horror, half in delight. The way the team had presented her revelation was so authoritative, no one could guess it was one woman's interpretation of a map.

The next section was almost an exact reproduction of their river trip to the village. From the prow of the boat, Damien's voice gave an introduction to the local people and offered an insight into how they lived. He translated a conversation with the chief and her distress at what was happening to their sacred ground. Scenes of hunting tribes, women mashing cassava in the circle of stones and dancing in the firelight painted the place with a vibrant beauty missing from the grim brown timber camp.

The angle wasn't subtle but the message hit home. Just as Veronique started describing the animal habitats under threat, Rocco's phone rang. Veronique paused the video and everyone listened to one half of a conversation.

Yes, he'd survive, Rocco assured his superior officer. A flesh wound and nothing more, although the hospital wanted him to stay overnight. Tomorrow? Of course. Both of them? But Inspector Maduro was flying to the coast this afternoon. A debrief? He locked eyes with Gil, who nodded once. First thing in the morning was an excellent idea. They both looked forward to it. He put down the phone and cursed.

"That bastard is playing politics and wants to cover his arse. You OK to stay the night, Gil?"

"I am. But Ann shouldn't be in Manaus a second longer than necessary." Gil stared at the frozen image on the screen, of a pink dolphin alongside a boat. "So the nature programme is actually an explosive documentary on rainforest destruction. You two had some guts to stay in that camp and factually record what they're doing right under their noses. Maybe you should consider undercover work."

Ann kept her expression neutral and her eyes fixed on the screen.

Gil continued. "When do you plan to drop this bomb?"

The Frenchwoman checked with her mummified colleague. "It needs another edit once we land in São Paulo tomorrow. What do you think, Damien? Could we go live by Thursday?"

"Thursday at the latest. As soon as the legal disclaimer is ready, this is going viral. The authorities have no choice but to close down the camp. If they find any stray bodies as part of their investigation, a prosecution is guaranteed." Damien's speech grew more distinct with every utterance, but Ann could see the effort caused him pain. "Thursday, we light the fuse and watch the fireworks."

"In that case, I'm taking Ann to the airport right now." Gil assumed control with ease. "Veronique, don't bring that fat bastard any beer, no matter what he says. Good luck with the documentary but keep yourselves safe, you hear? There will be some very angry and powerful people after you when this goes out. Ann, say your goodbyes but don't get too close to Rocco. He grabs every chance he can. I'm going to talk to the doctor."

While the other two made plans for the evening, Ann pecked Rocco's cheek. He beckoned her closer to whisper in her ear, "He's the finest man I know. You could do worse."

"I know. But he could do better."

Rocco snorted and offered his cheek for a kiss. "Just remember, I want to be godfather."

Veronique embraced Ann with tears in her eyes. "As the Americans say, let's do lunch."

Ann laughed. "So we'll never see each other again. You and Damien are incredible. You have such courage."

"Compared to yours? Another league, madame. No, we won't see each other again. That's the least I can do for you. *Bonne chance*, Ann. I will never forget *not* meeting you."

Ann placed her hands on Damien's shoulders and touched a cheek to both of his. She whispered in English, "Heal fast. You've risked a lot for a damn good reason."

"Thanks. Hey, if ever that handsome git falls under a bus, call me on the off-chance I might be available. Word is, scars are sexy. Look after yourself."

Gil returned to carry Ann's pack to the door and waved a hand to speed her up. Within ten minutes, she and Gil Maduro were in a taxi to the airport. His expression was closed and other than giving the driver their destination, neither said a word until they got out at the terminal.

"You can drop me here," said Ann.

"No chance. If I have to use my official ID to see you get on that plane, that's what I intend to do." He paid the driver and carried her pack into the building.

An idea occurred to Ann. "You played the police officer card at the hospital, didn't you? You asked the doctor about Edu."

He strode through the check-in desks without responding and Ann assumed the worst. She knew Gil would blame himself and the bumpy landing for whatever had happened to the logger.

Away from the crowds, he replied, "Yes, I did. Edu is out of intensive care, but he has multiple fractures and a detached retina. It will take him weeks if not months to recover, but then he can return to work."

Ann gasped. "But what about his amputation?"

"There was never any question of an amputation. I wondered how Dona Candida could possibly know so much, seeing as she and Telmo Carreira are sworn enemies. The answer is, she didn't. She made it up."

Ann stared out of the window, shaking her head in astonishment. "You said it from the start. Up there, it's cowboy country."

The Departures section of Manaus Airport was tinged with sadness, a leaden sense of imminent loss. A couple in a tearful embrace clung to each other while a family waved goodbye to a daughter, their smiles fixed until she went through the gates. Only then did the mother begin to weep, comforted by her husband and two sons.

"You're going to leave." Gil's voice was flat, with no question intonation.

Ann rotated her water bottle between her hands, unable to meet his eyes. The airport was air-conditioned and the change in temperature made her even more uncomfortable than his stare. She looked miserably around, wishing there was another way. Arrivals halls were different, filled with anticipation, flowers, balloons and the ecstasy of reunion.

"This time, I have no choice."

"When do you plan to go?"

"Tomorrow, I guess. Just enough time to pack up and make arrangements. Gil, I swear if I could stay, nothing would make me happier. But I can't. The guy they sent to kill me at the Rio Negro camp was actually an act of mercy. He told me so himself."

"I know. I heard him."

They sat on plastic seats, staring out at the row of aircraft on the tarmac in frustrated silence. A member of ground staff made an announcement, instructing anyone with a ticket to Soure to begin boarding. Around eight people started walking to the gate.

Ann turned to Gil. "I have to go." She touched his cheek and drew his mouth to hers for the gentlest of kisses. "I'm sorry." It was pathetically inadequate but the enormity of what she had to say defied words. She let him go and swung on her backpack.

He caught her wrist. "Stay till Thursday. I'm returning to Soure tomorrow and all I want is to say a proper goodbye. Promise me that, Ann. A car will be waiting to take you home when you land tonight and on Thursday morning, I'll take you to the airport myself. Please don't go before I get home."

She glanced out at her fellow passengers crossing the tarmac towards the little plane. Time to board. "I promise. I won't leave Ilha do Marajó until Thursday morning. *Até amanha.*"

He stood up, kissed her again and released her to run for the gate. As she pelted her way across the concourse, she glanced behind. He was smiling, or at least that was what it looked like. She couldn't see too clearly through her tears.

21

For the first few moments of Wednesday morning, Ann simply lay underneath her mosquito net and acclimatised. A night in her own bed in her own hut after the tensions of the previous days had delivered a sleep so deep she was still climbing out of it. Her joy in the familiarity of her surroundings was bittersweet in that she only had today to enjoy the place she called home. Her brain replayed the events of the last week as if it was a movie she'd watched and couldn't quite remember the details.

That enormous European city in the rainforest, dancing in the fairy-lit courtyard, the black silk hoods, confronting O Cabrito, tropical storms, unwelcome visitors, the river trip to the village and her intoxication, the night of passion in the darkness, a life-threatening boat journey, bloodied loggers and a mud-spattered boss, the stand-off at the Rio Negro camp, a killer hunting her through the jungle, the terrifying flight to Manaus, an emotional farewell at the airport, the weary journey home, one far less bumpy landing at Soure airport, a lift home from one of Gil's sergeants and finally, a walk down the beach to her shack. Her body grew heavier with each recollection. She could have slept for a week.

Coffee was the only thing capable of luring her out of bed. Her beach hut was as secure as she had left it, with everything intact. There was no sign of Branca. Ann could not decide if that was a good or a bad sign. She threw back the netting and boiled some water. In the exhaustion of yesterday, she had made no decisions as to her next move. Once she was fully caffeinated, she intended to plan. Packing up the hut would not take long, but making arrangements for a swift departure might be complicated. She sat with her feet propped up on the railing and stared out at the sea. One thing was certain. Wherever she landed next, she needed to be near water. Perhaps something calmer than the raging torrent of the Rio Negro and drier than Ilha do Marajó in the rainy season, but an ocean or a lake seemed absolutely necessary. The question was, where?

Above the squawks and screeches coming from the jungle, another sound penetrated the morning's peace. Fátima came into view around the side of the hut wearing pink shorts and a maraschino-coloured vest, and carrying one of her chequered laundry bags. She was already midway through a long speech.

"... days, you said! More like a week! I ran out of dog food but thanks to the Lord, well Zé, actually, I got some of that dried stuff. Smells like a dead boar, but she likes it. Branca! *Venha aqui!* Did you bring my camera back? I had a bet with Serena that you'd lose it. Anabela tells me a cop car dropped you in the village last night, so what happened to your boyfriend? If you were on your own, you should have come over. I was up till midnight, making adjustments to my new dress. Wait till you see it! Your line is, 'Why do you need a new dress, Fátima?' and I will tell you. Just as soon as you give me my morning brew. We're in luck because Baileys was on sale in the supermarket and apparently it's the perfect thing to liven up our coffee. Oh, isn't that sweet! *Que fofinha!*"

A white shape ducked past Fátima, raced up the wooden path, took the steps in one leap and writhed around Ann's legs. The dog's tail whipped back and forth so wildly it was border-line painful on Ann's shins. Embarrassed by how tearful she became at such an enthusiastic canine welcome, Ann buried her face in Branca's coat, scratching her ears and along her spine. A new bandana was tied around the dog's neck; a Brazilian flag this time. Ann swallowed the lump in her throat and told herself that was a good thing. Someone else cared enough for this animal to buy her a new collar.

"Good girl! I missed you. You all better now? *Bom dia*, Fátima, and thank you for looking after her. I'm sorry it took so long. Yes, I'll make some more coffee but I'll pass on the booze. What's Belize, anyway?"

"Not Belize, Baileys! It's comes from England and that's why I bought it for you. We're celebrating and how can we do that without alcohol? You may as well make a pot of coffee because I saw Serena on the way back from the padaria and told her you were home. She's coming down when she's finished surfing. I bought enough croissants for all of us, don't worry. Now tell me, what happened?" She plonked her bag on the table and took out a bottle of Baileys Irish Cream.

Ann debated whether to explain the drink came from Ireland, not England and the clue was in the name, but she didn't have the energy. She made coffee, found a plate for the croissants and sat opposite her voluble neighbour.

"Quite a lot, actually. The bottom line is I have to leave here. It's time to move on."

Fátima stopped in the act of unscrewing the bottle and stared at Ann in horror. "No! Leave the beach or leave the state?"

"Leave the country. I came here to hide. That's impossible when the wrong people know where you are. I have no choice but to get out."

"The wrong people," echoed Fátima. "The ones you're so scared of that you planted broken glass in the sand around your hut? But how come they found you when you weren't even here?"

Ann poured the coffee. "It's complicated. Just believe me when I say I love this place. I'm happy for the first time in I don't know how long." She swallowed her self-pity. "But that means nothing in these circumstances. Tomorrow, I have to run." She shoved her cup across the table for a slug of Baileys, but it was not forthcoming.

Fátima was pressing the heels of her hands against her eyes. "I don't want you to go."

Tears welled in Ann's eyes but the two of them sitting there weeping would solve nothing. "I don't want to go either. The only thing I want is to stay alive and in possession of all my body parts. What's worrying me most is what happens to Branca if I'm gone."

"Who do you think bought her that bandana?" Fátima's mascara was smudged and her expression hurt. "I'll mind the dog, of course I will. Haven't I just fed her for a week? Listen to me, Ann. My father always said you must stand up to a bully. What are you going to do, run around the world hiding and hoping he never catches up? What kind of a life is that? One of these days you have to stand your ground. Why not now?"

Giving her neighbour just a hint of Ann's reality required an encyclopaedia of explanations. She had neither the energy nor the time. "Because there's more than one. Pour us some of that whiskey and I'll fetch you some tissues."

By the time she came out of the bathroom with some cleanser, cotton pads and cleanser, Serena was on the porch, listening to Fátima's tearful rendition of the circumstances. The girl rushed to Ann and wrapped her in an embrace. Her swimsuit was still wet and she carried the scent of ozone in her hair.

"Dona Ann, you can't leave! You only just came home!"

"Hello, Serena. Sit down and have some coffee. Please don't get upset because I'm only just keeping it together myself. You two might tip me over the edge." She guided the girl to a chair and handed Fátima what she needed to repair her make-up. "The fact is that unless I get out of here tomorrow, I will wind up dead. Some nasty people are looking for me and unfortunately someone just let off a flare to tell them where I am. Listen, I've paid the rent on this place until the end of the year. Maybe you'd like to stay here, Serena? Give your mother some space, help look after Branca and quite literally live on the beach."

She took a swig of coffee. Noting how generous Fátima had been with the alcohol, she helped herself to a croissant. The three of them sat in silence; Fátima fixing her face, Serena pulling off little bits of croissant to pop into her mouth and Branca's, and Ann leaving the idea to simmer.

A fishing boat chugged past and a shout rang over the waves. All three women waved, even if Ann had no idea who it was or what he'd said.

"Until the end of the year?" asked Serena. "Is that when you're coming back?"

Ann took in the sun-bleached beauty beside her, so innocent and optimistic. "I honestly can't say if or when I might be back. Let's assume not. Meanwhile I hand over guardianship of this tatty white mutt to the pair of you. Serena, you can stay here for free until January, then you'll need to pay the rent yourself. Today I need to pack and change the way I look. Either of you any good at cutting hair?"

Swirls of long red locks lay around her feet, similar to the weeds trailing in the Rio Negro. Serena's fingers dabbed at Ann's temple, gentle as a butterfly, removing some of the hair dye. Her scalp burned as the chemicals did their work but Serena was careful not to let any of it near Ann's eyes. Fátima watched the process, offering her opinion at regular intervals.

"Dresses, that's what you need. No one will recognise you in a dress because you always look like a soldier. Dresses and jewellery. I've got some stuff I don't wear anymore. I'll go and fetch it when I've finished this coffee. You have the right kind of face for short hair. Mine's too round, which is a pity. With short hair, people see your earrings better."

"Talking of jewellery, I bought you something." She slid the two necklaces out of her pocket and across the table. Two pairs of eyes threatened more emotional outbursts so Ann changed the subject. "I hope it will go with your new dress, Fátima. Aren't you going to show us what you've got in your bag? Don't tell me you have another date."

Fátima clipped one necklace around Serena's neck and gestured for the girl to do the same for her. They each kissed Ann's cheeks.

"Thank you. It will suit my new dress very well and yes I do have another date. Alberto has asked me to spend the weekend with him while he visits some of those conservation projects inland. How about this for dinner on Saturday night?" She slipped a scarlet cheesecloth garment over her head and let it fall over her frame. Once she'd pulled the elasticated neckline down her arms, the shirred fabric clung to her curves, showing off her tanned shoulders.

Ann told herself it was the bleach making her eyes water. Her friend looked radiant, the colour complementing her skin and the style allowing her natural beauty to shine. The necklace added a natural simplicity to the whole ensemble. "You look fantastic!" she said. "That's the simplest yet most gorgeous thing I've ever seen you wear."

Fátima did a twirl. "Thank you. It's comfortable and cool, which is perfect if you want sex later in the evening. Let that be a lesson to you, Serena. Always plan ahead. Isn't it time you washed that shit off yet? It's damn strong stuff and we don't want to fry what's left of Ann's hair."

With some relief, Ann got into the shower, tilted her head back and let the water rinse away the out-of-date bleach Fátima had found in one of her cupboards. *Comfortable and cool, which is perfect if you want sex later in the evening.* She smiled, despite her stinging eyes, wondering where Gil Maduro was at that moment in time. She towelled herself and her head dry, amazed at how much lighter she felt. Without a mirror, she couldn't judge the colour but already loved the simplicity of an elfin cut.

She emerged onto the veranda, braced for the unvarnished truth from her friends, but instead encountered an edgy silence. Rather than two women awaiting her, there were three. Anabela, owner of the café/padaria, was standing at the top of the steps, her expression grim.

"*Olá*, Ann. Nice haircut."

"Anabela, is something wrong?"

"I don't know. Two men came to the café this morning, asking about a red-haired *gringa*, saying they were friends of hers. I asked them for a name and they didn't have one. Marco and I told them there were no *gringas* in Praia do Pesqueiro, but several were living in Praia do Ceú. They thanked us and the second they drove out of the village, I came straight down here. Who comes looking for a friend but doesn't even know her name? Marco said, and I thought the same thing, they looked like trouble."

Ann glanced up the beach. How had they found her so fast? O Cabrito? Juan-Carlos Ablos? Juliana? Rocco? Or perhaps Gil Maduro had played his last card under pressure. Whoever it was made no difference. They were around three kilometres away and closing in.

An idea flared and she went inside to rummage through

her rucksack. Fátima's camera was not in the pocket she'd stashed it. Neither was it anywhere else. The only time she'd been separated from her belongings was in Manaus, under the supervision of O Cabrito. Of course the old goat had taken the camera and identified her location from Fátima's photographs of Praia do Pesqueiro, Soure and their beach. *Leave no prints*, she whispered and returned outside.

"Thank you, Anabela. Can you go back to the village and spread the word I moved out early this morning? Then they'll look for me at the airport or on the ferry." She kicked at the russet locks on the veranda. "We need to get rid of this hair, it's an obvious clue. Could you burn it, Serena? Maybe down the beach a little way? Don't stay here tonight just in case they get the wrong woman. I'm going to pack and run through the jungle."

"Why don't I go with Anabela and find Zé?" Fátima offered. "He can drive you to the airport."

"No. No one can know where I'm going. Not you, not Zé, nobody. I'll handle this. Go home now, look after Branca and if they come knocking, tell them plenty but tell them nothing, OK?"

Once more Fátima's eyes filled with tears. "What does that mean?"

Ann clenched her fists, trying to keep control of her emotions. "Talk their ears off with all kinds of bullshit but tell them nothing about me. Maybe they're interested in your dresses?"

Without warning, all three women rushed her and for a second Ann's defences screamed RUN! But the tears and hugs were an attack of a different, less defensible kind. They clung to one another in a sniffly, sobbing group until Ann broke away.

"Go now, please. Take Branca; look after my tomato plant

and thank you for everything you've done. I won't forget you. I won't forget anything about this place."

Serena rested her chin on Anabela's shoulder and gazed at Ann with a downturned mouth. "You can trust us. We'll keep your secrets, but we won't forget you either. Your hair looks lovely, by the way."

Anabela nodded vigorously. "We want you to come back. We will think of you every day. But now we're going to the padaria to eat *natas* and cry and tell everyone you've gone. Maybe even the dog can have one." She whistled to Branca.

"*Até logo,*" said Fátima, stubbornly shaking her head. *See you later.* Finality was not in that woman's nature.

Ann pressed her hands to her mouth and blew a collective kiss. "Goodbye. Thank you. *Tchau.*" With one last stroke of Branca's head, she went inside. Crying would have to wait.

Packing all her belongings took exactly the forty minutes she had estimated. When her removal was complete, Ann locked up the shack for the last time. No lingering looks at her beautiful view, no loitering on the veranda to recall the memories but a careful survey of the beach and the jungle for any signs of a sniper or ambush. The heat was at its fiercest as she scuttled up the beach to the jungle path. At Fátima's back door, she left a paper bag containing the keys to her hut, and in lieu of the camera, the silver earrings Gil had bought her. It would be a nice surprise when she returned from the village.

Then she broached the jungle. If she walked along the road with a full backpack, she'd be an obvious target, regardless of how different her hair might look. Even if a friendly local were to pass and offer her a lift, he or she would know where she was going. No bike, no friends and no Gil Maduro, Ann was on her own. Again.

The walk into Soure usually took forty-five minutes, depending on the weather. In the midday heat when Ann had to duck into the forest every time a vehicle approached from either direction, while carrying all her worldly belongings on her back, the journey lasted around two hours. At least it gave her some time to plan. Her first instinct was to rush to the airport in the hope of meeting Gil, but that would be the first place her pursuers would look for a runaway. The ferries might be a way out but there had to be a more creative solution. She was scrambling out of the undergrowth for the third time in two minutes when she saw a neat wooden post with an arrow bearing the words Pousada Figueira.

It was a sign, in more ways than one. This was the hotel Gil Maduro had brought her to drink cocktails; the same place she'd suggested as their first date. She could get off the road, stay the night here and seek a way out of Soure in the morning. The sound of another car approaching galvanised her into action and she jogged across the track and up the driveway to the hotel. As the hotel complex came into view, a scattering of cottages around a central building with a pool, a sense of calm descended on Ann. This was a place she could hide, cool off and consider her options with a clear head. She needed it after two of Fátima's 'lively' coffees.

The receptionist had no free rooms in the main complex but one of the far more expensive cottages was still available. Ann paid in cash and used one of her fake passports, not in the name of Ann Sheldon. The photograph showed a pale-skinned female with long ash-blonde hair; bearing no resemblance to the woman she was today. It didn't bother the receptionist, who counted the cash and tried to sell her various excursions to buffalo farms, eco-parks and river trips. She refused them all and he handed over the key, wishing her a nice day with such deadened intonation, he might have cursed her with an early demise in the fishpond.

Shelling out cash hand over fist was beginning to be a

worry. With nothing more than her savings to live on, she'd chipped away at her nest egg after recent extravagances. Next place she landed, her first priority would be to earn some money. English lessons? A self-defence class? Poetry tuition? How she was supposed to do any of those things while lying low, she had no idea.

Her depressing thoughts fled like vampires in daylight the moment she opened the cottage door. It had a 'right place, right time' quality Ann couldn't exactly explain. Luxurious, light, spacious and decorated in shades of yellow, the room exuded the essence of sunshine. She dropped her pack on the floor and explored the security arrangements. When satisfied, she filled the sink with soapy water and dumped in as many clothes as would fit, including those she'd been wearing. When she'd washed every item of dirty linen, she laid it all out to dry on the little veranda. It was half the size of her own beach hut porch, but the perfect sun-trap. Finally, she took advantage of the massive showerhead and all the hotel toiletries. After all the days she'd only managed the occasional wash, now she couldn't stop.

Her appearance in the mirror came as a shock. When Serena suggested an elfin cut and Fátima provided some bleach, Ann's imagination had conjured Charlize Theron or Scarlett Johansson on the red carpet. That could not have been further from reality. She looked like an aged urchin. Her hair was ragged and uneven, its colour more scarecrow yellow than platinum blond, and her skin was reddened, peeling and dry. Her hope of a romantic tryst with Gil Maduro on clean sheets with the breeze blowing over their golden bodies was a fantasy, nothing more. She had to put him out of her mind and focus on her uncertain future.

While her clothes dried, she slathered her face and body with moisturising cream, wrapped herself in a towel and sat cross-legged on the floor, facing the open window to meditate.

Now was the time to gather her thoughts. Distracted and jumpy, she'd only make poor decisions. She closed her eyes and focused on her breath, reconnecting her mind with her body. Her temperature fell as she breathed, focusing on nothing but each inhalation and exhalation. Gradually clarity assumed control, cleansing her mind as thoroughly as she had scrubbed her skin. From now on, all decisions were her own.

She opened her eyes. A plan formed as if it had been waiting. Tomorrow morning, she would join an excursion from the hotel, blending in with other backpackers, until she reached a point where she could jump ship or bus or jeep. From there she'd take the ferry to Belém airport. Then two, maybe three or four flights until she landed in Mozambique. Or Angola. Even Cabo Verde might work. Anywhere they spoke Portuguese. She'd volunteer for an NGO, hide out, do some good and live by the sea. It was meant to be. Only then could she begin to analyse the layers of Uncle Jack's message.

Ann jumped to her feet, threw on a sundress and picked up the phone. When the receptionist finally answered, she booked a place on the Salvaterra bus at nine am. As she replaced the handset, a shadow crossed the window outside the veranda. Her breath caught in her throat. The silhouette of a man was coming towards her door.

In one move, Ann threw herself across the bed, switched on the shower and grabbed her knife. If this was one of the men from Praia do Pesqueiro, he had a partner somewhere. She had to be ready to fight two professionals with nothing more than a six-inch blade and her wits. Crouching beside the door, she waited for him to kick it in and enter the room. When he did, most likely with a weapon aimed at the bathroom, she'd cut the tendons in both his ankles with one slice. After that, she would snatch his gun and use it on him and his partner.

The last thing she expected was a polite knock.

"Ann?" Gil's voice was unmistakeable. She hunkered down

for a second longer, running through every scenario – he was at gunpoint, he was working with them, it was a clever mimic – until she uncoiled and looked through the spyhole. There he was, Gil Maduro, clean-shaven and wearing his classic blue shirt as if he were at work. Surely a mirage because wishes never came true.

She opened the door. Her heart swelled at the sight of him, armed with nothing other than a bottle of wine. "How did you know where to find me?" she said, incapable of hiding her smile.

For a second, he said nothing, blinking at her hair. "You said the location of our first date had to be here. So when you weren't home, I put two and two together. She's taken the initiative, I thought, and booked us a room." He looked past her at the white and yellow interior. "Not bad. There are worse places to spend the night. Can I come in?"

She nodded and took a pace backwards. He stepped inside and locked the door behind him, placing the wine on the table. Then he turned to face her, his gaze searching her face.

"Your neighbour, the one with the bright clothes, saw me coming away from your hut. She told me you'd left for good. She was wearing the earrings I bought you in Manaus." He glanced at the knife in her hand. "You didn't book us a room. You weren't expecting me. You were planning to leave without saying goodbye."

Ann folded her knife away. "Two men came to Praia do Pesqueiro this morning, looking for a red-haired *gringa*. The villagers sent them in the wrong direction but it won't take long before they work it out. I had to run, Gil, and get my head down. I couldn't risk coming to the airport or the police station, you must see that. Yes, I gave Fátima the earrings because I had nothing else of value to replace her camera. To be honest, if I kept them, they would always remind me of you."

"And that would be terrible."

"Yes, it would. To be constantly reminded of what could have been? Painful and unnecessary. It's better to move on and forget."

His stare bored into hers and in one sudden move, he took a step forward and pulled her to him, caressing what was left of her hair. "You cut it all off," he murmured.

"Yep, and dyed it blonde. What do you think?" Her heart fluttered as he kissed her neck.

"I loved the wild redhead, but this is also beautiful. I can see more of your face." His lips met hers and she closed her eyes. One arm pressed her against him while his other hand ran over her body, his touch awakening a familiar desire.

He broke the kiss and looked into her eyes. "You're not wearing any underwear."

"True. Subconsciously I must have been expecting you."

He slipped his hands beneath her dress and lifted it over her head. Her skin seemed hot and impatient, craving his touch.

"I can see you," he said, his voice husky. "This time I can see you."

She reached for his belt buckle. "I can see you too."

The sun was setting as they lay naked on the sheets, Ann's head on Gil's chest and his hand tracing circles down her spine. These were the moments she would remember, she promised herself, trying to memorise his scent, the texture of his chest hair and colour of his skin. In the afterglow of their lovemaking, their intimacy was at once fragile and infinite.

He kissed her forehead. "Are you hungry? Want to get room service?"

"Starving. Let's order something expensive that goes with white wine."

"With lots of bread." Gil dialled reception and ordered a seafood platter with a bottle of champagne. Ann feigned shock, while planning to enjoy every mouthful. *The last of your luxuries for this year, lady*. She collected her freshly laundered clothes and packed her rucksack while Gil showered. When a waiter delivered the food, they ate at the table with the veranda windows wide open to the vibrancy of the gardens, as blissed-out as a pair of honeymooners, exchanging smiles and sighs. Ann treasured every second of his company.

"My mother was a seer," said Gil, out of the blue. "She had a sense for when someone was pregnant, or sick, or troubled. The other trait she had was an ability to predict the future. Some of those skills she passed on to me."

Ann placed her knife and fork together on her empty plate, full and comfortable, ready to listen to Gil's story. "She *was* a seer? You mean she's no longer with us?"

"She died of emphysema two years ago. A lifelong smoker, she didn't need a sixth sense to see that coming. When I was around thirteen or fourteen years old, she said something I never forgot. She told me that in order to be happy, I would have to work harder than I ever imagined to hold on to someone extraordinary." He smiled to himself. "Driving down the beach in the rain that day to interview some flaky foreigner about a murder, I felt my mother's presence. Not in a calm, benevolent way, but as she used to be, clapping her hands and laughing in anticipation. The minute you opened the door, I've never had a stronger reaction to anyone or anything in my life. Ann, I swear I will do whatever it takes to hold on to you. Even if that means letting you go."

She swallowed, stunned by the intensity in his voice. "Gil, the thing is ..."

"Let's close the windows. I don't want to be overheard." He shut the veranda doors, cleared the plates and put them on a tray outside the front door. Then he poured them both another glass of champagne and reached for her hand.

"I know who you are. Not all of it, but I'd already done a lot of digging. Rocco spilled the beans last night and with everything I've learned in the last week, I think I pieced together your story. You don't have to confirm or deny any of what I'm about to say, I just want to lay out my conclusions."

The champagne in Ann's stomach grew acidic. "What's the point? It makes no difference. I'm leaving here tomorrow, Gil. Your conclusions, real or imagined, are irrelevant."

"I want to know who you really are." He drew her hand to his lips.

"Even if you don't like what you find?" Her tone came out harsher than she intended.

Gil searched her eyes. "You already told me your real name is not Ann Sheldon. You've demonstrated your knowledge of how drugs gangs operate and what a police operation entails. You can handle a gun, find your way around the dark web and if I'm not mistaken, kill a professional hitman with your bare hands."

Ann said nothing, maintaining a poker face.

"I'm not sure on which side of the law you stood, maybe that changed over time. At least once, I believe, your operations involved narcotics. I couldn't identify the organisation at first, but when O Cabrito recognised you, it wasn't much of a leap."

"Don't, Gil. Don't say it."

They sat holding hands, separated by a wall of silence. Outside, the wind picked up and a light rain began to fall. Ann's eyes avoided his and came to rest on her pack. *Run*, said a voice in her head. *It's not just your enemies who are dangerous.* She pulled her hands from his grasp and rubbed them over her shorn hair.

"You were working ..." Gil began.

"Undercover. Yes, I told Rocco as much, but only because

he compared himself to me. Rocco's alliance with organised crime might be the only way for him to survive, I don't know. But I have a different ethical outlook. I play by the rules. Sorry, that should be past tense. I played by the rules until they changed the rules."

She took a swig of champagne, a righteous anger bubbling. "I refuse, present tense, to be compromised. As a fellow cop, Gil, you must respect the fact I can say nothing more."

His index finger circled the rim of his glass, much as it had traced lines down her spine less than two hours ago. "You don't need to. I heard what that guy said and I connected the dots."

Even though she knew what he meant, she asked the question. "What guy?"

"You know who. Uncle Jack." He slipped his phone from his pocket and played a recording.

'You can't blame them. Bad enough when one mole gets away but two? They've been humiliated and they want revenge. On both ideally, but you don't have police protection, which makes you the easier target. At least for now. They'll get him in the end. Long story short, your ex is doing you a favour. Jack, he said to me, put a bullet in her head. Clean and tidy. Let that be an end to it. All I want, he said, is a picture to prove she's gone. Quite romantic, if you think about it. So that's what I gotta do.

'That's the message? He wants me dead? Like I didn't know that already.'

'Oh, no. That was me managing your expectations. No, his message is this. Wait now, he made me promise to get this right. Tell her I've taken care of her sister.'

The hitman's voice curdled Ann's stomach. Not just gazing down the barrel of his gun but the cruellest torture of knowing her family was at risk.

Gil put his phone away and leaned towards her, his face full of sympathy. "One, you have a sister. Two, there was a pair of detectives working undercover and only one got police protection."

Ann hadn't even got around to processing those details herself. "Please let's not talk about it. That's for your benefit. The more you know, the greater the danger. You shouldn't have gone digging."

"Digging is what I do. The operation is the subject of rumours, Ann, in police forces around the world. We all know it went wrong, or perhaps it went right. Depends on your point of view. For some reason, you ran from the repercussions. That's where I get confused. To grow close enough to the heart of the operation, you must have been intimate with one the kingpins. Which means you were an invaluable asset to the police. In that case, why didn't they give you a new identity like they did for Thanh Ngo?"

Two words were all it took to pierce Ann's emotional shield. She stumbled to her feet, banging her knees against the table. "What the hell do you know about Thanh?"

"The information is available if you know where to look and have the right clearance. At least two cops infiltrated that organisation, you and Thanh Ngo. When everything collapsed, Ngo was removed and given protection. The trail I followed goes as far as Hong Kong and then he vanishes. New documents, surgery maybe, anything is possible. But on paper, Thanh Ngo no longer exists."

A quivering began in Ann's legs. She grabbed the chair to steady herself. Uncle Jack had told the truth. Thanh was alive. The crippling guilt about bolting and leaving her team mate at the hands of those sadistic bastards was a pointless waste of energy.

Like her, Thanh had escaped.

Unlike her, he'd had help.

Her gaze ranged around the room but she saw nothing. She walked to the window and looked out at the rain, rearranging her perspective on the world. It took a while before she could trust her voice.

"When the op started to collapse, I ran and I hid. Nothing will ever make me tell you why, but I had my reasons. I left everything behind to save myself: my family, my career, my friends and the finest man I ever worked with. Knowing Thanh is alive ... that changes things. But it will never erase the knowledge I abandoned him, throwing him to the wolves." Her voice cracked. "I thought he was dead. But he's not because they got him out."

Gil came to stand behind her, wrapping his arms around her waist. "Listen to me. I'm not stating any of this as a threat. It's the opposite. Your life is complicated and I'm beginning to understand a little about why. The more information I have, the more I can help. All I want is for you to live a normal existence. Because I'd like to be part of that." His cheek brushed hers. "Let's not forget I saved your life."

She stiffened for a second, the gulf between her past and her present an impossible leap. Then she relaxed into his embrace. "About bloody time. I've saved yours twice."

"Touché," he murmured.

The heat of his chest against her back and his breath in her ear aroused her all over again. But she had to set boundaries. "Gil, you're right to say you understand a little, but you don't have the whole picture. Even I'm in the dark about certain elements. What's crystal clear to me, and it should be to you, is that I am being hunted. Staying in one place too long, making friends, adopting a dog and falling in love are all hazardous choices which not only endanger my life but those of others. I'm leaving Brazil tomorrow and it's unlikely I will return. I won't tell you where I'm going for both our sakes. If you have the smallest affection for me, you'll let me go."

He rested his chin on her shoulder. "You said 'falling in love'. With me?"

"No. I was talking about Rocco." She turned to face him.

"Of course with you. But it makes no difference whether I love you or hate your guts. We can't be together. That's a fact."

His jaw jutted forward, reminding her for a second of O Cabrito.

"We can't be together. Yet …" he said, placing his hands on her waist.

"You have to let me go."

He dropped his hands immediately.

"No, not now." She snaked her arms around him. "You have to let me leave Ilha do Marajó. Tomorrow morning, I'm getting out of here on a tourist excursion bus to find a way out of the country."

"Not the bus. We'll leave here before it gets light and I'll take you wherever you need to go. The airport is so small you'd be easy to spot and the express ferry too obvious. I'll drive you to Camará for the six o'clock slow boat to Belém. From there, you're on your own."

"Thank you." She rested her forehead on his chest then looked him in the eye. "Gil, if you try to follow me, you'll get us both killed."

His fingers brushed her cheek. "I will let you go and I promise not to follow. But sooner or later, I am going to find you. We're meant to be together. I feel it in my heart."

She opened her mouth to comment but he covered it with his own and she completely forgot what she was going to say.

22

Neither suggested a silent departure the next morning, it just came naturally. Ann dropped the cottage key in the post box, glad Gil had paid for room service in cash. The police Jeep was the furthest vehicle from the main building and he eased it down the driveway, causing the minimum of disturbance. They encountered no other cars, even as they drove through Soure and the sky began to lighten. A thundercloud lay over them reflecting their oppressive emotions.

Ann coached herself, repeating her mantras, but the presence of Gil at her side contracted her throat. To spend one night so close, so intimate and vulnerable, only to tear themselves apart the next morning was akin to ripping a plaster off her whole body. She couldn't bear it. He was right. They were meant to be together.

Raindrops, light at first, soon became a battering on the windscreen. The Jeep's wipers worked at top speed to clear enough visibility. The port loomed into view in the dawn light. Trucks, cars and pedestrians assembled on the docks and harsh lights illuminated the double-decker car ferry.

Gil drove past and parked further along the quay, out of sight. "I'm going to let you out here. A passenger arriving in a police Jeep will attract attention you don't need. Goodbye, Olivia, and good luck."

She unclipped her seatbelt, desperately trying not to cry, and realised what he had just said.

"You called me by my real name."

"Why not? It's beautiful. To me, it sounds like 'I love you' in English."

His arms reached for her and she lost her battle, sobbing into his shirt. He stroked her hair and held her tight. "Take good care of yourself. Because one of these days, I'm going to turn up on your doorstep. I love you, Olivia. Nothing will change that."

The sound of the ferry horn announcing its departure intruded on the moment. Olivia wiped away her tears and kissed Gil. "I love you, Inspector Maduro, and if you don't find me, I'm coming back for you. Deal?"

"Deal."

Olivia jumped out of the Jeep and ran to the ferry, glad of the rain disguising her face. The song started up in her head and made her laugh-sob. She wasn't walking, but running. Her tears were falling and the pain physical. And once again, she was running away. The man at the ticket booth sold her a ticket and tapped at his watch. She scrambled up the gangway and found a seat at the back of the middle section, away from the lashing weather, beside two women already dozing on each other's shoulders.

She stowed her backpack under her seat and scanned the gloomy dock for any sign of a police Jeep. Cars and lorries moved in and out of the port, but all looked uniformly grey in the downpour. Until one vehicle tooted its horn and used its hazard flashers: once, twice, three times.

Olivia didn't react, aware she might be under observation

and knowing Gil would not see her tiny wave through the sheets of rain. But his goodbye embraced her as warmly as his arms. She rested her feet on her backpack and started humming under the sound of the starting engines.

'Runaway' by Del Shannon.

Dad's favourite song from 1961, the source of her pseudonym and the story of her life.

Dear Reader

I hope you enjoyed **BLACK RIVER**. If a snake can shed its skin, why can't a woman? Ann has become Olivia again.

In the next novel, **GOLD DRAGON**, Olivia can no longer hide. She must trace an old acquaintance to Southeast Asia. Finding him is vital if she wants to right the wrongs of the past.

ACKNOWLEDGMENTS

With sincere thanks to Florian Bielmann, Jane Dixon Smith, Julia Gibbs, Katia Ackermann and Sebastião Salgado

ALSO BY JJ MARSH

Other titles in the Run and Hide series

WHITE HERON

GOLD DRAGON

My Beatrice Stubbs series, European crime dramas

BEHIND CLOSED DOORS

RAW MATERIAL

TREAD SOFTLY

COLD PRESSED

HUMAN RITES

BAD APPLES

SNOW ANGEL

HONEY TRAP

BLACK WIDOW

WHITE NIGHT

THE WOMAN IN THE FRAME

ALL SOULS' DAY

~

My standalone novels

AN EMPTY VESSEL

ODD NUMBERS

WOLF TONES

And a short-story collection
APPEARANCES GREETING A POINT OF VIEW

For occasional updates, news, deals and a FREE exclusive novella, subscribe to my newsletter on www.jjmarshauthor.com

~

If you would recommend this book to a friend, please do so by writing a review. Your tip helps other readers discover their next favourite read. Your review can be short and only takes a minute.

Thank you.

Made in the USA
Monee, IL
18 October 2021